RALPH COTTON

D0017396

"GUN-SMOKED, BLOODSTAINED,
GRITTY BELIEVABILITY...
A HARD HAND TO BEAT."
—TERRY C. JOHNSTON

BAD RIVER

BERKLEY

$7.99 USA
$10.99 CAN

ISBN 978-0-593-43772-8

DYNAMITE!

"All right, I can see you're getting hungry," Sam said quietly. "Let's go get you fed."

He unwrapped the stallion's reins from the iron hitch rail. Doc jerked hard against the reins.

"Okay, take it easy," Sam said.

He would have said more, but before he could . . .

In the shack behind the saloon, JR Claypool wrestled with the crate the men had left there. "Damn it!" he said aloud, fumbling with a long wooden match he'd taken from his swallowtail coat pocket. He struck the match on the crate and held the flaring tip up to read the large red letters one at a time. "D-y-n-a—!"

"Oh! Hell no!" he shouted.

. . . On the dirt street, Sam and Doc both felt the earth explode and hurl them forward, end over end. The street rippled and writhed beneath them like some monstrous snake, uprooting the iron hitch rail, sending horses and all tumbling, rolling and sliding on their sides. Flaming pieces of building material showered down, littering the street.

Broken glass and slivers of wood framing blew past like wind-driven rain from where the saloon had stood seconds before. Tumbling horses screamed in fear and pain. Cave bats out foraging in the night fell dead on the ground amid broken furniture and burning fabric.

"Doc!" Sam shouted into the fire and falling debris.

The big stallion, shaking, rose from the dirt on wobbly legs. As Sam struggled to lift himself to his feet, he realized he couldn't hear a sound. The world around him had turned as silent as death. He fell back down on his stomach, watching from ground level as Doc plodded toward him, silently, slowly, unevenly. The world turned black. . . .

BAD RIVER

—◆—

Ralph Cotton

BERKLEY
New York

BERKLEY
An imprint of Penguin Random House LLC
penguinrandomhouse.com

BERKLEY and the BERKLEY & B colophon
are registered trademarks of Penguin Random House LLC.

ISBN: 9780593437728

First Edition: October 2021

Printed in the United States of America
1 3 5 7 9 10 8 6 4 2

For Mary Lynn, of course

Part 1

Part I

Prologue

Arizona Ranger Sam Burrack, known by many as simply the ranger, looked around the bleak, dusty yard of Yuma Prison. Midday sun beat down mercilessly from a glaring white sky. On a high catwalk some thirty yards away, two guards stood looking down at him, their rifles at port arms as he walked across the hard, hot ground. Horses were forbidden inside the main wall surrounding the compound.

Understandable, Sam thought.

Inside the compound, there were no hitch rails, no water troughs—nothing to accommodate either man or animal sharing an interest in sudden flight. His horse Doc, a big, rangy dapple roan stallion, stood at an iron hitch rail. Doc stared after the ranger through a stone archway lined with thick iron grillwork.

From a black patch of shade beneath a roof overhang, sweaty faces watched the ranger cross the yard, their eyes moving slowly, keeping pace with his footsteps. A dirty hand in the shape of a pistol reached up and pointed through the blackness. A lowered voice behind it whispered, *"Bang!"*

Another voice whispered, "You missed!"

Other voices chuffed in the darkness.

"If I had a gun, I wouldn't miss. I'd kill him so quick, his shadow would still be standing in the street," the first voice added with bitterness.

"Is he the one who put you here, Dallas?" another voice asked.

"No," the bitter voice replied. The voice belonged to a New Mexican–Sonora outlaw named Dallas Curio. "But he's wearing a badge. That draws him a killing straight up, far as I'm concerned." Curio grinned in the blackness. "I'm out of here in two weeks. Any lawman gets in my sights, I can't wait to burn him down."

Across the yard, the ranger walked onto a board-walk, through an open door, into a long barrack-style adobe building reinforced with block and steel rods. As he walked down a long hallway, every sound carried an echo of metal.

A guard stood up from a low wooden bench and stared at the ranger. "Let me guess, Ranger," he said with a slight Mexican accent. "You're here to see Hueto Escalante again, eh?" His tunic was unbuttoned against the smothering heat. Sweat streaked down his bare chest. "I'm guessing you've brought him more tobacco."

"You're right on both counts, Victor," Sam said.

The big guard nodded him down the long, shadowy passage.

Sam took off his pearl gray sombrero and ran his free hand back through his wet, sweaty hair.

The guard, Mexican-American Victor Cafferty, gave a weak smile. "Hot, ain't it?" he said. He gave a dark little laugh and seemed to take some strange satisfaction in others being as hot and miserable as himself.

Sam nodded and walked down the hallway to where

Hueto Escalante stood against his cell door, his hands sitting at chest height, wrapped around the bars.

"I thought it was you I heard out there, Ranger," he said. "Have you brought me some smoking tobacco?"

"I have, same as always," said Sam.

He reached into his shirt pocket and pulled out a bag of chopped tobacco. Hueto watched with eager eyes. Sam added, "I'm told you have information for me this time."

He jiggled the tobacco bag in his hand for Hueto to see. Hueto almost reached through the bars, but he hesitated, then stopped when he saw the look on the ranger's face.

The ranger extended the bag to him. The outlaw took it and opened the drawstring with trembling fingers. He sniffed the contents of the bag and closed his eyes for a second. Opening them, he smiled and said, "No matter what others say about you, Ranger, you do all right by me."

Sam watched him take a crudely carved four-inch-long wooden pipe and dip it into the bag.

When Hueto was ready, he held the pipe close to the iron door. Sam struck a wooden match and held it through the bars. Hueto lit the pipe, drew a deep breath of smoke, and held it in his chest before letting it go in a gray stream.

"*Santa Madre . . .*" he whispered, savoring the smoke. He crossed himself, pipe in hand. "You always bring me good tobacco, *mi amigo*."

"Not after today I won't, Hueto," Sam said. "I've looked out for you the whole year you've been here. But I'm not your amigo. Today you either point me toward your Cowboy pals—Cree Sims, Giles Tillis and Earl

Dupree—or I won't waste my time coming back here.
¿Comprende?"

"*Sí*, I understand," said Hueto. "Take it easy." He
drew on the smudged wooden pipe and let out another
breath of smoke. "Today, I will tell you everything. All
you want to hear about where my pards are lying low."

Sam nodded. "Go on. I'm listening."

Hueto raised a grimy finger for emphasis. "First, I
must tell you why I tell you today, but never before."

"If I leave *right now*, these matches go with me,
Hueto," Sam said, warning him to get on with it. He
took a step back and added, "Unless you prefer a good
chew . . ." He let his words go unfinished.

"All right, Ranger!" Hueto said, speeding up. "I tell
you today because I have learned that Kura Stabitz is
now riding with them.

"Stabitz," said Sam, "the Russian Assassin."

"You have heard of him, I see," said Hueto. He gave
a sharp smile of contempt. "Now that the Russian is
riding with the Cowboys, I will tell you where they
are—but only because I know now that if Cree Sims
doesn't kill you, Stabitz will. He will kill you and bleed
you like a pig at slaughter."

"That's an ugly idea, Hueto," Sam said with a flat
expression. "Now tell me where I'll find these men, and
I'll leave you here to enjoy this *warm* weather."

"That is not funny, Ranger," Hueto snapped. He
stepped in closer to the bars. "The Cowboys will kill
you when you go there, and I will laugh and smoke my
pipe when I hear about it!"

"Then tell me where they're hiding," Sam said.
"We'll see how this all pans out."

Hueto glanced all around the long hallway and lowered his voice as he spoke.

"They are in Río Malo," he said.

"Bad River," Sam translated. "I've been through there. What a quiet little place to hide."

"*Sí*, but even so, they are no longer hiding. They are living in the caves above the old Quaker mission. They have started a new gang there. The Bad River Gunmen they call themselves. Many others have joined them. They are robbing banks, payrolls and trains on both sides of the border." He paused with a longing expression. "If only I could be riding with them these days."

"You would give up your Cowboy's red sash to be a Bad River Gunman?"

"*Sí*, right now I would," said the outlaw. "What good is it for me to be a Red Sash Cowboy if I am stuck in this sweat hole for four more years?"

"I always knew Bad River to have a strong company of *rurales* there, not to mention a company of *federale* cavalry nearby."

"You are right, Ranger," said Hueto. "But times have changed in the Mexico Valley. The surrounding hombres who made up the *rurales* have gone into the cities for jobs or off to work in the French silver mines. The cavalry has gone to fight the roaming Apache. All that's left are the local *políticos*." He grinned. "The Cowboys have always found local officials eager and willing to take bribes and allow them to do as they please. The new Bad River Gunmen have learned their crooked skills from us Cowboys—we are the best there is!"

"So this new gang has bought off the local leaders," Sam said, "and the longer your pals live there, the worse it's going to get."

Hueto shrugged. "And what you need to know is that anytime the law gets close, the town leaders warn the Gunmen." He grinned. "The gang spread out into the limestone mountains until their pursuers gave up their search. It is much better treatment than they get on this side of the border."

Sam watched him grin again and say, "It is unfortunate for the citizens, but what is unfortunate for some, is always good for others, eh?" He thumbed his sweaty chest. "I'm one of the *others*. I only hope it lasts long enough for me to get out and get my hands in this sweet pie," he said.

"If I were you, Hueto, I wouldn't count on the Bad River Gunmen being there when you get out. Not if the law on either side of the border can help it." He backed away a little, knowing that information was all he was going to find out today. What more did he need to know? He'd already heard stories of what was going on up in Bad River, in and above the wide Valley of Mexico. Hearing it from Hueto was just sound confirmation—as good as he would find anywhere at this point.

Hueto eyed him up and down, watching as a spark of interest lit up the ranger's eyes at the mention of Bad River.

"So what do you do now, Ranger?" he said. "Are you going to stick your nose to the ground and go after the Bad River Gunmen with a mad-on that hell would not have?"

"No, Hueto," Sam said. He ran his fingers back through his damp hair and placed his wide sombrero atop his head. "When I leave here today, I may quit being a ranger. I told my captain I'd come see you today— one last trip to find out what you might want to tell me. Now I might take off my badge."

Hueto stared in disbelief.

"You might leave the rangers?" he asked.

"That's right," said Sam. "I just wanted to hear what you had to tell me before I go."

"Where will you go?" Hueto asked, fishing for any new information he might be able to pass along.

"I'm taking myself a horse spread outside of Nogales. I might settle down and take it easy. Get some time for myself."

"For yourself? *Ha!* I don't believe you, Ranger." Hueto said.

"Suit yourself," Sam said. He half-turned to leave, before adding, "Don't tell anybody what I've told you here today."

"No, of course not," said Hueto. He looked shocked. "I never tell anybody anything."

"Gracias," Sam said, satisfied the tidbit would spread, obscuring his real plans.

"Hey, wait a minute, Ranger," Hueto said quickly, stopping him. "Give me the matches in your pocket. Call it a farewell gift?" He gave a wider grin.

"I don't think so, Hueto," Sam said. "If you fooled around and set yourself afire, I'd never forgive myself." He drew the sombrero's string up under his chin.

"No, wait, Ranger! Hey! Listen!" said Hueto, watching the ranger walk away down the hallway. "I'll be careful! I swear I will!"

Without reply, Sam made his way to the open front door. He nodded at the guards inside the iron-grilled archway, then continued out across the boardwalk, onto the hot, dusty street. Moments later, he was on his way to Coyle Siding, seven miles away, the nearest telegraph facility outside of Yuma Prison. The prison had its own telegraph room and operator, but there would have been too many watching eyes and listening ears among guards and convicts alike to suit him. He needed to let his captain know *in private* what a nickel bag of tobacco had just bought him.

In Coyle Siding, when he'd finished wiring his captain and received an answer, he stood beside Doc at a water trough while the big roan drew his fill of tepid water. His captain's wired reply had given him two options. Either withdraw and abandon the Bad River case until other rangers could be sent to assist him. Or ride into Bad River, maintain a low profile and keep a close watch on the gang. If their next robbery was on the American side of the border, there would be more rangers or federal deputies sent to assist him, the captain's reply assured him.

So much for that. . . . He shredded the telegraph, wadded it up and shoved it inside his shirt for now. He had no idea how many gunmen might be waiting in Bad River or on which side of the border their next robbery would take place. He thought on it for a second. Anything else he needed to know, he'd have to hear from someone in Bad River. A piece of information here and there. Soon the pieces would all come together like a mental road map.

There were already several murderers and thieves on a Wanted list that he carried in his saddlebags. If he could eliminate any of those names on his way to Bad River, he would, but Cree Sims, Giles Tillis and Earl Dupree had been at the top of that list for the past year. He wanted to get to Bad River while his information on their whereabouts was still fresh. He would add the name Kura Stabitz to the list tonight by the light of his campfire.

He knew he wouldn't ride into the town of Bad River and find these gunmen standing there waiting for him. But with some effort, he would find them nearby, maybe on the limestone mountaintops. He'd smoke them out like rats if he had to. "All right. . . . that's the work," he told himself, "like it or not."

"Doc," he said to the roan in a lowered voice, "it sounds like Captain Jamison is telling us we're on our own."

The big roan raised his wet muzzle from the trough. He gave Sam a curious look, then stood staring straight ahead, feeling the familiar draw of the cinch as it came up snug and comfortable against his full belly. He could hear the familiar sound of metal on metal as Sam checked his rifle and slid it into its boot against Doc's side and swung up easily into the saddle.

The roan gathered himself at the slightest touch of the reins, the slightest shift of the ranger's knees on his sides. He turned onto the dusty street.

"At least there's plenty of water where we're headed," Sam muttered to him.

They rode out of Coyle Siding at an easy gait, horse and rider outlined against a red-streaked evening sky.

Chapter 1

———

"Shoot him again, Earl!" Giles Tillis shouted, jerking his horse to a halt beside Earl Dupree. They stared down at the wounded guard struggling in a bloody belly crawl up the rocky hillside toward the trail. A moment earlier, Earl Dupree's rifle shot had sent the guard flying from his saddle, tumbling down over the rocks. A French pistol had flown from the guard's hand; it lay just out of his reach.

"I've got him," Dupree replied, jacking a fresh round into his rifle chamber. He looked down at the struggling guard and chuffed. "Crazy bastard. What does he think, if he gets that gun he'll come back up here and shoot all of us?"

"I don't know what he's thinking," Tillis said in a sharp tone. He glanced around at the roar of gunshots on the mining plateau behind them. Bodies of two mine workers and a guard lay scattered down the rocks. "Are you going to shoot him or not?" He cocked the big Colt in his hand.

"Hold your water, Giles. I said I've got him." Dupree raised his rifle and took aim, wondering for just a second if Giles Tillis meant to aim his Colt at *him* or the wounded guard.

The guard had managed to reach his pistol and place a weak hand on it. Dupree's shot ripped through his chest and slammed him backward.

"You were fooling around," said Tillis as the sound of the shot echoed across the rocky mountainsides. "People fool around, things go wrong. We need to make a good showing here."

He motioned his Colt toward the mine office, where their gunmen were loading bags of cash and silver onto a freight wagon. Guards and workers watched in silence as rifles pointed at them threateningly.

Earl Dupree chuckled behind his bandanna mask. "Jesus, Giles! *Fooling around?*" he said. "What are these workers going to say? 'While *some* gunmen loaded the wagon, others were out here *fooling around*, playing a harmonica and dancing a jig'?"

Tillis took a breath and tapped his pistol barrel against his masked cheek. "Watch your bandanna, Earl," he said to Dupree. "Take this *serious.*"

"Hellfire, I reckon *I will!*" said Dupree, straightening his mask higher up on his nose. His rifle swung up to his shoulder and he fired shot after shot into the dead guard's body. When his smoking gun finally clicked on an empty chamber, he propped the butt of it on his thigh. "Is that serious enough, *pard*?" he asked. Gray smoke curled up from his rifle barrel.

"It'll do," said Tillis. "Reload. Let's get going."

He turned his horse toward the mine office as their gunmen stood around the loaded wagon and waited for orders.

Inside the office building, mine manager Bob Udall stared out through the dusty window in the direction of the rifle shots. In the room behind the window, the Gunmen's leader, Raeburn "Cree" Sims, stood at ease, a hip propped on the edge of a large oaken desk. He'd pulled his mask down below his chin. A Colt hung loosely in his right hand.

"Bob. Hey, *Bob!*" he said to the manager, raising his voice to get the man's attention. "Look around here."

When Udall turned from the window and faced him, Sims tipped his gun barrel up and down toward him. "You've got to keep your hands up and stay away from the window," Sims said. "This is supposed to be a robbery, remember?"

"Oh, I'm sorry! I forget myself!" Udall said, nervously raising his hands chest high.

The Russian Assassin stood near the office door, a big Remington revolver cocked, aimed and ready. The look on his face indicated he was well prepared to shoot anybody for any reason. A stiff four-inch-long black spade goatee covered his chin. He spoke in a gruff tone to the manager. "Maybe next time I shoot you in the head—you won't forget?"

The manager's face turned stark white. His lips trembled.

"*Damn*, Stabitz!" Sims cut in. He looked the Russian up and down. "Take a breath. Ease up some."

"I am eased up," said Stabitz in a coarse tone. He stared hard at Bob Udall as he spoke to Sims.

"Okay, better still, go on outside with the others, check the wagon," Sims said. "We're fixin' to go."

Stabitz only nodded, still staring at Udall. But he let the hammer down on the big Remington. Without reply, he turned and stepped out the front door.

"*Holy God!*" said Udall as the door closed behind the Russian. He clasped a hand to his chest, catching his breath. "What was the meaning of all that? I had no warning he was coming with you!"

Sims gave him a level stare. "We don't ask your opinion on how we pull off a robbery, Bob."

"No, of course not," said Udall. "But there're bodies lying out there. I was told there would be no killing!"

"That's too bad," said Sims. "But I don't know how to stop it without tipping our hand. Some people have to be martyrs."

The manager was still shaking terribly. Sims took note of it and said, "You ain't going to die on me, are you, Bob?"

"No, I'll be okay now," Udall said. "It's just that I wasn't expecting him to be with you. What was I to think, he shows up in my office? He's a known *assassin* after all."

Sims considered Udall's words for a moment, then gave a little chuff and said, "All right, I see how you might have thought I brought him here to kill you to make this look good. But you were wrong. If I wanted you dead, I wouldn't need Stabitz. I'd kill you myself."

"I can see that *now*," said Udall, settling a little. He swallowed a lump in his throat and pointed at his desk. "There's a bottle of whiskey in the drawer there. . . . Would you, please?"

Sims nodded. Stepping around the desk, he took a bottle from the top drawer, walked back and handed it to Udall. Udall threw back a long swig and let out a whiskey hiss.

Sims watched him intently with a slight smile. "I'll be better at this next time," said Udall, settling, wiping a hand across his mouth. "That man just gives me the willies, is all."

"*Next time* won't happen for a year or more," said

Sims. "We have to keep things staggered out, not draw attention too much to any one place. There're likely a hundred mines or more up here within spitting distance. One's as fat and rich as the next." He took the bottle back from Udall, corked it and stood it on the desk.

"I understand," said Udall. "You set it up with the manager, rob some of the better ones about once a year. Rest of the time, you keep the other bandits away." He grinned. "It's a pretty sweet deal."

"Yes, it is," said Sims, "so long as everybody keeps their mouths shut and doesn't let themselves get rattled if anybody comes asking questions."

"If they ask, one gang of masked riders looks the same as the next," said Udall. "All these mines get robbed every once in a while anyway. It's a business cost these Frenchmen know they have to pay. But robbers don't have to get all of it. So what if we take something for ourselves once in a while?"

"That's the spirit, Bob." Sims grinned. "This is our third French mine. We'll get things running smoother in no time."

"Yes, sir, we will," said Udall. He gave a shaky grin, still settling his nerves. "You needn't worry any about us managers on this end keeping our mouths shut."

"I know that, Bob," Sims said in a peaceful tone. "Believe me, I'm not worried about any of you at all."

Outside the mine office, two men resting double-barreled shotguns across their laps sat on the wooden seat of the loaded freight wagon. Five other gunmen, including Kura Stabitz, had mounted their horses and gathered around the loaded wagon, ready to go. Their rifles still covered the miners and guards. All of the captive employees still held their hands up at chest height. One man let his hands droop a little, until he caught the eye of a mounted gunman named Harry Hanson.

"Keep 'em up!" Hanson shouted. "We're about done! You don't want to die this late in the game!"

Every captive's hands rose six inches higher.

Hearing Hanson warn the captives, Tillis and Dupree rode in from the edge of the mine yard.

"The hell's taking so long?" said Dupree. "We ought to be down the road by now."

As if on cue, a single gunshot roared from inside the mine office. All heads turned in unison.

"Uh-oh," Dupree said in a lowered tone.

All eyes watched Cree Sims step out of the office onto the dusty plank walkway. He corked the bottle of whiskey he'd taken from atop Udall's desk as he walked to his horse and stepped up into the saddle.

"Driver!" he called out in a strong voice to the man holding the wagon reins. "Turn this rig around. We're burning daylight!"

The driver, a new outlaw named Eli Denton, let down the long wooden brake handle and slapped the reins on the backs of the four big wagon horses pulling the heavy load. The animals stooped low into the weight to get the wagon moving, then pulled forward, raising dust in a quick wide circle, and headed out of the yard toward the trail.

The mounted gunmen set their horses, keeping the captive mine employees covered until the wagon was thirty yards away.

"All you squareheads, get back to work!" Sims shouted at the miners and guards. As he shouted, he turned his horse and rode a few yards away while the employees hurried to the mine office to get under cover and to see what the gunshot was about.

The rest of the mounted gunmen rode along with Sims. They stopped and gathered around him when he reined his horse down and looked back at the mine office.

Giles Tillis gave Sims a questioning look.

"That's right, Tillis," Sims said in a harsh tone. "He's deader than hell." He looked from face to face among the horsemen gathered around him. "Everybody hear that? The man back at the mine is *deader than hell*! He's dead because he was too *damn nervous* to live. Think about it on the way home. If you're born of a nervous spirit, you're riding with the wrong bunch."

The riders nodded in agreement. Their bandanna masks came down from their faces.

"We're none of us what you would call born of a nervous spirit, are we, pards?" Earl Dupree called out.

The horsemen laughed.

"Not a back-shooting one of us!" a strong voice shouted in reply as the contingent rolled on.

Near dark, the men on horseback followed the wagon as they weaved through a labyrinth of broken limestone boulders streaked with ancient lava spills. The men began looking all around, confused and suspicious. Instead of staying on the same trail they had followed to the mine from Bad River, Cree Sims had ridden in front of the line and gestured to the wagon driver to turn the rig into a steep, wide ravine. Above, on both sides of the ravine, riflemen stepped into sight.

"This is a straight-up ambush!" Dupree whispered

to Tillis, riding beside him. He started to swing his rifle up from his boot toward Cree Sims.

Giles Tillis stopped him. "No, wait. It's not an ambush!" Tillis said.

He spoke loud enough for not only Dupree to hear him, but the rest of the men as well. Everybody's hand froze on their guns. But they held their fire, glancing back and forth at one another, tense, ready.

At the sight of the gunmen on the upper edges of the ravine, Cree Sims seemed to have vanished. The men looked around as they wondered what was going on. Now that they had listened to Giles Tillis and not started shooting, Sims reappeared from a rocky crevice and held his horse steady at the front of the wagon.

"All of you, listen up!" he called out. "This is the best part of this whole deal!"

The men watched him closely. Sims put his horse into a slow walk along the trail beside the wagon, right in the midst of the mounted gunmen, something no one would have done if this really were an ambush. He held sheets of paperwork above his head.

"Here is the value of all the smelted silver, raw ore and cash ingots we've got riding in this wagon. There's also a hefty amount of U.S. dollars and Mexican *pesos* that were headed to the bank in Bad River." He grinned. "The French mining company demanded it all be taken somewhere *safe*!"

Cautious laughter rose among the men. Sims continued. "Everything I totaled up here comes to a little over two hundred thousand dollars!" The men fell silent, stunned by the large amount. Sims waved the paperwork overhead with a dark chuckle. "That's the whole day's pay on paper," he added with a dark laugh. "Any of you want to go over all this, just say so. I'll bring it right to you. Otherwise, you can take every word I'm telling you as the living gospel."

A hand went up. All heads turned toward a newer gunman named Gus Baker, a killer out of Missouri. "I'll take a look at it," Baker said, "since you don't mind."

"Mind? Hell no, I don't mind," said Sims. "I was hoping somebody would ask." He gigged his horse back to where Baker sat on his mount, giving him a level gaze.

Two other riders backed their horses a step to make room.

"You Missourians always like being shown, don't you?" said Sims.

"Not that I don't trust you, Cree," said the new man with a half-smile.

"Here it is," said Sims. "Check it out good."

He held the shipping papers out with his left hand. When Baker reached for them, Sims's right hand pulled the trigger on his big Colt, blasting Baker from the saddle.

In the dead silence that hung over the roar of the shot, Earl Dupree leaned in his saddle toward Giles Tillis, who was mounted right beside him.

"I saw that coming a mile away," Dupree whispered, muffling a laugh.

"Good for you. Now shut up," Tillis leaned over and whispered in reply.

With his Colt smoking in his hand, Sims called, "Anybody else want to check all this out?" When no one replied, he called out, "Good. Looks like we all understand one another."

He gestured at a wide crevice in the rock wall of the ravine. As the men looked on, an elderly Mexican wearing a long serape led a large black-and-tan donkey and two saddled horses out onto the rocky path. Two sets of saddlebags hung across the mule's back. The two horses looked rested and ready for the trail.

"Everybody listen close so you won't have questions later on," Sims said. He motioned at the gunmen along the sides of the ravine. "These hombres are going to give us a hundred and eighty thousand U.S. dollars in exchange for this two hundred-thousand-dollar shipment. We leave here with all cash. We don't have to transport this heavy stuff. We don't have to hide it, protect it or nothing else. We'll be done with it." He looked from one silent face to the next, then said, "If anybody has a problem with that, raise your hand like Gus Baker did, and we'll straighten it all out."

No hands were raised.

"Good," said Sims. "When we get to Bad River, we're going to cut this money up and everybody takes their share. Until we get there, I'm standing personally responsible for keeping our money safe."

He paused for a few seconds. When he heard no objections, he continued. "We're making a couple of stops on our way home. The last couple of miles we're going to ride into town one and two at a time from different directions."

As Sims spoke, the old man handed the mule's reins to him. Sims pulled the mule to the side. The old man led the two horses over to the wagon. Seeing him coming, the wagon driver set the long wooden brake handle and hooked the wagon reins on it.

"*Caballos para ustedes,*" the old Mexican man said to the two in the wagon seat.

"*¡Gracias, viejo!*" said the wagon driver with a wide smile. He and the shotgun rider hurried down from the wagon and took the two horses from him. He looked at the shotgun rider and said in a lowered tone, "I thought we'd be stuck on this hard seat all the way home."

"I'm damn glad we're not," said Chaz Campo. "I think I'm going to like riding with the Bad River Gunmen."

"Yeah, me too," Denton replied. He looked toward the tall donkey, the saddlebags stuffed with cash. "Looks like the pay ain't going to be nothing to complain about either."

"I do feel a little bad that the new man got himself shot to hell," said the shotgun rider.

"No job is perfect," said Eli Denton. "Anyway, you won't feel so bad about it once we're back in town, with some fancy woman with shiny nails and smoothed-down legs rubbing all over you."

"Hellfire, stop it," said the shotgun rider. "I feel better already, just thinking about it."

They laughed. Two men from the old Cowboy Gang, Jake and Hugh Barret, laughed with them.

"It's going to be a hoot," Hugh said.

Chapter 2

———————

Above the Mexico Valley

Five miles outside of Bad River, on a secluded ledge of limestone and ancient volcanic lava rock, the ranger and the big roan camped out for three days, taking in the town's usual comings and goings. So far, Sam had seen nothing out of the ordinary—that was, nothing looking or sounding like a town with its arms spread in welcome to a bunch of gunmen.

Patience, he reminded himself as he had every time he looked down on the switchback trail below, or scanned the rugged, junglelike valley foothills and shimmering lakes through his battered telescope. *Nothing going on . . .* He squinted and spit, then closed the telescope between his palms and shoved it into his duster pocket.

Yes, patience, he repeated.

On the inside edge of the stone shelf, Doc stood picketed in the shade of an overhang, grazing on wild grass that, true to its name, had taken purchase in a long, soil-filled crevice and propagated from there. Other overhangs and grass-filled fissures dotted the mountainside, but none was as wide as this one. Iron and wooden wheel scars had worn trail ruts across the thick limestone shelf, showing signs of wayfaring humanity from hundreds of years past.

The impressions left by wheel and hoof on hard stone were not as distinguishable as the countless deeper trails cutting across distant miles of low, sunken plain lands and soft, marshy green flora.

The Old Spanish trail? Conquistadores . . . ? Sam speculated.

He sat observing the deeper-cut trails across the valley from his lookout spot between two broken boulders. Broad patches of wild yucca stood at random on the mountainsides, their bayonet-like blades stirring on a soft breeze.

Taller cacti stood on thick, stiff carpets of spiky barrel cacti and boot-ripping ground cover. Yesterday, a large desert hawk had swooped in and landed silently on the boulder to Sam's right to take up watch. The big bird appeared to share an interest or curiosity in the same comings and goings on the steep mountainside. Sam did nothing to chase the bird away, yet when a gunshot rang out farther down the mountain, the bird gave him a hard, sharp stare, rose effortlessly on its big wings and was gone.

All right! Rifle in hand, Sam stood in a crouch and looked around the edge of a boulder toward the waning echo of the gunshot. *A pistol shot*, he told himself. As soon as he identified the type of gun, he saw a thin rise of gun smoke drift up from behind the cover of rock near a switchback trail below. *Here we go*, he told himself, dusting the seat of his trousers, hurrying to where Doc had stopped grazing and stood looking at him.

The big roan stallion stood still as Sam slipped off the rope picket, raised the bridle onto his head and saddled him. One pistol shot in an otherwise silent land was no cause for alarm, but it was reason enough to ride down the hundred-yard distance and see what had brought it about. When he'd snugged the cinch and shoved his rifle into the saddle boot, he led Doc across the stone shelf and down onto a steep, perilous path where no horse should have been ridden. Doc took the path in careful yet unhesitant stride.

"That a boy," Sam whispered, keeping the sound of his and Doc's walking as quiet as he could.

When they stopped at the switchback where the ranger believed the gunshot had sounded from, Sam stopped the stallion and rubbed his nose. Doc had not been with him long. Sam's usual stallion was a big Appaloosa named Black Pot, who was enjoying a well-earned rest in the ranger stables back in Nogales. It had taken only a short time for Sam to realize this roan was one smart, trail-savvy cayuse—the kind of horse that always seemed to know what was going on around him with little or no guidance.

You'll see, Ranger, Doc's former owner, gambler turned road agent Henry Wise, had told Burrack. *Doc will never let you down! Will you, Doc?*

Sam recalled Wise reaching out for one last rub on Doc's nose. Sam thought he'd seen the old gambler's eyes water. That was the day Wise had climbed aboard a railcar wearing handcuffs while Sam led Doc to a hitch rail where Black Pot stood waiting. Two big, tough stallions at the same rail, neither of them balking at the sight of the other.

Sam thought about it.

"Good job," he whispered to the big roan. He often wondered what accounts Doc might give of his life, if only he could talk.

He led the horse off the hillside, onto the trail, staying to the softer inner edge where their steps were muffled. But before they had gone twenty feet, the shrill sound of a woman's voice called out fearfully, "Help, please! Somebody! *Help!*"

Doc's ears perked up at the sound. Sam hurried, drawing his Colt and keeping it in hand. He kept his eyes on everything around him. When he reached a turn in the trail, he picked up his pace and saw a young woman kneeling over an elderly man lying flat on his back.

Seeing Sam and Doc hurrying toward her, the woman called out louder, "Father has been *shot*! Please help us!"

"Now, now, my daughter," the man said, "I'll be all right. There's been an accident . . . just an accident." He looked up at the ranger as Sam and Doc halted.

Sam lifted a canteen from his saddle horn and stooped down beside the young woman. *An accident . . . ?* Sam looked at the bloody wound on the man's shoulder. A small pool of blood seeped and spread beneath him.

Sam watched the man lift a hand toward the woman as if to comfort her. Sam noted the man wore a faded black collarless shirt.

"Who shot you?" Sam asked, looking back and forth between the man and the young woman.

Together Sam and the woman helped the older man sit up. Once Sam made sure the bullet hadn't hit anything vital, they raised the man to his feet and assisted him over to the buggy wheel, where they leaned him against it.

"It wasn't her," the man said as if he needed to make that crystal clear. He nodded toward the lower hillside. "It was a young man. . . . He's gone now."

"Do you know the man?" Sam asked.

Neither the man nor the young woman replied. The man gestured toward the buggy. "Under the seat there," he said, speaking to the woman. "My bag of supplies . . ." His voice trailed off.

"Yes, Father." The woman hurried to the buggy, brought back a leather drawstring bag and opened it.

The man took the canteen, drank from it and handed it back. He watched the woman raise a handful of bandages from the bag with one hand and a small, ornately engraved silver flask with the other.

"Careful, my daughter," the man said quietly, gesturing to the small flask.

The woman dropped the flask back into the bag and pulled out more bandages.

Sam took the bloody shirt from the man's back and laid it to the side. As he folded some bandaging to press against the bleeding wound, he asked, "Are you a preacher, mister?"

The man saw the ranger's badge on Sam's chest.

"I am a retired priest, Ranger," the man said. "That is to say, I am retired from my order." He offered a pained smile. "My name is Lawrence Merita. Many people here still call me Father Lawrence. This is where I live and where I served many years." He glanced at the young woman. "This is Sara."

"Ma'am," the ranger said, touching the brim of his sombrero.

The young woman gave him a courteous nod in reply.

"Mexico is home to us both," the old priest continued. "I have more family and friends here than anywhere else on earth."

"I see," Sam replied, placing pressure on the bandage he'd pressed to the man's bleeding wound. He hadn't asked for such a broad explanation, but it was good to see the man holding up well, talking, sounding clear minded. He looked at the young woman.

"When I first heard you call him Father, I thought . . ."

"Yes, I understand," the young woman said. She turned her eyes away from him and looked down.

Something wasn't right about all this, Sam decided. He wrapped bandages around the man's chest firm enough to exert pressure and slow the bleeding. Was the gunshot really an accident? He looked down the mountainside toward the next lower switchback. The young man who'd been involved was gone. He hadn't stayed around to see if this retired priest, Father Lawrence, was all right. He'd left the old man lying wounded on the ground. The story didn't fit.

Sam looked at the young woman as he finished bandaging the old man's wound. She seemed to read the growing doubt in his eyes.

"He's my betrothed, Antonio Villa," she said. "He didn't mean to shoot Father. They were both trying to—"

"No, he's *not* your betrothed!" the old priest cut in adamantly, raising his voice. "Antonio Villa is not your betrothed! You were raised together like brother and sister. You are both too young to be married! And what you are about to say is not what happened here, daughter!"

But the young woman went on. "They were both trying to take the gun from each other. Neither of them meant for the gun to go off."

"It's true, Ranger," the man agreed, quieting a little. "Antonio is a well-meaning young man. I raised him. I raised them both."

Sam foresaw that a long story that they had no time for was about to emerge. This man needed help—not trail help, but *doctor* help.

"Listen to me, both of you," he said. He picked up his canteen and stood, then poured water over his hands.

Doc stepped over for Sam to hang the canteen on the saddle horn.

"I don't know what went on here," Sam said. He gave a rub on Doc's nose. "If it's none of my business, so be it. But right now we need to get to town and have this wound taken care of." He looked pointedly at the old priest. "Am I going to have trouble with this *well-meaning* young man if I escort the two of you to Bad River? I don't like being ambushed."

"No, no!" the young woman said quickly, shaking her head for emphasis. "Antonio is a good man. He would do nothing to hurt any of us. I swear it." A trace of a Spanish accent came into her voice.

"Don't swear, Sara," the old priest corrected her. Turning to the ranger, he added, "What she says is true. Antonio is a young man from a good Mexican-Irish family. He is somewhere right now, feeling terrible about what happened." He turned a strong gaze to the young woman. "I forbid this betrothal you speak of. But I know the boy's heart and spirit are good. I myself raised these two in the teachings of the Holy Mother Church." He crossed himself quickly. "There is no ambush awaiting us."

"Good," Sam said. "I'll escort you into Bad River, right to the doctor's front door." He liked the idea of riding into town with two well-known residents, instead of conspicuously arriving as a lone gunman.

"But what about you, Ranger?" the young woman asked. "How can we impose on you to ride with us to town?"

"You're not imposing, Miss Sara," the ranger said. "I'm riding through Bad River anyway."

"Why are you riding through Bad River?" the old priest asked, now looking at the ranger closely.

"I've come to the Valley of Mexico on business," Sam replied.

"Law business?" the old priest asked.

There was no point denying it, but if Sam could play it down, he would. "Yes, *law* business," he said. "Can we keep that between us for now?"

"I am used to keeping secrets, Ranger." The old priest smiled. "And I am familiar with the Matamoros Agreement between the United States and Mexico. You are allowed to come here and take back a fugitive from *Americana* law."

"You're right," Sam replied. "I'm taking some outlaws back to the States." He stopped there, hoping that was the end of it, but he quickly saw it wasn't.

"These fugitives," the old priest said, "who are they?" He watched the ranger's eyes closely.

"Just some cowboys," the ranger replied casually.

"*Cowboys?*" The old priest considered the word.

Sam saw there was more coming.

"These fugitives," the old priest asked, "are they working cowboys, like our Mexican vaqueros—honest range hands? Or are these the kind of Cowboys who wear red sashes and work only when it comes to taking something that does not belong to them or to gun down their fellow men?"

"I'm not the judge," Sam offered. "I only bring them to someone who is."

"Always do they come with you *peacefully*?" the priest asked.

Sam realized the priest knew better, so he wasn't going to mince words. "Seldom ever," Sam said flatly. "But they are always peaceful and quiet on the ride home."

Bad River—in Spanish, Río Malo—lay on a bed of deeply broken stone, surrounded by clinging evergreens, piercing assortments of ground cover and a patchwork of wild grass, which spread halfway up one of the taller mountainsides. At one end of town, a bullet-scarred boulder with the faded name Río Malo painted on it stood sixty feet high. It sat atop a deeply cut bank above the raging river of the same name.

Southern gambler J. Radlear Claypool stood out front of the German Ale and Whiskey House, smoking a thin Mexican cigar and taking in the pattern of evening shadow that stretched long on the dirt street. Across the road, he caught a glimpse of Antonio Villa walking his tired horse along an alley toward the livery barn. *What have we here . . . ?*

First checking to see if anyone else had spotted the young man, Claypool walked casually over and into the alley. Then he hurriedly caught up with Antonio near the big livery barn on the back edge of town.

"Kid, wait up," he called out in a lowered voice. "What are you doing here?"

"They sent me on ahead," said Antonio, without stopping.

"Sent you on ahead? Why? And just where are Sims

and the others?" Claypool asked, before the young man could answer. "I daresay every sporting man and painted woman in town has been waiting all day for them."

"I don't know why they sent me on in," Antonio said. He had an idea it was because he was new to the gang and Sims was stopping along the way at a place he didn't want a new man or any outsiders to know about. Antonio looked gravely at the gambler and said, "Something bad happened out on the trail, JR."

Claypool saw the ashen, frightened look on his face. "What are you saying? Did things go wrong? Was there no money?"

"No, nothing like that," said Antonio. "The job went well. We made plenty. You'll see."

"Thank goodness!" Claypool breathed relief.

"I shot Father Lawrence," Antonio blurted out. He started to cross himself but stopped, fearing it might look weak to a worldly man like JR Claypool.

"Wait a minute!" Claypool shook his head as if to clear it. "You . . . *shot* the old priest? Did you kill him?"

"No, but he is badly wounded. I didn't mean to shoot him," Antonio said. "We were arguing over a gun. It went off and shot him." He raised a hand slightly. "So help me, God, if he—"

"Shut up, kid," said Claypool. "Listen to me. Where was all this? How did it happen? I always thought you worshipped the old man."

"I did— I mean, I *do*!" said Antonio. "He has been a father to me since I was a baby! When my father left and my mother died, it was Father Lawrence who raised me." His face started breaking up. "Holy God, what have I done?"

"Easy, kid. Come with me," said Claypool. "Let's get

off the street. Start from the beginning. What happened?"

"I came upon Father Lawrence and Sara along the trail—"

"Came upon them?" said Claypool. "You mean, in the woods along the trail on a blanket or something?"

"No, they were in Father's buggy coming down the trail. I know what some people think about Father and Sara, but none of it is true."

"I know it's not. And if it is, whose business is it but his and hers?" Claypool gave a strange little smile as they walked along, evening growing darker around them.

"But it's not true!" Antonio said. "Anyway, we talked. Father knows Sara and I wish to marry. But he forbids her." He took a deep breath. "We started to argue. I drew my gun in anger to scare him. We struggled with the gun and it went off."

"You left them on the trail?" asked Claypool.

"Yes, I did," said Antonio. "But a lawman came along and was helping them."

"A *lawman*? This gets worse and worse," said Claypool.

"Yes, a lawman from Arizona," said Antonio. "I saw his badge. And I thought, 'What if Sims hears about all this?' I heard the lawman and Father talk as I hid behind a tree on the hillside. When I heard the lawman say he would ride with them to town, I slipped away and found my horse. I started to go back and find Sims and the others on the trail, but then I thought that might not be a good idea. So here I am."

"You did well coming here, kid. If I can say anything to the priest on your behalf and keep this from blowing up, I will. Sometimes it's best to stop something like this before it starts rolling downhill. The longer it rolls, the more cuniculi it uncovers."

"Conicu—*li*?" Antonio looked lost. "I don't know what that means."

Claypool chuckled a little. "Don't worry. Neither do I exactly. I am a bit drunk. Let's get out of sight before that sod-poling old priest and sweet lady Sara get here."

"I don't like you calling either of them names," Antonio said. "Stop it!"

"Consider me *stopped*," said Claypool, "and with sincere apologies." He patted Antonio's sweat-damp shoulder. "If you will allow me to say so, kid, I have learned in my many wanderings that the more you reveal the intricacies of your life to a person, the less command you have over their comments on it, be they kind or cutting."

"Should I not have told you anything?" Antonio asked. "I didn't know you were drunk."

"On the contrary," said Claypool. "If you can trust Father Lawrence, you can certainly trust me, drunk or sober."

"What does *sod-poling* mean?" Antonio asked as they walked along the alleyway into the livery barn.

Claypool grinned, staring straight ahead. *Just how dumb has the old priest raised this boy to be?*

"Never mind, kid," he said. "If you don't know by now, let's hope you never find out." He changed the subject by looking at the splatter of dried blood on Antonio's shirtsleeve and a streak of it smeared across his chin. "Is that the priest's blood?" Claypool asked with a lift of his chin.

"Yes, it is!" said Antonio, seeming to have noticed it for the first time.

"Here, give me your horse." Claypool took the reins from him. "Go to my room and clean yourself up. Borrow one of my shirts. When our wounded holy man arrives, I'll start trying to soften this mess. Nothing looks worse than you showing up with his blood on you."

Chapter 3

When JR Claypool had watered Antonio's horse and led it into a clean stall, he poured a heaping scoop full of mixed grains into a feed trough. While the horse ate with an enormous appetite, Claypool gave the animal a quick rubdown with a handful of fresh straw, and left. On his way to the Bad River Saloon, he looked up at his room in the Frenchman Hotel and saw lamplight glowing in the window. *Good* . . . The young man was doing as he'd been told.

Claypool didn't mind lending him a hand, taking his side in a matter such as this. He'd always found the boy likable, respectful. Now that Antonio was riding with the Bad River Gunmen, it went without saying that any favor given was a favor to be returned. But Claypool would deal with that later, he thought.

Inside the Bad River Saloon, a few men and bar girls half-stood at their tables. He saw disappointment when they recognized it was him, not Sims or any of the Bad River Gunmen returning to town.

"Damn the waiting!" said a Mexican teamster, plopping back down in his chair.

Patrons along the bar turned back to their glasses and bottles.

"It's only me, folks," Claypool said, walking to the bar. "Soon as I see our boys come riding, I'll stick my head in the door and tell yas." He motioned for the bartender and said, "Estez, *por favor*."

Before serving Claypool, the Mexican bartender Miro Estez looked at the saloon owner, Irish Mike Tuohy, who stood farther down the bar. The owner gave him an approving nod, knowing that once the Gunmen arrived and started spending money, Claypool's gambling would more than pay his bar tab.

Knowing Claypool's brand and its location on the shelf behind him, Estez reached back without looking and pulled down a bottle of Eagle Talon Whiskey. He stood it on the bar only a second before it vanished behind Claypool's swallowtail evening coat. In a flash, man and whiskey bottle were headed out the door.

"My tab, Estez," Claypool said in parting. The bartender tapped the side of his head.

"*Sí*," said Estez, "I got you, up here."

Irish Mike shook his head and went back to looking at recent shipping invoices.

Claypool left the saloon and walked quickly to the doctor's home, a modest wood-frame-and-adobe structure standing back off the street. Two cacti stood like sentinel doormen on either side of a stone walkway. An oil lamp glowed dimly on a front porch above an MD sign. Claypool sipped the whiskey and stood back off the street in the shadows.

For twenty minutes he watched the shadowy streets and buildings until he finally saw Father Lawrence's buggy come into sight. The young woman Sara was driving as the old priest slumped against her, his face

lowered. Looking all around—beside the buggy, behind the buggy and a few yards farther back on the
dusty trail—Claypool saw no sign of the Arizona lawman Antonio had told him about.

Even better, he told himself. *Here we go. . . .*

He corked the Eagle Talon bottle, stuck it back inside
his loose evening coat and leveled his medium-brimmed
straw skimmer atop his head.

"My goodness, Sara! What has happened? Is that Father Lawrence? Is he dead?"

"No, he is alive," Sara said, stopping the buggy.

"Yes, I am alive by God's grace," the old priest said,
straightening up.

"Thank God," Claypool said, still glancing at the
trail behind them, even as he hurried to help the priest
down from the buggy. "Let's get you inside, have the
doctor take care of you."

Together, JR and Sara helped Father Lawrence down.
As if seeing what was going on in the gambler's mind,
Sara said, "An *Americano* lawman from Arizona met us
on the trail and bandaged Father's wound."

"Oh?" said Claypool. "And where is this lawman
now?"

"He turned off the trail a ways back. I told him I
could get us here. He seemed to have things to do."

"Let's hope he's headed a long way from here," said
Claypool.

Sara and he gathered the priest between them and
started helping him along the stone walkway. The doctor's live-in Irish-Mexican housekeeper, Irena, came
from the front door with a large spotted hound at her
side and a raised lantern, which she held at shoulder
level.

"Who's there?" the woman called out.

"It's Father Lawrence, Irena," Sara called out to the other woman. "He's been shot!"

At the sound of Sara's voice, the hound gave a low growl, but stopped as the housekeeper touched the top of his head to silence him.

"Glory be to the Father!" the woman said with a lingering Irish brogue. "Get him in here! Dr. Jorgenson is asleep, but I'll wake him."

Looking around again as they continued along the walkway, Claypool said under his breath, "I'd feel better if we knew more about that lawman. This town already has a good sheriff, Showdown Art Forbes."

"Sheriff Forbes is retiring," Sara interjected.

"Yes," said JR, "but things being as they are here, with our new town council, we don't need any more lawmen snooping around."

"The ranger rode on, Mr. Claypool," Sara said. "I'm sure he has other things to do."

"That's good to hear," said Claypool as they and Irena helped Father Lawrence through the front door and onto a cot in one of the doctor's treatment rooms.

"I'm glad I was here to help you inside, Father." Claypool looked at Sara. "If everything is under control here, I must excuse myself long enough to take care of a little piece of business that has fallen upon me. That is, if there is nothing else I can do here for now?" He had already half-turned to the front door. "I shall return shortly, however."

"Go, please. We have things in hand here," said Sara, who did not see why Claypool had been there in the first place.

Claypool gazed at the priest. A knowing looked passed between them.

"Go, JR," Father Lawrence said. "I'm sure what you

must do is just as important as watching the good doctor treat this *annoying* wound."

"I assure you I shall return hastily," Claypool said.

He touched his hat brim and left. Of course, he would return in time to listen to the priest and Sara's version of what had happened—to make sure the word *accident* was used many times in telling it. He hurried up the dark street on foot and slipped into the door of the livery barn. He threw a bridle on the first horse he came to, led it from the barn and rode it away bareback out of town.

When he returned, he would smooth away any hard feelings caused by Antonio Villa's actions. After all, even the wounded party himself had called it an accident. *Lucky no one was killed,* he reminded himself, riding hard. Bad River had far too much good going on right now to let an accident like this cause a rip in the town's unified social fabric.

Once again, the expectant patrons of the Bad River Saloon half-stood when they heard someone enter. It was a young, well-armed stranger. As Sam walked in, he looked all around before making his way to a spot the drinkers had cleared for him at the far end of the bar. The disappointed patrons sat back down, but all eyes stayed on the newcomer, with his wide-brimmed sombrero and a big Winchester rifle hanging in his right hand.

Estez, the bartender, walked down the other side of the bar and glimpsed the shiny ranger badge on Sam's chest behind the lapel of his duster.

"What'll you have, Ranger?" he said, raising his voice for everyone to clearly hear the word *ranger*.

Sam was used to being publicly identified in such a manner. *"Agua fría, por favor,"* he said quietly.

"Agua fría." The bartender gave a sidelong glance at the drinking patrons. "We also sell alcohol, you know—whiskey, cerveza, mescal. . . ." A slight smile showed behind his thick mustache.

Quiet laughter rose along the bar. Sam just stared at the big bartender until he finally gave a half-shrug.

"Okay. Cold water it is, Ranger," he said. He walked away and took up a wooden cup from under the bar and filled it from a wooden bucket with a gourd dipper. He brought the cup back and set it in front of the ranger.

Half a dozen drinkers sat at the bar, three on either side of Sam. They watched him raise the wooden cup to his lips, drain it and set it back down. He wiped a hand across his mouth, looked back and forth at the drinkers and gave everybody a courteous nod.

"That's a fine-looking Winchester, Ranger," said an elderly man on his immediate right.

"It dang sure is," another old man said, leaning in a little closer for a look.

"It goes where I go," Sam said in a sociable tone, straightening the rifle on the bar to give the men a better view. He motioned for the bartender.

"More water, hombre?" Estez asked.

Sam stirred a finger in the air in front of himself and said, "Cerveza for these six gentlemen and me." Whatever tension they might have felt toward the stranger eased away.

"Sí, Ranger, coming up," said Estez.

The six drinkers drew closer to Sam, thanking him, raising frothy mugs and glasses of beer in their hands. Other drinkers rose from the chairs around the tables and gathered closer to Sam and his new friends at the end of the bar.

No sooner had JR Claypool reached the outer edge of town than he saw the dark silhouettes of riders coming toward him on the narrow trail. Seeing the riders stop, he also reined the bareback bay he was riding to a sliding halt, and sat for a moment.

One of the silhouettes called out, "Who's there?" A silent second passed; then the same voice said, "The next thing you'll hear is the sound of a rifle shot. *¿Comprende?*"

"It's me, JR Claypool," the gambler called out. "I rode out here to warn you?"

Now it was Sims's voice that called out, "Well, come on in and warn us, Claypool."

"My God!" said Claypool, out of breath, riding in closer on the bareback bay. "It is a damn good thing I found you this quick. I was prepared to ride all night if I had to!"

"We're all happy as can be that you didn't have to," Sims said in a harsh tone. "Are you going to give us the warning you brought us?"

"Of course I am," said JR. "There's a lawman—"

"He rides bareback, this one," Kura said gruffly, cutting Claypool off.

"I see that, Kura," said Sims. He said to Claypool, "Who does the chestnut bay belong to?"

"I don't know. I grabbed the first horse I could from the barn." He hurried. "I didn't want you riding in tonight unawares. Antonio Villa shot the priest on the trail earlier this evening. Everybody's all right, but an Arizona Ranger rode to town with them. That's what I'm here warning you about. The ranger."

Sims thought over what the gambler had told him.

"Damn it all," he said casually. He asked Claypool in a cool tone, "Anything else you want to warn us about?"

"Well, no, I expect not," said Claypool, feeling let down. He had expected something more than *Damn it all*, but now he saw that was all he would get.

"Then get hauling," Sims said, jerking a nod toward the dark trail back to town.

Claypool hesitated for a second. *What is this? Nobody says, "Thanks a bunch, JR" or "Much obliged, amigo"? Nothing?*

He glanced around and noted there were only six riders. None of the other gunmen had ridden up as they sat there talking in the half-moon light. *What the blue living hell . . . ?* He looked at the mounted riders—Sims, the Russian, Tillis, Dupree, and the two new men, Chaz Campo and Eli Denton. He heard the metal click of Sims's Colt hammer being cocked. It was still in the holster, but Sims's hand rested poised on the gun's bone handle.

"Did you hear me say, 'Get hauling'?" Sims said in a low, menacing voice.

"I'm hauling!" said Claypool. "See you in town!" He jerked the bay's reins, made a fast half-circle and batted his heels to its sides.

"Yeah, Claypool, see you when we get there." Sims gave a muffled laugh under his breath.

Beside him, Tillis and Dupree gave him a look. Campo uncocked the Colt he'd cocked when Claypool had ridden up.

"We're not riding into town, are we?" Dupree asked.

"We're sure as hell not," said Sims. He grinned, turning his horse around on the trail. "Antonio shot a priest, there's a ranger there poking around and bounty hunters are on the prowl. A man ain't careful, he could get himself shot."

The other five turned their horses too and followed.

Tillis rode up beside Sims and said, "If we stay on this trail, we'll run back into Jack Swift and his bounty killers."

Sims replied sharply, "Or we can ride into town and bring a bunch of bounty hunters behind us. How will the town like that at a time when we're trying to show everybody how well we can run things?"

"We lost good men back there tonight," Tillis added. "We owe Swift and his men some hard killing."

"The way our Cowboy pards are showing up in Bad River, we'll replace the men we lost tonight within a week. The important thing is, we didn't lose the money." Sims paused, then said, "Losing those men means more money for the rest of us, right or wrong?"

"Right," said Tillis, "but still—"

"There's no *but still* to it," Sims said, cutting him off. "Right now we're ahead of the game. We'll stay away from the town, the ranger and the Swift bounty men a while longer." He grinned. "The longer the town waits for us to feed this money to them, the more they'll love us for bringing it in."

"I have to say," said Tillis, "swapping out all that heavy silver ore was a smart move. It would've been hard getting away with the big wagon."

"Well, thank you," Sims said, half sarcastic. "I'm glad you agree." He pulled a small white business card from his shirt pocket and handed it to Tillis, who adjusted it in the moonlight until he could read it aloud. "'Jack Swift Detective and Tracking Service.'" He gave Sims a questioning look.

"I found it on the ground back there on the mountaintops while we were getting ambushed," Sims said.

Reading the business card again, Tillis thumbed it on the corner and said, "Ain't this real punchy?"

"Yeah, punchy as hell," said Sims. "Jack Swift always was slicker than socks on a rooster."

"You figure he dropped it by mistake?" Tillis said, handing the card back to Sims.

"That old Indian scout never did anything by mistake. I learned that from riding with him. But he's gone, I hear, and his grandson is ramrodding the company. If this was the old Jack Swift, he would've dropped this business card for one of two reasons. Either he's declared war on us, or he's wanting to talk." He grinned. "Either way, I've got him covered."

Racing back to Bad River on the big chestnut bay, Claypool rode straight to the livery barn, led the horse inside and put it in the same stall he'd taken it from. He sat a full water bucket in front of the horse and grabbed up a handful of straw to rub the horse down. Then he changed his mind and let the straw fall from his fingers.

"What the hell?" he whispered to the bay. "You'll just get out and get dirty again." He jerked a handkerchief from his lapel pocket and wiped his face as he walked out and headed toward the saloon.

Hearing voices and laughter coming through the doors, he stopped out front and tried to look in through a dust-coated window. Unable to identify any new faces who'd shown up since he'd left, he tried to see why so many drinkers were now gathered at the far end of the bar. *Damn it!* He couldn't see anything in the dim lamplight and looming cigar smoke. He turned away from the window and searched along the hitch rail for any unfamiliar horses. Catching sight of a big roan stallion, he batted his eyes and stared at it curiously for a moment.

"Doc?" he said finally. "Is that *you*?" He adjusted his glasses, stepped off the boardwalk and ran a hand down the stallion's neck. Doc swung his head away, but then looked back at Claypool and let the gambler look him in the face. "I'll be tied down and whipped! It is *you*, you old bounder!"

Doc sawed his head up and down a little and blew out a breath; then he swung his big head around and let Claypool rub his nose. "Oh, yeah, it's you all right," Claypool said. "You always had a soft spot for a good nose rub." He looked around at the saloon doors while he continued rubbing the big roan.

"Where's Henry?" he asked as if the stallion would answer. "Is Henry Wise inside there?"

"Hey, you, horse talker," said a gruff voice from the middle of the dark street.

Startled, Claypool sprang to attention. A huge man wearing a long nightshirt stood in the moonlit street, carrying an ax handle in the crook of his.

"That young livery hostler said he saw a man in a swallowtail coat leading *my* chestnut bay into the barn a while ago! Was that you?"

"No, sir," said Claypool, "that would not have been me at all!"

The man kept walking closer, taking the ax handle from the crook of his arm and letting the ax swing freely at his side.

"Yeah? Well, my bay is worn out, and either you or that hostler is lying." The mountain of a man stepped right up to Claypool, almost nose to nose. "I ain't seen a swallowtail for the longest time. I'll wager the one you're wearing just earned you a cracked head!"

"Whoa! Hold on, mister," said Claypool, appearing to search his memory as he constructed a story on the spot. "Did you say a big chestnut *bay*?"

"I did," the man said. He stared hard at Claypool.

"Whatever was I thinking?" said Claypool. "Yes, sir, that was me he saw! I was walking past the livery and saw a *beautiful* bay running back and forth like he was lost. Seeing he had a bridle on and seemed intent on getting into the barn, I figured he belonged there. I lent a hand, led him inside and put him in the first empty stall. The stall door was already open, come to think of it."

"That's the stall I left him in," the man said, relenting, but still looking suspicious. "Some sumbitch must've opened it."

"Then there you have it," Claypool explained, smiling, spreading his hands. "Somehow your horse got out. I won't accuse anybody of leaving his stall door open, but I brought him back, as any honest man would do."

"Maybe . . ." the man said, looking Claypool over, recognizing him from around the saloon gambling tables and the German Ale and Whiskey House. He looked off along the empty street, patting the ax handle on his palm, as if making up his mind whether or not to give Claypool a beating.

Claypool, wanting none of it, saw his chance and slipped a little five-shot Harcourt pocket pistol from his swallowtail coat and cocked it as silent as a newborn's breath. He raised it behind the big man's thick neck, pointing it level to the base of the man's brainpan.

"Adios, big hombre," he said to himself. His finger was fixed on squeezing the trigger when suddenly the big man turned back around to face him. Claypool brought the gun down, slick and swiftly, and hid it out of sight. He quickly adjusted his glasses.

"If you walked my horse back inside and put him in the stall, I expect I owe you an apology, not a beating, mister. I should not have come out here accusing anybody of anything. I don't know what's been troubling me. . . . I ain't been sleeping well at all." He let the ax handle hang loosely at his side. "What an ass I've made of myself."

"No harm done," Claypool said, having slipped the Harcourt pistol back inside his swallowtail. "My nature is to practice forgive and forget anytime I can." He smiled and stepped toward the door. "And now, if you'll excuse me, sir. I'm headed inside to see an old friend."

As he turned toward the saloon doors, he caught sight of two men leading their horses into an alley between the saloon and a tack shop next door. One carried a small wooden crate on his shoulder, while a canvas bag hung in his hand.

What is going on here? Claypool watched, adjusting his glasses and slipping away from the saloon doors. Silently, he followed the two men, staying back in the shadows far enough to keep from being seen.

As he watched, one of the men took the small crate to an empty shack across the narrow alley behind the saloon, while the other man sat holding their horses.

"Is that shack deserted?" the one holding the horses asked when the man came out without the crate or bag.

"Yes," the other replied, "it'll all be safe there, so long as nobody comes snooping around. Little Jack said to find a safe place until Sims and his bunch show up here. That's what we've done."

The one on his saddle handed the other man the reins to his horse. "I hope I ain't around to ever hear you call him Little Jack to his face," he said.

Claypool watched the man step up into his saddle.

"Do I look real worried to you?" the second man asked with a smug grin.

"No," said the other man as they turned their horses back toward the dusty street. "But you don't look real smart either."

Chapter 4

With no sign of Cree Sims or his Bad River Gunmen, the drinking crowd at the bar and the gamblers at the game tables soon began to drift away. At the end of the bar, only one of the patrons who'd gathered around the ranger was still there. He wore a wrinkled suit with shiny elbows and lapels. Sam could tell the man had something on his mind. Whatever it was, he must've preferred keeping it to himself.

Both Sam and the man in the suit waited until the bartender had removed all of the empty mugs and wiped the bar top with a damp towel. Then the man looked around and inched closer. The mug of beer Sam had first ordered sat with only one sip missing. Empties sat abandoned on the end of the bar.

"Ranger Burrack," the man said quietly, "I won't reveal my name or what business I'm in. If you are here on business as you said you are, that's fine." He gave Sam a questioning stare.

Sam only returned it.

"Okay, I see," the man said. "But if you're here because of an unsigned letter to the Mexican consul in Matamoros, I just might be the one who wrote it."

"Go on . . ." Sam encouraged him.

He had no idea what the man was talking about, but he listened intently. He'd heard stories, both from his captain and from the prisoner Hueto Escalante. Now this man. Yes, this man had his attention. He wanted to hear from someone firsthand what was going on with Cree Sims and his new gang.

The man took another guarded look around. His voice dropped to a low, cautious whisper.

"I'm risking my life telling you this, Ranger. But I don't feel like I have a choice," he said. "Sims has put our town council in his pocket. He owns them! He and his men are robbing the French mines and paying our town council big money to look the other way. They've robbed three so far, and they're just getting started. Even some of the mine managers are getting in on it. Before long, it will be so well organized, it will be next to impossible—"

"Hold on, mister." Sam stopped him. "Before you go any further, let me explain what I'm doing here. It has nothing to do with a letter to Matamoros. Under an agreement with the Mexican government, I'm allowed to cross the border to arrest wanted outlaws and take them back to stand trial. If these outlaws are the same men who are doing what you're telling me about, I'm glad it helps this town. But that's not what brings me here. I have no legal authority to stop them. That's the job of local law officers."

"I know that. But if these men are involved in crimes when you come to arrest them—"

"I still have no authority to bring them to justice for *other* crimes committed in Mexico," Sam said, stopping the other man short again. "The government here can be real touchy about that."

The man fell silent for a moment, considering what the ranger had said.

Finally, he said with resolve, "All right. I'm certain we both know the names of the men we're talking about."

"I believe we do," the ranger agreed.

"If only there's something I can say that would make you understand—"

"I do understand," Sam said. "If it helps you any to know, the kind of men I hunt seldom go back across the border without a fight."

"So once these men put up a fight . . ." He let his words trail off, trying to get an answer without coming out and actually asking the question.

"That's right," the ranger said. "When they decide not to go back with me, it won't matter what they might have been doing here. They won't be doing it again."

"I suppose that helps some," the man said. He took the last drink from his beer mug. "Suppose I told you there are good people here who would pay you well if Sims and his men started dying off. What would you say?"

"I'd say someone needs to show them a pathway to better health," the ranger said flatly. He paused, then added, "We're through here. It's time I grain my horse and get him into a stall for the night."

The man started walking with him to the doors.

"By the way, you and I never talked," he said.

"I figured as much," the ranger replied.

Out front, the man eased away and disappeared with a bowler hat brim pulled down to partially hide his face. Sam stepped off the boardwalk at the hitch rail and shoved his rifle down into the saddle boot. Doc gave him a look. Sam patted his neck.

"It wasn't my fault," he told Doc in a low voice. "I couldn't shake him loose."

Doc let out a breath and chewed at his bit.

"All right, I can see you're getting hungry," Sam said quietly. "Let's go get you fed."

He unwrapped the stallion's reins from the iron hitch rail. As he turned to lead him to the livery barn, he saw two riders cantering out of town, their silhouettes clear against the darkened sky as they disappeared around a rocky turn. He wanted to stop and see which way they were headed once they came back into sight, but Doc jerked hard against the reins.

"Okay, take it easy," Sam said.

He would have said more, but before he could . . .

In the shack behind the saloon, JR Claypool grabbed hold of the crate the men had left there, tipped it up into a crack of moonlight and adjusted his glasses on his nose, but still could not read the faded label on its side. Reaching into the canvas bag, he pulled out a length of white cord. *The hell is this . . . ?* He pulled again and more cord uncoiled from within the bag. It had a strong odor to it.

"Damn it!" he said aloud, fumbling with a long wooden match he'd taken from his swallowtail coat pocket. He struck the match on the crate and held the flaring tip up to read the large red letters one at a time. "D-y-n-a—!"

"Oh! Hell no!" he shouted.

In a panic, he shook the match hard. But instead of going out, it flew from his fingertips. Arcing like a small shooting star, the flaming match bounced off a support post and landed atop the crate. It flipped off and fell into the bag full of cord. The bag started sizzling.

"No, no, no!" Claypool screamed. His glasses flew off. He could do nothing but dive out the back door into the alley. But instead of landing on level ground and making a run for it, he fell headlong off of a cutbank and tumbled, face-first, two feet down into soft, watery mud.

. . . On the dirt street, Sam and Doc both felt the earth explode and hurl them forward, end over end. The street rippled and writhed beneath them like some monstrous snake, uprooting the iron hitch rail, sending horses and all tumbling, rolling and sliding on their sides. Flaming pieces of building material showered down, littering the street.

Broken glass and slivers of wood framing blew past like wind-driven rain from where the saloon had stood seconds before. Tumbling horses screamed in fear and pain. Cave bats out foraging in the night fell dead on the ground amid broken furniture and burning fabric.

"Doc!" Sam shouted into the fire and falling debris.

The big stallion, shaking, rose from the dirt on wobbly legs. As Sam struggled to lift himself to his feet, he realized he couldn't hear a sound. The world around him had turned as silent as death. He fell back down on his stomach, watching from ground level as Doc plodded toward him, silently, slowly, unevenly. The world turned black and calm. For how long? Sam had no idea.

He awakened to the face of Sara, who was stooped down beside him in the dim light of a lantern, wiping his forehead with a cool wet cloth. On either side of her, guards with rifles stood looking down at him. He'd felt himself being dragged from the street and dropped against an adobe wall. Were these the men who had dragged him here? He squinted up at the two and tried to straighten himself up against the rough wall. He couldn't.

"Lie still, Ranger," Sara said, leaning close.

"Did you call him Ranger?" one of the men asked.

"*Sí*, I did," Sara said. "I met him earlier on the trail today when Father Lawrence had his accident. He escorted us to town."

Sam's duster fell open enough for the men to see the badge on his chest. They looked at each other in surprise.

"Whoa!" one guard said. He stepped away, moving quickly to their horses, which stood at a hitch post on the edge of the boardwalk. He hurried back, opening the cap on a canteen of water.

"Here, give him a swig," he said, handing the canteen down to Sara. Sara held the canteen to Sam's lips and let him sip. Then the guard said, "Go get Mr. Swift. Tell him we've got a lawman here."

"Right away!" The other guard turned and hurried off through the smoking debris to where six more gunmen, carrying torches, were talking to townsmen, passing canteens around and checking buildings along the dark street.

"Can you hear me, Ranger?" Sara asked. Sam blinked and she repeated, "Can you hear me?"

Her voice sounded a long way off. "Sort of," he said. He felt his ear to see if something was blocking it. "Not very clear though," he added. He looked around the debris-strewn street, noting a bucket brigade passing pails of water from the horse trough and throwing it on the smoking skeletal remains of the saloon. He searched the street with his eyes. "Where's my roan?"

"He's all right," Sara replied. "Irena took him to the livery barn."

"I'd better go see about him." Sam tried to push up. "He'll be shook up by all this."

"No, Ranger," said the guard, holding Sam down with a hand on his shoulder. "You're staying here until Mr. Swift tells us what to do with you."

"Do with me?" Sam said, his hearing coming back a little.

The guard looked down the street at the men carrying torches, then back at the ranger.

"Mr. Swift is coming right now," he said.

"Are you one of Jack Swift's detectives?" Sam asked above a dull ringing in his ears.

"I am indeed, Ranger," the guard said proudly. "We're lawmen too."

"And I, sir, am Jack Swift, in the flesh," an approaching voice called out from behind a glowing lantern that was swinging back and forth in the moonlight.

Three men walked to the boardwalk where Sam lay. One held a lantern above their heads. They stopped and gazed down at Sam, rifles hanging in their hands.

Sam eyed the young man as Sara stood and took a step back.

"Last time I saw Jack Swift was back in Nogales, over a year ago. He's an older man, part Comanche." Sam said, his voice rose a little against his difficulty hearing. "You're not that Jack Swift."

"Oh, I certainly am not." Smiling, the young man took out a business card and held it down toward the ranger. When Sam didn't take the card, the young man handed it to Sara.

"I daresay you met my grandfather," he said to Sam. "Sadly, the old fella passed away a year ago. I now own the company."

Sam gave him a dubious look. But then he took a breath and said, "Sorry about your granddad."

Swift gave a slight shrug. "We weren't close," he said.

Sam gave him another look. "Even so," he said quietly, "I knew him to be a good man. Good for his word, good in his trade."

Swift looked at Sam as if he might be joking. Seeing Sam wasn't just trying to flatter him, he nodded and thanked him. Then he stood, looking all around the blown-up street, his hands propped on the gun belt around his waist. With a flat stare he reflected for a moment on the violent efficiency of the dynamite.

"I suppose you're wondering three things. Why are my men and I here? What just happened? And what might my men have to do with it?" He gestured around the charred, littered street. "Huh? Am I right?"

"Those questions have crossed my mind," Sam said. He ran his eyes across the destruction, the smoldering remains of the Bad River Saloon.

"*Ha*, that's funny." Swift gave a little chuckle. So did the men standing behind him, one still holding the lantern up at shoulder level. Swift took the canteen back from Sara, capped it and passed it to one of his men.

"The fact is," Swift said, "the French mining project has hired my company to provide security and to find the people responsible for the recent mine robberies." He lowered his voice. "I can tell *you* it's Raeburn Sims and some of the Arizona Cowboy Gang—three robberies in the past few weeks." He paused and took a deep breath. "They're calling themselves the Bad River Gunmen."

"So I've heard," Sam said quietly. He wondered if Swift's information also came from Hueto Escalante.

He had a mental image of Swift sticking a bag of tobacco through the bars into the prisoner's sweaty hand. *Huh-uh, not Swift himself,* he decided. *One of his men, more likely . . .*

"All right, Ranger, that's my story," said Swift. "What's yours?"

"My story is simple enough. . . ."

Before continuing, Sam reached a hand up to the guard who'd been there when Swift and his other two men arrived. Before taking Sam's hand, the guard looked at Swift for approval. When Swift nodded, the guard lent a hand and helped Sam pull himself to his feet.

"I'm here to take back three wanted men," Sam said.

"I supposed that to be the case, Ranger," Swift said. "Lucky you're wearing that badge. We could have mistaken you for one of the men we're after."

"Yes, lucky for me," Sam said. "You're using dynamite on them?"

"We had word they were coming here," said Swift. "They robbed a mine thirty miles back along the mountain line. Had they been here, we would have likely wiped them out with one large, powerful blast!" He grinned, appearing excited at the prospect of using explosives.

Sam looked around, then back at the other man.

Swift dismissed all the damage with a wave of a hand. "This was accidental," he said. "I don't know what set it off. My men were supposed to have the dynamite hidden until Sims and his men showed up. Imagine, if we had caught them here all in one spot!" He waved his hand again at the debris and damage. His grin widened. "We could have cooked enough outlaw stew to feed every wolf in these mountains!"

He roared with laughter. His men joined him.

"You got that right, Mr. Swift," said the one holding the lantern.

"Damn sure did!" said another.

The guard holding the rifle smiled only enough to be a part of the group. He avoided Sam's eyes.

"What say you, Ranger?" Swift asked.

Sam looked away for a moment, declining to comment. Then he looked back at Swift and said, "I'm after Sims too. Him, Earl Dupree and Giles Tillis."

"I thought as much," said Swift. He dropped his laughter and put on his business face. "But it makes me no matter. Now that I have established that you're a lawman like myself and all of us, let's talk serious," Swift said. "What's the chance of you joining forces with me, kick us some outlaw butt together?"

"I have no forces to offer," Sam said, wanting to get off the subject. "It's just my stallion Doc and me. Sometimes I have a partner, but mostly not."

"Come now, Ranger, you're far too modest," Swift said. He took a cigar from his coat pocket. "I've heard of you, Ranger Burrack. What detective or bounty hunter hasn't?"

He bit the cigar tip off, stuck the cigar in his mouth and glanced at his men. One of them struck a match, cupped it in his hands and held it over to his boss. Swift puffed the cigar to life and blew a long stream of smoke.

"I can make man hunting more lucrative than you've ever imagined it could be."

"I understand," Sam said. "Thanks for the offer, but I have to decline." He wasn't going to discuss it. He looked at the young woman. "Obliged for your help, Miss Sara. I'll gather Doc and get out of here."

She stood gazing at him with concern. "Your ears are bleeding!" she said.

"They are for sure," said Jack Swift with a curious look.

"I'll be all right," Sam said, his voice sounding muffled to him, "soon as I get on the trail." He reached both hands up to his ears. When he brought them down, he saw blood streaked across all of his fingertips.

Chapter 5

"Sims knew we were headed to Canto Alto when we rode on past Bad River," Earl Dupree said to Giles Tillis. The two sat atop their horses, looking down through a lingering morning mist at the Canto Alto mine site on a wide cliff below.

"Hell, 'course he did," said Tillis. "Look around us."

He nodded at the riders camped among the rocks behind them. More riders had joined them one and two at a time along the high trails the night before—one of them was Antonio Villa.

"When we headed past Bad River two nights ago, there were only a few of us. Now we're a dozen strong." Tillis grinned. "None of it was by coincidence." He gave a half-shrug. "The kid maybe, but these others were planned on ahead."

"More than enough to rob another mine if we took a notion to," Dupree said, putting the idea together with the prodding from Tillis. He thought about it for a second. "You think Sims is going above the man on top of all this?"

Tillis gave him a look. "I think Sims *is* the man on

top," he said. "I figure he took over that position the minute he killed that mine supervisor."

Tillis looked all around before he spoke again. "I'd like to know who he's been answering to," he said quietly. "There'll come a time soon enough when he's worn out his welcome. When it happens, I'd like folks to know I'm here just waiting to take the reins."

"If you took this over from Sims," Earl Dupree said, "where does that put me?"

Giles Tillis gave him a sharp look. "We've been pards a long time, Earl," he said. "If I didn't already figure you'd be on my side, do you suppose I'd be saying what I just said about taking over?"

"I'm just asking." Dupree shrugged. "Never hurts to ask, does it?"

They both glanced around and saw Sims and Kura the Russian riding their horses forward at a walk through the narrow campsite.

"Here comes our dashing leader now," Tillis whispered to Dupree.

"Yeah. Always with our Russian Assassin riding right at his rump," Dupree said in contempt. "If they got any closer, they'd be more than just pals." He turned his head sidelong and spit.

The tall black-and-tan donkey walked along with Kura holding its lead rope.

"Well, well," said Tillis, "looks like the donkey has lost weight since we saw him yesterday." He looked away from the Russian and the donkey as he spoke.

Lost weight . . . ? Dupree wondered. *"Damn!"* said Dupree upon doing a double take. "The saddlebags are gone!"

"Oh? Do you mean the saddlebags that held all of

our money inside?" Tillis said sarcastically. "Why, yes, Earl, I believe you're right."

They watched Sims and the Russian ride closer. In the campsite behind them, the men were rising from blankets and gathering their gear.

"I see you two have found the Canto Alto mine," Sims said as he and the Russian stopped their horses beside them.

"It would be hard to miss," Tillis said. "We looked down and there it was. Was it meant to be a surprise?" He let himself be seen looking over the bareback donkey.

"Not a surprise." Sims gave a slight smile. "But I thought we might rob it, seeing's we're here."

Tillis and Dupree both nodded.

"Why not?" said Tillis. He nodded toward the donkey. "I hope he didn't lose our saddlebags."

Sims kept smiling. "Naw, I know where they are," he said. "I thought putting them out of sight for a while might keep everybody wishing me good health down there if shooting starts." He gestured toward the mine site.

"We knew it had to be something like that," Tillis said with a flat stare. "Right, Earl?" he said to Dupree.

Dupree gave Sims the same look. "Right as rain," he said to Tillis.

Without taking his eyes off the two, Sims said to the Russian, "Go wake the kid up, Kura. Tell him I said to stick close to you on this job, to do what you tell him. We need to start finding out where he stands on things. We don't need some soft-footed mission boy. We need hardcase gunmen who'll kill quick as a rattlesnake." To Tillis and Dupree, he said, "You two agree?"

"It's what this kind of business calls for," said Tillis. "Otherwise, I wouldn't be in it."

"Nor would I," Dupree agreed.

"That's good to hear," said Sims.

"Why do you ask?" said Tillis.

Instead of answering, Sims turned his horse and said to them both, "Come back here with me."

The two gave each other a look, but turned their horses and rode behind him through the campsite. When they stopped at a narrow crevice in the rock wall, they saw Kura and Antonio Villa standing over a mine guard who lay on the ground, hands and feet tied, with a bandanna around his mouth. He looked at them, wild-eyed with fear. He stared from one face to the next, frantically shaking his head. Even wearing the gag, they could hear his muffled, distorted voice pleading, *"No! No!"*

Sims ignored the bound, terrified man. He looked at Antonio, who had been awakened only moments ago by the Russian. Antonio gave Sims a questioning look.

Sims patted his shoulder and said, "Kid, these two are wondering if you have the grit to kill a man who's staring you in the eyes, like this poor poltroon lying here."

Tillis and Dupree knew better than to comment.

Antonio's eyes flashed anger at the two. He stiffened his chin and started to draw his gun. Sims laid his hand on Antonio's gun, stopping him.

"No gun, kid," he said. "It's too damn noisy. They think anybody can put a bullet in a man." He looked at Tillis and Dupree and grinned.

"What do you want me to do?" Antonio asked. He looked down. The man lay sobbing and praying behind the gag.

Kura pulled a big knife from his boot and threw it down hard, sticking it into the gravelly ground at Antonio's feet.

Antonio bent and picked up the knife; then he turned to Sims in disbelief.

"That's right, kid," Sims said. "Cut that sucker's throat. Show these two jakes what you're made of."

"Come on," Dupree said, trying to cut in quietly, "there's no need in—"

"Did I say a damn word to you?" Sims shouted at Dupree. "You think because this man was raised by a priest, he's too damn good to look a man in the eyes and cut his throat?"

Dupree took a step back and shut up, knowing when to back off and let a killer like Sims have his way.

In silence, the four men stood watching Antonio go about his grizzly task. The dying guard jerked and convulsed on the gravelly dirt as blood flew. Kura stared intently, a strange gleam in his eyes. When Antonio finished the killing, he started to wipe the big blade dry across the dead man's chest.

"No," Kura said, stopping him. "Give it here. Let me see it!"

"Crazy bastard," Tillis whispered sidelong to Dupree.

Antonio looked at Sims as he handed the bloody knife to the Russian. "Any other throats you want cut this morning?" he asked Sims, a quiet tone of pride in his voice.

"You did good, Antonio," said Sims. "Get ready for some more hard killing today. Kura and you are riding together on this job. Pay attention to our Russian Assassin." He beamed with pride. "Learn how he does things. You'll do all right."

Kura smiled a flat, mirthless smile at the mention of his name. "Listen to me, kid," he said, "and I teach you everything real good." Looking up from the body on the ground, where the dead man's head had been nearly severed from his body, he added, "I see your work. You will become the best among the Bad River Gunmen."

Sims chuckled and said, "The Bad River Gunmen. I like the sound of it. We're going to make the Cowboy Gang look like a bunch of left-foot amateurs." He gave Tillis and Dupree a pointed stare. "You two get ready to ride," he said. "This is going to be bloodier than last time."

The mounted Bad River Gunmen fell upon the Canto Alto mine site in the first full light of morning. Tall stone chimneys above the smelting furnaces were already streaming thick orange-black smoke into a clear blue sky. The attack was sudden, fast and relentless.

"¡Santa Madre!" cried one of the first miners to see the wild horde pounding nearer. He made the sign of the cross on his chest and ran for cover.

Four armed mine guards had leaned their rifles against the wall of a tool shack. They'd rolled up their shirtsleeves and started carrying crates and canvas bags of smelted silver ingots from a cooling shed and loading them onto a large freight wagon.

When the thunder of hooves and the first hard volley of rifle fire erupted on the narrow stretch of flatland behind them, three of the four jumped toward their rifles. The fourth fell dead before taking a step, a bullet exiting through his heart.

"Mr. Moe! *Mr. Moe!*" a worker shouted, running toward the mine office through a steady roar of gunfire. Men fell to the ground before they could reach cover of any kind.

Moe Bridges, the mine manager, ran out onto the boardwalk around the office shack, a double-barreled shotgun in hand. But before he could raise the gun, three bullets hit him almost as one, slamming him against the shack.

He shouted, "*Son of a—!*" but his words were cut off as a fourth bullet slammed him harder against the shack and he slid down the wall as if he'd decided to rest there. He was still alive but only barely.

Within seconds, the Gunmen had hit the mine site and spread through it as easily and violently as a flash flood. From their camp on the stone ledge, Sims had pointed out with a short, dried juniper branch who should go where once they'd gotten inside the site and taken control.

"It looks like everybody did their jobs just right." Sims sounded amused, almost surprised. He looked all around, realizing that the attack was over as quick as it had started.

Sitting their horses as the rest of the men rode forward, Sims and Tillis watched as the gunfire settled down. Dupree had ridden forward with Kura and Antonio. Tillis had meant to ride forward with them, but Sims had held him back.

"I've been thinking about Jack Swift and what we talked about," he said.

"Yeah? What do you figure?" Tillis asked. "Is he declaring war or wanting to talk?"

"He wants to talk," said Sims. "We know he's a tracker in a detective company. Why warn us unless he's simpleminded? We already know he's after us." He gave a little chuckle.

"I'm with you so far," said Tillis, "But talk? Talk about what?"

"Now *you* sound simpleminded," Sims said. "If he's as smart as his granddad, he sees what a sweet setup this is. The French are hanging in these mountains with their asses in the wind. Biggest army in the world. They ain't *allowed* to send troops to protect their investment? Damn! Figure that out!"

He laughed aloud as they nudged their horses forward. Tillis laughed a little too.

As they rode up to a small clearing and looked at the few men gathered around the boardwalk of the office shack, Tillis looked over at the sound of a single gunshot and watched a miner fall limp as a bullet from Antonio's gun hit him point-blank in the back of the head.

"What's this?" Tillis asked Sims, nodding toward Antonio.

"Nothing much," said Sims. "I just figured the kid needs some practice."

Three other miners stood in a line where the first miner had been shot. The Russian and Dupree stood watching as Antonio stepped over behind the next miner in line.

Tillis kept his mouth shut. He stepped down from his saddle beside Sims and followed him over to the manager, who was lying mortally wounded against the wall of the office shack. The other men parted to let Sims and Tillis step in closer.

"Great job, all of you!" Sims said to the men around him. "Now go help load the rest of the silver and take all cash out of the office. This place has a big iron safe."

"Does it have a combination?" Tillis asked.

"Of course it does." Sims grinned, pulled a piece of paper from his shirt pocket and handed it to Tillis. "Here it is. Go with them. I'll be right along."

As the men hurried away, some to load the wagon while Tillis and a couple of others went inside to clean out the safe, Sims stooped down beside the dying manager.

"Look at you now, Moe Bridges," he said quietly. He looked around on the bloody plank boardwalk. "You're bleeding like a stuck hog."

"Go . . . to hell, Sims," the dying man said in a weak, barely audible voice. He tried to mumble a few more words, but a surge of dark blood prevented him from doing so.

"Easy, Moe." Sims laughed a little. Seeing the man had more to say, he leaned in closer.

"Next . . . month," the man managed to say.

"Next month . . . ?" Sims considered his words. Then, as if it came to him, he said, "Oh. You're wondering why I'm here today instead of next month like we planned?"

The man gave a weak nod of his blood-splattered head.

Sims shrugged and said, "No reason really. I just pushed the date up some. I hope you don't mind. We were in the area, thought we'd stop by."

The man choked back another surge of blood.

"I . . . I hope Melford . . ." He gasped. "I hope he . . ."

Sims chuckled, seeing the man's eyes go blank. "Just couldn't get it all said, could you, Moe?"

He stood up and stared down at the dead man for a second before reaching out with the pointed toe of his boot to close the man's eyes. "Ashes to ashes, and all that," he said.

He turned and walked inside the office, where Tillis and the two men had hefted three heavy bags of cash from the safe and pitched them atop the dead manger's desk.

"This is a lot of cash, Sims," said Tillis. "I'm betting it's close to—"

"Let's not start guessing," Sims said in a sharp tone. He opened the rope drawstring on one of the bags and took out a stack of bills, U.S. currency. "My, my," he said, "all this money and not a saloon in sight."

As he spoke, the Russian and Dupree walked in and stood looking at the cash bags and the money in Sims's hand.

"Where's the kid?" Sims asked.

"He's right outside," said Dupree. "I think he doesn't feel so good."

"Oh?" Sims called out, "Kid, get in here. I've got something for you."

Antonio stepped in slowly.

"Come here," Sims said. "Here's some of the money you earned today. Five hundred American dollars."

Antonio looked in excitement at the bundle of cash Sims took from the stack in his hand and held out to him. "Take this to your family, that little señorita you're sweet on."

Antonio took the money and gazed at it until Sims laughed and said, "Get out of here with it before one of these jakes robs you." He and the men laughed. Antonio started to say something, but Sims cut in. "Go on, get out of here. Be in Two Forks next week to get the rest of your money and be ready to go to work."

Antonio just stood there for a moment. Then, as if coming out of a trance, he turned, went out the door, climbed up into his saddle and headed for the trail.

"We've seen the last of him," Dupree commented.

"He'll be back," said Sims. "If he's not, I don't need him. If he is, he'll *belong* to me forever."

Chapter 6

———

Ranger Burrack awakened in a small, clean bedroom inside the stone walls of the priest's rectory behind Bad River's modest cathedral. Cut into each thick timber window shutter was an ornate Spanish cross. They served not only as symbols of God's love, but also as shooting ports for the countless rifles it had taken to kill thousands of Apache.

"Ranger . . ." Sara whispered near his cheek as he began to stir, his eyes shifting about the room. "Can you hear me?" she asked.

Sam nodded only as she took his hand and held it. Her hands were damp from wiping his face with a cool wet cloth.

"Where's Doc?" he asked. "I want to see him."

Before Sara could answer, Father Lawrence, who had been standing across the room, stepped closer to the side of the bed. His forearm rested in a sling, owing to his wounded shoulder.

"My son," he said, "our doctor is very busy today. Limited though I am, anything I can do to assist you, please tell me—"

"Father," Sara cut in quietly, "the ranger's roan is named Doc. He is asking about his stallion."

"Oh, I see," said the priest. He went on. "Our house-keeper, Irena, has watched over him these past three days."

"I've been here three days?" Sam asked, looking at Sara.

"Yes," Sara said, "and you are not yet back to your strength. You need to let your body rest and repair itself."

"I'm afraid I can't do that, Miss Sara," Sam said, making a failed move to push himself up in the bed.

Father Lawrence leaned in and pressed his good hand firmly yet gently on Sam's chest, pushing him back.

"You must listen to us, Ranger Burrack," he said with the same firm gentleness. "Over the years, we have helped miners who lived through just such a dynamite blast as you have. Always, they think they are well and are eager to leave. Yet in many cases, they were in far worse shape than they thought. The blast misguides a person's senses. One miner told us that the blast was like being struck by a fast train, only without physical impact." He smiled. "Perhaps that is why it fools people."

"I have an idea," Sara said. "If you please, I will have Irena bring your roan here from the barn and let you see him."

A slight look of apprehension crossed Sam's brow.

Sara smiled. "Don't worry, Ranger," she said. "Like so many of our young Irish-Mexican women in Bad River, Irena is a horsewoman, heart and soul." She smiled. "Is Doc of good temper?"

"He hasn't been with me long," Sam said. "From

what I know of him, he's as levelheaded as any animal I've ever ridden. I'd trust him with anybody so long as they're horse people. ¿Sí?"

"Sí, I understand," Sara said. She picked up a cloth from the pan of cool water on a small lampstand beside the bed, squeezed it and laid it back across Sam's forehead. "You go back to sleep and rest. Doc will be here when you awaken."

"Gracias," Sam said, already relaxing back onto the soft feather mattress.

In less than a half hour, he awakened again, this time to the sound of Doc nickering at the open window near his bed. Sam smiled at Doc's big head and sparkling eyes as the horse nosed in through the window, looking at Sam.

"Miss Sara, you did it," he said. He looked a little surprised.

"Sí, just as I told you I would, Ranger—or may I call you Sam?"

"You surely may, Miss Sara," Sam said.

"And you will please just call me Sara," she said.

"Yes, Sara, I will," he replied. With her help, he sat on the side of the bed and this time shoved himself to his feet.

"You can't come in, Doc," he said, seeing the stallion pressed tightly against the window frame. Sam rubbed the stallion's nose and patted him under the chin. "You are a sight, pal," Sam said, one arm around Sara's shoulders for balance.

Irena, a beautiful, capable-looking young woman, sat in a saddle atop Doc.

"Here," she said. "He loves these."

She leaned forward. Through the window, she handed Sam a handful of dried apple slices wrapped in a clean handkerchief. As soon as Sam took the handkerchief, Doc poked his nose closer, sniffing at it.

Sara stood close, but she let Sam get his balance and give Doc the apple slices one at a time.

"He seems no worse for the wear," Sam said, looking at Doc's eyes, seeing they were still clear and bright.

Irena stepped down from the saddle and stood at the window, Doc's reins in her hand. "He was foggy the first day. He didn't want to eat and couldn't stand real steady. But he came around quick."

"Miss Irena, I'm much obliged for all you've done," Sam said.

"I was happy to do it," she replied. "Satisfied?" She motioned at Doc.

"Yes, I am, *very*," Sam said.

Irena stepped back into the saddle and said to Doc, "Come on, fellow, we're going back to the barn."

She and Sam nodded at each other. Doc hesitated but only for a second, looking at Sam in the window as if to make sure it was all right. Then he turned at the slightest tap of the woman's heels and loped off across the yard.

"Irena said she loves him," Sara said to Sam, standing close to him.

"Doc has his ways," Sam said.

He started to turn away, but Sara didn't move. She stood close, almost pressed against him. He realized it was intentional, not at all to help him keep his balance.

"Sam, you have been so kind to Father and me. I want you to know how much I appreciate it."

"Likewise, Sara," Sam said, wanting to play this down, whatever her intentions. "The two of you have been most gracious."

"And we are honored to have you stay with us—"

"Perhaps you sleep with this man now?" an angry voice said from the open window.

They both looked around quickly. Antonio sat on the window ledge, one leg crossed over the other, his gun hanging in his hand.

Sam stared; Sara gasped.

"Antonio!" she said. "You startled me!" She stepped back from Sam.

A bad sign, Sam decided. He thought about his holstered Colt hanging on the bedpost, his rifle under the edge of the bed. Even in his addled state, he remembered seeing the priest placing them there.

"I *bet* I startled you both!" the enraged young man said to her without taking his cold stare off of the ranger.

Sam reminded himself that he was not startled. He'd been surprised a little, he supposed. But he was over that. He was busy now considering possibilities. Was he strong enough to make a leap for the bed, grab his Colt and shoot this man back out of the window—all without hitting the woman?

Before Sam decided what move to make, Sara stepped toward Antonio.

"Is that what you think? You shoot Father, leave us on the trail and run away like a dog! You are gone for a week! Now you show up accusing me of unfaithfulness?"

Antonio started to speak, but she wasn't through. "This is Arizona Ranger Sam Burrack. Thank God he showed up when you left us stranded!"

Sam eased up on his thoughts of grabbing his Colt as he saw the young man's anger slowly recede. He took a breath, waited, watched.

Antonio looked him up and down. "You helped them?" he asked Sam.

As soon as he asked, Sam realized Antonio had been watching them that day. Afraid to come forward and show himself? *Maybe . . .* Sam kept his same firm expression, not giving anything up, not about to say anything to gain favor. What the priest and Sara had said about Antonio didn't fit him. He was not the young man Sam had expected. He was Sam's age, give or take a couple of years; and there was a hardness in his eyes that no savvy lawman would have missed. It crossed his mind that shooting the priest might not have been accidental.

"Put the gun away," Sam said sharply.

Antonio didn't put it away, but he let it slump an inch, his interest in violence appearing to wane.

"I apologize for coming here and accusing you— both of you." He looked from one to the other. "Forgive me, Sara," he said. He looked at Sam and gave a respectful nod.

Sam returned it and took a step back. He felt a weakness move over him again. But he made himself stand strong. He was out of the bed, and he wasn't getting back in it.

Antonio moved like a cat, stepping down out of the window and over to Sara. He leaned in and whispered something in her ear.

"Sí," she whispered in reply. She turned to Sam and said in a polite voice, "If you will excuse us, please . . ."

Sam nodded and watched them walk out of the room. When the door closed behind them, Sam went to the bed, bent down and pulled out his rifle. He checked it, sat down on the edge of the bed and laid it across his lap. Maybe Antonio was just hotheaded under these circumstances, but he was not the good-spirited, well-mannered young man Sara and the priest had described.

A rifle in hand never hurts, he reminded himself.

When Antonio and Sara left the small bedroom and started walking along the stone hallway, Antonio suddenly took her by the wrist. He turned her almost roughly and pressed her against the wall, his lips covering hers. She did not struggle as they kissed long and deep. Even when the kiss ended, their lips lingered close. They breathed each other in.

"My God, I thought you might have been killed, Antonio. The sort of men you ride with," she gasped. As they hugged and kissed, tasting each other, she pounded her small fist on his shoulder. "What would I do if anything happened to you? Please, don't go to join them—never leave me again. Men like these will get you killed!" She paused, then added, "They blew up the saloon!"

"The ones who did that were not Bad River Gunmen. They were bounty hunters."

"Still, they are violent men. The kind of men who hunt all of you down to kill you for whatever price is on your head."

"There is no price on my head, Sara," he said.

"Not now," she said. "But there will be if you keep riding with them." Tears filled her eyes. "There is something I must tell you, Antonio."

He looked into her eyes as she gathered her words. She looked away, then back at him. "I am carrying our baby, *your* baby." Her hand went down and rubbed her belly gently.

Antonio stared, at first not seeming to understand. Then slowly, a tender smile came to his face. "A baby . . . Are you sure?" he whispered, his face close to hers. "How do you know this?"

She gave him a flat stare until he got it.

"Oh, yes!" he said. He stopped and gazed warmly into her eyes.

"Are you happy for us, Antonio?" Her hand cupped his cheek as she spoke.

"I am very happy, Sara," he said.

She said, "So do you see why I can't have you riding with these men? Our child must not grow up without a father. You can work the fields here—we both can. We will need money for our child." Again, her hand went to her belly.

Antonio's face hardened a little. "Our child must not grow up ragged and hungry either," he said. "I cannot make a living for us here, sticking seeds in the ground. Not like the money I can make riding with Sims and his men."

He took out the roll of cash from inside his shirt and handed her two hundred dollars he'd separated from the five hundred Sims had given him. "Look at this, Sara. This is the kind of money we need for our child."

At first she appeared to be afraid to even touch the money.

"Take it, Sara," he coaxed her, pushing it into her hand. "U.S. dollars, Sara! And there will be more. I give you my word."

"But—but what if something happens to you?"

"Stop it, Sara. Nothing is going to happen to me," Antonio said.

Suddenly, he jerked around, startled at the sound of something echoing in the distant hallway. His hand went to his holstered pistol and stopped. He collected himself quickly and held her at arm's length.

"What does a man do that pays so much money as this?" she asked. "I know these gunmen break the law."

"Yes, Sara, but it is the French whose money we take. Remember how they ruled over our people, taking our resources while our people did without." He offered a smile. "We are taking some of it back."

He wasn't going to tell her he had killed innocent men for the money. He wasn't going to tell her that on his way here, he had decided he would never go back to the Gunmen. The killing had been so terrible, it had made him sick, had made his hands tremble. He'd decided to take the five hundred dollars and make a way for Sara and him. But now, with a baby coming, that idea was gone. They would need money for the baby, for a home, clothes, food. He regretted what he'd done, but now he knew he had to go back to the Bad River Gunmen.

"Tonight, I must go back, Sara," he said.

"No, not tonight," Sara said. "Please stay here with me. I have missed you so much."

"I came to bring you the money," he said, "and to see how Father is doing. I feel bad for what happened."

"Father knows you do, Antonio," Sara said. "He is doing well. He misses you too. But we both are doing well."

"What about this ranger?" Antonio asked. "He helped you on the trail, but he is down here hunting wanted *Americanos*. I cannot trust him." He looked toward the door to the bedroom where Sam sat with the cocked rifle on his lap. "Why is he staying here?"

"He was in the explosion," Sara said. "Irena and I brought him here to stay until his senses settle back in place. The explosion caused both his ears to bleed. Father and I have washed out the dried blood, but he is still unsteady. As soon as he can ride, he will go back on the trail."

"Who is he hunting?" Antonio asked.

"I don't know," said Sara. "The men who blew up the saloon maybe. He said he hunts only the men the court in Nogales sends him to bring back."

Antonio thought about it. "You mean even if I am with the men he is hunting, he is not interested in me?"

"Only the men the court wants him to bring back," Sara said. "They are wanted for breaking laws in the United States. Mexico allows their lawmen to come here and take them back. But it is against the law of Mexico for them to arrest Mexicans for crimes they commit here."

Antonio considered that information some more. "All right, I understand," he said. He smiled. "It makes no sense to me, but I understand."

"Must you leave right this minute, Antonio?" she asked in an inviting voice.

"No, not this minute," Antonio said. "I have time to make love to the mother of my son."

"It can be a girl just as easily," Sara said, taking his hand.

They walked along the hallway. In the small bedroom, Sam had laid the rifle alongside him and pulled a cover over himself. He could barely hear their footsteps, Antonio's leather boots and ringing spurs moving closer, then passing the closed door and fading down the long stone corridor.

When the sound of footsteps fell away, Sam cupped a hand over his rifle as he uncocked it in the silent darkness. Under his pillow, he laid his right hand on his big Colt, out of habit. Then he closed his eyes and fell into a half-sleep, the kind he could snap out of easily, should he suddenly find cause to do so. He had a feeling sleep was about to get scarce in his world.

Chapter 7

Late in the night, Antonio slipped out of Sara's bed and dressed in the dim moonlight shining through an open window. He put on his gun belt, adjusted his pistol. Carrying his boots, he looked down for a moment at Sara, who slept with an arm lying across the side of the bed that was still warm from his body. He stood wishing, praying that somehow he could change the direction fate had laid out before him.

Seeing Sara move gently in her sleep, he realized he could change nothing. The lives of the men he'd killed had set him on this path. If he stopped now, it would somehow feel blasphemous. No, he knew he had to go. He almost crossed himself but stopped. After a moment, he stepped back, away from the bed and the woman he loved. He reached down into one of the boots in his hand. He took out the big knife the Russian had given him and moved along the hallway as silent as a ghost to the ranger's bedroom.

Opening the door narrowly, he eased in the room and stepped barefoot over to the bed, knife poised to raise quickly and strike. But looking down where the dim slanted moonlight lay across the bottom half of the bed, he saw the ranger was not there. The bed was made, the pillow in place. *No ranger . . .*

At the window, he saw the iron latch that could be locked only from inside. It lay open, *useless,* as if mocking him for coming here in the first place. *Me and my ill intent,* he thought. He set his boots down quietly and pulled them on one at a time.

Perhaps this is for the best.

He did not believe the story the ranger had given Sara and Father Lawrence. No ranger, or any lawman, would come here and take back wanted men without facing the rest of the gang they rode with. There was no man with courage such as that. Only a fool would try such a thing. He allowed himself to smile a little. The ranger knew he could convince an aging priest and a young woman like Sara of such a thing, but not a man like himself.

At first Antonio had not planned to kill the ranger, but the man was a danger to him, not to mention what killing him would do for his status among the Gunmen. If he was destined to be a killer of men, so be it. And now he felt as if fate had betrayed him somehow. But he took a deep breath, realizing that this time his hands were not shaking as they had before. He was getting used to this work.

Antonio nodded, looking out into the endless night sky. Maybe the ranger had realized what he was up against and decided to turn tail back to Arizona. Anyway, the ranger was gone and that was that.

"Adios, Ranger . . ." Antonio said to himself, confident he would never see the man again—it suited him fine.

* * *

In the light of the moon, the ranger made his way to Bad River, using a back trail that ran along the rocky back edge of town. His thoughts had felt thick and diminished when he'd first slipped out through the window beside the small bed; but as he breathed the cool, crisp night air along the way, his lungs felt cleansed, his dulled senses stimulated. He'd started off using his rifle as a cane to keep his balance in check, but by the time he neared the livery barn, his balance had greatly improved.

Two sets of eyes watched from a darkened window on the upper floor of the Frenchman Hotel as he opened the barn door wide enough to slip inside and pull it shut behind him. At the sight and scent of the ranger standing in the moonlight, laddered by the cracks in the planked barn wall, Doc rocked his head up and down.

"It's me, pal," the ranger said, walking up close.

He stopped long enough to rub the stallion's moist nose above the stable gate. Then he reached over the gate, leaned his rifle against the inside of the stall and walked to a saddle rack. He lifted his saddle, threw it over his shoulder and walked back to Doc. He opened the gate and started to walk inside when he heard a quiet sound behind him and saw the stallion's ears stand straight up.

Instead of stopping right then, he walked to Doc and tossed saddle, blanket and all onto the stallion's back. He laid the bridle over the saddle and hooked it on the horn for the time being. He took a step back toward his rifle when he heard a man's gruff voice.

"Mister! Wherever you think you're going with that cayuse, you're wrong."

Sam heard the hammers of a shotgun cock.

"Easy now," he said. "This is my stallion, Doc. I'm Ranger Sam Burrack."

"Hold on," the man said, "and keep your hands in sight."

Sam stood still, his hands held chest high while the man took down a lantern from a hook and lit it with a match. He turned up the light and looked at Sam closely. Then he let out a breath of relief.

"Ranger," he said, "I'm sure glad it's you. I was wondering how I was going to burn down a horse thief without taking a chunk of side meat off that fine roan."

"I'm glad you didn't have to," Sam said. He recognized a slight Irish brogue in the man's voice. "You're Irish Mike Tuohy, the saloon owner?"

"*Huh,*" said the big man, lowering the shotgun. "I'm Tuohy for sure, but I'm the former saloon owner now, as I'm certain you know."

"I know," Sam said. He gestured with his head at his hands.

"Yes, bring 'em down, Ranger," said Tuohy. "I'm surprised to see you up and around. Folks said that explosion left you looking like a smokehouse scarecrow."

"I took a big blast," Sam said. "It could have been worse. I'm glad it wasn't."

"Right you are, boyo," said Tuohy. "I know my explosives from the silver mines in the old days. That was some old dynamite. Otherwise, none of us would still be here."

Tuohy walked into Doc's stall as he spoke and began saddling the big roan for Sam.

"I can saddle him," Sam said.

"I know you can," said Tuohy. "But I own this livery, and I like to keep my hands busy." He went on. "I found JR Claypool facedown in the drain-off ditch of the men's outhouse." He gave a dark chuckle. "He caused all this, so I expect he deserved a good face washing. Lucky he didn't drown."

Tuohy took the bridle from across Doc's saddle and put in on the big roan. Doc sniffed at Tuohy's shoulder until the big Irishman rubbed his nose. "I learned about his nose rub from Claypool. He said he almost won Doc in a poker game from Henry Wise a couple years back."

"So I heard," said Sam. "Henry turned him over to me while he's in prison."

"That was thoughtful of him." Tuohy said. "It'll be tough giving him back."

When Sam didn't comment, Tuohy went back to talking about the blast.

"We lost a good town selectman, Ed Cherry," he said. "The blast sent a sliver of a chair leg through his heart." He looked closer at the ranger. "He's the man you were talking to before you both left. Ed lingered too long on the front boardwalk." He shook his head.

"Sorry to hear it," Sam said.

"Who knows why a good man like Cherry dies and a scoundrel like Claypool goes on living?"

"He was upset about how things are going here," Sam said, wanting to find out as much as he could.

"Sure was," said Tuohy. "Ed Cherry spoke for a lot of us."

"What about all the money the Gunmen are bringing to Bad River?" Sam asked. "Isn't that what everybody wants?"

"At first, yes," said Tuohy, "but it got to where nobody was seeing any of the money. It was always coming, but it never quite made it into anybody's cashbox." He handed Sam the reins to the stallion. "I made more money, but some went here, some went there. By the time it was all divided up, I made about the same as before! Only, I was having to work twice as hard for the same amount. I always say, when a saloon can't make money, there's something bad wrong going on!" He took a breath and settled a little. "Hellfire, I should've known better. No crook ever shared anything with anybody. It ain't in their nature. He's all about taking everything for his greedy self. If I've learned anything, it's never trust a damn crook!"

Sam just looked at him.

"I reckon that sounds a little foolish," Mike said, "but you know what I mean."

"I do," Sam said. He went on to ask, "With Ed Cherry gone, who takes his place?"

"We had three selectmen," said Irish Mike. "One disappeared mysteriously, if you get what I'm saying. Now with Cherry dead, a no-good skunk named Clement Melford is the only one left until we can rustle up an election." He added, "To the Mexicans' credit, they have been good and fair to all us *Americanos*. They let us run our town to suit us, so long as we run it right."

"So you're saying no Mexican officials are in on any of this?" Sam asked.

"Not that I've seen," said Irish Mike. He chuckled, then said, "I don't know why I'm bothering you with all this. I know you're under strict orders to take back your wanted men and leave everybody else alone."

"That's true," said Sam, "but if I know Cree Sims, he's not letting something go on without taking a big share off the top."

"Yeah?" Tuohy listened curiously.

"He won't go back with me without a fight," Sam said.

"Meaning?" said Tuohy.

"Meaning he'll only go back tied dead over a saddle," Sam said bluntly.

Irish Mike looked taken aback, but only for a second. "Oh . . ." he said, getting the picture.

"And that will leave Melford," Sam said. "What kind of man is he? Is he going to give this place up without a fight?"

Irish Mike considered it.

"He used to be a gunman," he said. "But if everybody else is done for, there're plenty of us here who will beat Melford into the ground. But how will we know what you're doing out there?"

"Word travels quick," Sam said. "You'll know when I finish what I'm here to do." He paused, then asked, "Do you have a map of the locations of the French silver mines up here?"

"You know what?" said Tuohy. "I sure do!" He reached inside his shirt and took out a folded map and opened it. "I drew this off of the original in the courthouse. If you can read my scribbling, you're welcome to it. By the way, the three mines marked with an X are where the dynamite likely came from." He grinned. "Not that you would want to blow anything up."

The ranger unfolded the map, looked at it and made mental note of the Xs. "Why would the French leave dynamite in these three mines?"

Irish Mike shrugged. "Probably hoped they might reopen them someday. Who knows what these corporations were thinking?" He paused, then said, "I'd give anything to go with you, Ranger."

"It sounds like the town needs you right here, Mike," Sam said. "You've got a saloon to rebuild."

"Ah, well, I know you're right," Mike said. "Plus, I

lost my good bartender. Truth is, the little lady, my dearest Marlene, would skin and salt me alive if she thought I was hitting the trail hunting for Sims and his miscreants." He motioned at the map. "I'll be with you in spirit though, surely so."

"Much obliged," Sam said. He folded the map and put it away. "This will give me an idea what Sims and his gunmen might be up to next."

Sam led Doc from his stall and out the front door. In moments, he was in the saddle and headed for the trail leading up to the mines. The map Irish Mike had given him looked like a long snake crawling from the earth to the sky. That snake lay broken in the middle, where the mountaintop stopped, but it restarted its winding way up the next mountaintop.

No wonder Sims and his men settled here. . . .

Sam rode until the first rays of dawn seeped up like molten gold on the mountainous horizon, and he stepped down from the saddle on a narrow, flat clearing overlooking a lower mountain ridge.

Loosening the cinch under Doc's belly, he dropped the saddle from the horse's damp back. Doc blew out a breath and reached his nose around for a rub. Sam rubbed his nose, then dropped his bridle and fashioned a hackamore-grazing halter and walked Doc to a clump of wild grass standing tall between two boulders. Doc dug right in, ripping and crunching the tall, sweet stems.

"Unless you've got other plans," Sam said, "why don't we rest here and carry on after daylight?"

Part 2

Chapter 8

———————

At daylight, the ranger and Doc pushed upward to where an abandoned mine sat back from a trail scarred by wide ironclad-wagon ruts. A stripped and broken-down freight wagon sat on three wheels, one of which had scooted off the trail and sat as if looking for any reason to plunge off the edge and tumble more than two hundred feet into a deep rocky chasm.

"Easy, pal," Sam said, seeing Doc eye the sweet wild grass growing up through the wagon bed and along the trail. "Don't let a hungry belly push you off the edge."

Doc settled and blew out a breath as if he understood.

Sam opened Irish Mike's map across his lap and compared it to the trail below. Mike had a good eye for detail, not to mention a mining engineer's memory. He folded the map, put it away, stepped down and led the roan stallion farther from the edge. He tied Doc's reins to a hitch post and walked into the mine opening.

He traveled only far enough inside the shaft for a look around, but seeing the mine timbers were in good shape, he decided to venture on. Lighting a lantern he found hanging from a wall peg, he traveled downhill with the lay of the mine. When he found a spool of cord, he stopped and looked closer.

What have we here . . . ?

He walked over and looked at the crate of dynamite lying on the floor. He saw an electric-ignition plunging device. By indentions in the dirt, he could tell that other crates of explosives had recently been removed. *Okay.* He'd expected that. He bent and took up the electric device. He wrapped the extra wiring around it and loaded it up under his arm.

Much obliged, Irish Mike Tuohy, he thought.

He roamed the lantern-lit floor a few moments longer until the sound of voices came down through the shaft. These were young voices. *Children?* He headed up the shaft to find out. He heard Doc grumbling—not angrily—as if he was making sure Sam had heard the voices. He quickened his steps, turned out the lantern and set it aside.

Where stripes of sunlight slanted into the shaft opening, he slowed his pace to cautious steps and looked around. A young girl stood patting Doc on his neck. But Doc was looking away from her to where two young boys bounced around inside the abandoned wagon bed.

Uh-oh! Sam saw where the bare wagon sprocket on the rear of the wagon had scooted three inches through fresh trail dirt.

"Alto! ¡Quédense donde están!" Sam called out in Spanish. The two boys looked at each other in wonderment.

"¿Qué?" one said.

"Why stop?" said the other. "We play here all the time."

"It is true. They do," said the little girl at his side.

"You, stay right here!" Sam said to her. He yanked

down a long leather-braided lariat from Doc's saddle horn.

"Come on, Doc!" he said as he hurried closer to the wagon, sorting the lariat as he went.

He saw the wagon sprocket scoot another inch. Now the boys looked worried, feeling the wagon jar up and slam down in the dirt.

The larger of the two boys leaped out of the wagon bed and grabbed its rotted sideboard with both hands, as if that was all it would take. "I've got you, my brother!"

But Sam knew better. He spun the lariat and lassoed an exposed side post. Then he turned to Doc, who had followed him closely. He quickly spun the lariat around the saddle horn and immediately felt the big roan bear down against the weight.

"Good boy!" Sam said to the stallion, feeling the lariat draw tight.

The wagon squeaked and slowed to a halt. He hurried to where the young boy stood watching, wide-eyed. He held his arms up to the boy.

"Jump!" he shouted.

The boy hesitated but only for a second. When the wagon shuddered unsteadily, the boy leaped out into Sam's arms.

Sam grabbed him and quickly pitched him aside. "Stay back," he said.

The boy backed away even farther. The wagon scooted farther and quicker off the edge. Sam pulled his big knife from his boot, and with a wide swing of the blade, the lariat flew apart. He watched Doc almost collapse under the sudden release of the wagon weight, and the wagon plunged downward. It floated silently and easily through the air until it touched the side on the sheer stone wall and blew apart in a thousand pieces.

Sam stepped back in great relief—thankful he hadn't had to see the child's face as the boy rode the wagon to his death. He raised his sombrero, adjusted it and looked around at the three children's frightened faces. He put his big knife out of sight.

"Everybody all right?" he asked quietly. The children all nodded as one. He smiled and said, *"Bueno."*

He raised a hand to Doc, causing the big stallion to plod over, shake himself off and stand beside him. "Good work, pal," Sam said, rubbing Doc's nose.

Seeing the big roan at the ranger's side and how well he and the ranger had worked together, the children gathered closer around the two, patting Doc's neck, his bowed head.

"¿Ama usted a su caballo, señor?" the elder boy asked.

"Do I *love* my horse?" Sam said. "Yes, I like my *caballo* very much. He is a strong, smart stallion." As he spoke, he patted Doc's withers.

"But for a stallion, he is so well-tempered," the boy said.

"I know," said Sam, "and I like that about him. I don't want to travel around on a horse that doesn't get along with both people and other horses, eh? *¿Comprende?"*

"Sí, I understand," said the boy. The other two children nodded their scruffy heads.

The little girl leaned close to the elder boy and whispered.

Seeing the ranger's curiosity, the boy said. "My sister said we like you better than the other *Americanos* who come up here, like they did yesterday." The boy gestured toward a length of cliff edge obscured by clumps of juniper and barrel cacti.

"Oh?" Sam said quietly, stepping over to the edge as the children watched.

Right away, he saw a half dozen horses and riders gathered at a hitch rail near the entrance of another French mine that looked only slightly different from the one he had just exited. He stepped over to Doc, took a telescope from a saddlebag and walked back. He looked down through the lens. Near the horsemen at the hitch rail stood a large two-wheel Mule Killer cart. A tall black-and-tan mule stood calmly, twitching its huge ears against a spinning horde of flies.

Upon looking closely from face to face, Sam began to realize these men represented two groups: the Jack Swift Detective and Tracking Service and, of all things, the very group young Jack Swift had been hired to put out of business—the Bad River Gunmen.

All of them together looked like fish swimming in the same pond. Sam smiled to himself and shook his head. Swift had offered him a deal. He could've taken it. He was glad he hadn't. At the hitch rail sat Cree Sims, next to the Russian Assassin, Kura Stabitz. The other two wanted men, Giles Tillis and Earl Dupree, weren't far away.

As Sam watched, four men carried crates of faulty, outdated dynamite from the Mule Killer cart into the mine shaft. One of the men was a big burly man by the name of Benibar Greenly, whom *old* Jack Swift had always kept on the payroll owing to his cruel treatment of prisoners. Once in Benibar's custody, nobody tried to escape, Sam reminded himself. He and Benibar had little respect for each other.

Sam was certain that with Swift and his bunch in town, none of the Bad River Gunmen were going to show their faces there. Until the time came for him to gather his wanted men and leave town, he was going to have to maneuver carefully. Meanwhile, it wouldn't hurt for him to gather as much dynamite as he could and keep it on hand and out of sight. He looked over at the children as they stood playing with Doc's mane.

"Niños, es hora de que se vayan a casa," he called out to them. They stared at him curiously. *"Sí,"* he said. "I must go to work now. You can all three come back and play with Doc another time."

In the afternoon, the ranger had finished what he'd set out to do. He'd moved the dynamite crates he'd watched the Jack Swift men and the Bad River Gunmen handle, hauling them to a different cave on the next level down the mountains. He'd put himself in a good spot, having taken control of something that apparently both sides wanted badly. Four crates had no dynamite in them. What they had instead were well-stacked packs of cash.

What he needed to do now was go back to town and let Swift know what he'd seen and what he'd done so that Swift and his boss, Melford, knew that if they ever wanted the dynamite or the money, everybody had better back off and let Sam do his job. He intended to slip into Bad River and deliver his message while the Gunmen weren't there. *Simple enough . . .*

Sam gazed straight ahead as he rode back into Bad River amid laughter, fiesta music and a strong, rollicking turnout.

"Hey, *hey*!" said Benibar Greenly, seeing the ranger seated atop Henry Wise's roan stallion. "Looks like it's true. Wise turned Doc over to this ranger before he went away." He poured back a swig of Mexican whiskey and let out a hiss. "I would have paid him big money for Doc!" he said to the Swift detective drinking beside him. "Some folks don't know it, but Doc started out as a *fighting horse*. Here in Old Mex, I would have made a fortune."

"Is that a fact?" the other drinker said, uninterested. He managed to move away from Greenly.

"Wise ought to have given that stallion to me," Greenly mumbled to himself.

A crowd had been gathering all day, packing in around the large barrels and planks that served as a horseshoe-shaped bar encircling half of the street and much of the former location of the Bad River Saloon. Pork, goat and lamb lay roasted—falling off the bone and served in a high steamy pile. Overhead, canvas tarps flapped and fluttered above the makeshift bar on the warm evening wind.

At an iron rail across the street, Sam stepped down from his saddle and hitched Doc near a long water trough that sat a few feet away. He dipped a large gourd full of fresh water and carried it to Doc.

"Look who's here!" Greenly called out, walking up beside him. "Ranger Sam Burrack! Am I right? The man known for killing his outlaws from a mile away! Never gets a drop of blood on his boots!"

Now, this *idiot*, Sam said to himself.

He only glanced up from the water gourd, nodded in a minimal show of respect and looked back down.

"Hey, that's ol' Doc, ain't it?" said Greenly. "I heard somewhere that you took Doc off of Wise's hands," he added. He paused, then said, "What say I take him off *your* hands. I can give a good home to an old bounder like him. He's still got colts in him. A few good fighting rounds too, I'll wager."

He reached a hand out to Doc's nose. Doc chuffed and turned his head away.

"Don't turn your damn head on me, you ornery, flea-bit cayuse!" Greenly said. He started to grab Doc's bridle, but Sam clenched his forearm.

"I don't think he likes you, Greenly. Neither do I," Sam said with a flat stare. "Get your hand out of his face." He thrust the man's big hand away. "Doc's with me now. He's not for sale. I know he was a fighter. That was long ago. Horses never get a choice in the matter."

Greenly looked ready to throw a punch, but he settled, rubbed his wrist and gave a sour grin. "Lucky for you I've been told to stand back some. Else I'd break every bone in your *ranger* head. If I wanted that cayuse, I'd take him. You would not be the man to stop me."

Sam pitched the empty gourd over into the water trough. "Would you, then?"

He stared at Greenly for a moment, silent, poised, his hand an inch from his big Colt holstered on his side. *Ready? Yes.* But he knew this was headed for trouble and it was trouble at a time when he didn't need it. *Put a stop to it*, his inner voice cautioned him.

"Why do you want Doc so bad, Greenly?" he asked, keeping his voice level. "Are you still fighting horses?"

"So what if I am, Ranger?" said Greenly, taking a stiff defensive stand, but also showing some restraint. "It's legal here. Anyway, Doc wouldn't be doing nothing he ain't done before."

"If we're through here, why don't you go on about your business, Greenly?" Sam said. "I know if we keep this up, we'll end up hurting each other's feelings."

Greenly started to say more, but he caught himself and stopped.

Oh, yes, he's been reined in, Sam thought.

He watched as the big man gave him a sneering look, then turned and stomped away into the rollicking party crowd.

"It's okay, Doc." Sam reached his hand up to the stallion's forehead. "I already knew about your dark, sordid past," he said jokingly to the big roan. "I don't hold it against you, I promise."

Greenly looked back through the crowd, then worked his way to the plank bar to order himself a beer.

"To hell with the both of yas!" he muttered. His thick right hand rested on his holstered Remington. Under his breath, he repeated what he'd said to Sam, "If I wanted that cayuse bad enough, I'd take him and ride away"—and this time he added—"or leave him lying dead in the street!"

Chapter 9

Through a dusty upper-corner window of the Frenchman Hotel, Jack Swift watched as the ranger weaved his way through the festival crowd toward the hotel's porch. Behind him, in the hotel room set up as an office, Clement Melford stood at his desk, placing stacks of American cash into a canvas bank bag.

"Speak of the devil, Mr. Melford," Swift said. "It looks like you are about to meet our young ranger, Sam Burrack."

Melford only half-turned, a cigar in his teeth and a stack of cash in his hand.

"Oh?" he said, jiggling the cash. "Maybe I should keep some of this out, just in case he thought about joining us?"

"Mr. Melford, if I might say so, this ranger appears to have a limited understanding of what's going on around him—"

"As do many lawmen—at first anyway," Melford cut in. Again, he jiggled the cash. "Until we can properly *enlighten* him," he added, gesturing at the door. "Meanwhile, have your man outside the door there step inside and join us once the ranger is here." He gave a wide smile.

"Yes, sir, of course," Swift said obediently, stepping over to the door. He gave a series of short, quiet taps. In a moment, his tapping was answered, and he turned and smiled at Clement Melford.

"Message *relayed* . . . message *received*, sir."

"Brilliant system, Jack Swift," Melford said. He chuckled and drew on his cigar. "I trust that your man on the door is one of your best?"

"*The* best, sir." Swift beamed. "If the ranger starts any trouble here, I promise you he will be shut down so quick it will make your head swim—"

The two turned at the sound of a light knock on the door. Swift gave Melford a nod.

"See him in," Melford said with authority. Stepping around behind his desk, he sat down quickly as Swift turned the big brass door handle.

"Ranger Burrack," Melford almost gushed. "I have to say, I have long looked forward to meeting you!"

His hand came out. Sam reached across his desk, shook his hand, then saw the look on Melford's face as Swift's man Harvey Rhimes stepped forward and laid Sam's rolled-up gun belt on the edge of the desk.

"What's this? The ranger's Colt?" Melford asked Swift, who was standing nearby.

"Yes, sir, Mr. Melford," said Swift. "That is our ordinary security procedure—to take our guest's weaponry. Temporarily of course." He smiled at Sam. "But we can make an exception for Ranger Sam Burrack if you'd like."

Sam just watched. He knew they were trying to ingratiate themselves, and it wasn't working.

"Yes," said Melford, "seeing as this man is an Arizona Ranger, I feel it unnecessary to—"

"Quite all right," Sam said, holding a hand up to stop Rhimes from handing him the gun belt. He offered a thin smile. "We're a civil bunch here. I won't take much of your time."

He liked his gun belt right where it lay, the butt not too close to his hand, but a quick twist would remedy that if need be. He sat down in the chair Melford motioned to, straight across the desk. Melford offered him a cigar; Sam accepted it, pocketing it for later.

Swift stood ready for a cigar, but Melford made him no offer. He took a chair next to Sam. Rhimes stepped over to the ranger's other side. Sam glanced up at him and saw a trace of a sneer on his pockmarked face.

After a silence, Melford narrowed his brow at Sam. "Now, then," he said, "what can I do for you, Ranger?"

Sam looked around at the others, then at Melford, indicating this was not a conversation to be shared.

Melford just gave a little chuckle and watched to see how Sam was going to handle it. "Come now, Ranger, out with it," he said.

"With all respect," said Sam, "I think it'll be better if I come back another time."

Melford was becoming more interested in what the ranger had to say.

"So if you'll excuse me—" Sam started to stand up, but Rhimes's hands came down on his shoulders, shoving him back into the chair.

"You'll leave, Ranger, when Mr. Melford says you can leave— *Argggh!*" Rhimes let out a pained, tortured squeak.

As soon as Sam had touched down in his chair, he'd sprung forward from under Rhimes's hands, drawn his Colt from his holster on the desk and swung the big gun sidelong and up. He buried the Colt, chamber, barrel and all, high in the detective's exposed crotch. When Rhimes jackknifed at the waist with the prolonged squeak rattling in his tightened windpipe, Sam stepped back and stared down at him as he slung his gun belt on and hitched it.

"He might need some water," Sam said calmly.

The other two stared at him almost dumbfounded as he raised his right foot onto the chair and tied down his holster.

On the floor, Rhimes struggled to pull himself up the side of the desk, but all he managed to do was scratch his nails on the varnished finish like some wounded dog trying to paw open a screen door.

"I won't have your man ruining my desk, Swift!" Melford said in a huff. "Do something about him."

Swift hurriedly tried to lift Rhimes into a chair, as Rhimes was unable to do anything for himself but squeak in a high, strained voice. Sam stepped over to Swift and helped him.

When they settled him in the chair, Swift turned to Melford. "Sir, I don't know what to say—!"

"There's nothing you can say," Melford said. "I hope you have noticed my head is not swimming!"

"No, sir, I see it's not," said Swift. "I will trounce this man soundly and get him out of town—!"

The ranger pulled away as Harvey Rhimes tried to grasp him by his trouser leg. "Well, if we're all done here, I'll take my leave and come back sometime when we can talk over some very *private* business."

"No, Ranger, please," said Melford. "After all this, I must hear what it is you're being so closemouthed about."

Sam made a cursory glance at Rhimes, then all around the office.

"Don't worry about this one," said Melford. "Swift will drag him out of here right this minute."

"Yes, sir, Mr. Melford!" said Swift. "He is on his way out!"

Swift tilted Rhimes's chair back and pulled him, chair and all, across the floor. Another one of Swift's men opened the door and stared down at Rhimes as Swift dragged him into the hallway. Sam heard Swift talking to the other man. "Get this worthless fool into a wagon and get him out of town, Adams—you'll keep me from killing him with my bare hands!"

Melford stepped over and quietly closed the door between Sam and the men in the hall. With a hand on Sam's shoulder, he guided him back to the desk.

"I hope you can appreciate how difficult it is for a man like me to find good help, Ranger. It's tiring, very tiring," said Melford, shaking his head a little. Hiking his coattail behind a polished holster, which housed a bone-handled Colt covered with ornate engravings, he gestured toward the chair where Sam had sat moments earlier.

"Please. Sit down," he added. "Let's start over."

Swift walked back in, wiping his hands on a large white handkerchief. Melford motioned him to a chair. As Swift started to sit down and Melford stepped toward his big chair behind his desk, Sam stood on the same spot.

"Gentlemen, I won't need a seat," said Sam. "I'll keep this short and straight to the point."

Both men looked at him with anticipation.

"Here it is," said Sam. "I saw some of your men out on the mine trail earlier today. They were taking crates of dynamite from a loaded wagon and hiding them down in the mine—"

"How do you know they were our men?" Swift cut in, trying to be shrewd.

"For God's sake, Swift, shut up, or I'll strangle you!" Melford shouted. His face reddened to a dangerous glow.

"Let's be straightforward here," Sam said. He looked at Swift. "Your men are a ruse to make it look like Sims and his gang are being dealt with, should the Mexican government come snooping. But right here, right now, in the walls of this room, we know the deal."

Melford ignored everything the ranger had just said and smiled.

"And that was it, Ranger?" he said, "You just saw some men handling faulty dynamite?" He spread his hands in an unconcerned gesture, playing it off.

"That and the company both of your employees have been keeping." Sam pointed first at Swift, then at Melford. "The lot of them working together like beavers building a dam. Except in their cases, instead of building a dam, they were working together, carrying crates of cash into the old mine." He paused and watched their faces for a moment. As they appeared to settle a little, he added, "I meant to mention, after they left, I took out all of the money they hid inside the mine—four wooden crates' worth and some stuffed canvas bank bags. A sizable amount." He stopped for a moment to let his words sink in.

Swift gritted his teeth. He needed to make some sort of show. "I will have you shot and bled, Ranger!" he said.

Melford drew his ornate Colt and cocked it at Swift's chest.

"Easy," Sam cautioned him. "Nobody here needs to die. Listen to what I've got to say. I'm not after the French mine's money or the mine's dynamite. I came to Bad River to take back three wanted men and a paid killer who works for them." He focused entirely on Melford as if Swift were no longer in the room. "Are you interested or not?"

Melford lowered his fancy Colt from Swift's chest, uncocked it and slipped it down into his holster. He let out a breath and said, "You're mighty damn right I'm interested."

Sam continued to persuade them that he had no interest in their stolen mine money or assets. At first, Melford had a hard time believing him. "Where I come from, Ranger, a man puts nothing before money. Why should I believe you?"

"What am I doing here?" Sam said. "I could have left today with the money and nobody would know it was me who took it."

Melford considered that, then said, "It does not strike me as natural." He gave Sam a piercing stare. "You steal our money—"

"Your *stolen* money," Sam cut in.

"All right, our stolen money," Melford conceded. "You hide it again. Then you come here to tell us we can have it all back?"

"That's the long and short of it," Sam said. "You get your money when I leave here with my outlaws in chains *or* wrapped in canvas." He added, "We all know when you deal with outlaws, there comes a time when either you or they take a fall." He focused on Melford.

"Yeah?" said Swift, trying to insert himself in the conversation. "What's to keep you from taking your prisoners and keeping the money?"

Sam shook his head at this stupidity. "Let's not start all over, Detective. It's too simple to have to keep explaining." He looked at Clement Melford as if for an agreement.

"Keep talking, Ranger. Pay Swift no attention," said Melford. "He doesn't seem to get it, but I do. You want your outlaws. I want the money." He turned to Swift. "Good Lord, Swift! Are you a complete imbecile?"

Swift still didn't seem to understand. Sam thought it might be because he saw no place for himself in the deal.

"Anyway," Sam said to Melford, "that's the whole deal, no tricks, no swindles. When I have my wanted men cuffed and seated in saddles or tied down dead across some, I'll tell you where to find the cash. I'll wait until your men signal you that they've found it. Then we all ride away."

A silence fell across the room. Sam looked steadily at Melford, waiting for a decision.

But before Melford could speak, Swift blurted out, "This all sounds good, but what about—"

"No more *what abouts*, Swift!" Melford shouted, the taste of big money starting to sweeten his palate. "It's so damn gut simple, my son could understand it—and he's as dumb as his uncles on his mother's side, of course."

Sam picked up his sombrero from atop Melford's desk and leveled it atop his head. "I'm glad we've worked it out," he said.

"As am I," said Melford. "Let me know when you're ready to take your wanted men." He appeared to relish the idea of double-crossing Sims and his three gunmen out of the big mine money. "We'll put this plan into motion as soon as I hear you're ready."

"It won't be long," Sam said. "A couple days maybe. You'll break the news to Sims that I have all the money. I'll give it up when I mark him and the other three men off my list."

"You're going to let him know up front that it's you?" Melford said. "This is like inviting him, Tillis, Dupree, and Stabitz to a gunfight!" He grinned. "Hell, I kind of like it."

"Good," said Sam. "When I'm ready to make my move, you tell him I have all the money. Tell him and his men to come meet me and take it. It shouldn't be hard to convince them—one ranger against the four of them. He'll look like a coward if he turns down a deal like that—"

Sam froze as he heard a horse whinny in pain out on the street below.

Doc . . . ? He glanced toward the window as the sound of pain blared out again. *Yes, it was Doc! No question!*

Without another word, Sam raced out the door, down the stairs and out onto the boardwalk. Across the street at the hitch rail where he'd left Doc, he saw a big blood bay stallion up on his hind legs, a death grip on Doc's nose. Doc, still reined to the rail, had hunkered under the big stallion's weight. Sam raced across the busy street, shoving onlookers out of his way. Ten feet away from the horses, he leaped forward into the air, Colt drawn, and landed hard against the other stallion's trunk.

The force of the ranger's weight slamming the big bay's side forced the stallion to turn Doc loose. Sam swung the big Colt and struck the blood bay a full powerful blow. The impact staggered the bay but only for a second. As the horse stomped and bellowed, preparing for his next assault, Sam knew he couldn't leave

Doc tied up with no way to defend himself. The cayuse was already bloody in several places. Sam jerked his knife from his boot and sliced Doc's bridle, reins and saddle and jerked them to the ground.

The bay made short lunges at Doc, the ranger right between them. Sam saw nothing was going to stop the big raging bay. Irish Mike Tuohy came running up with his ten gauge, but Sam motioned him back.

The bay's threatening lunges had grown closer, his front hooves brushing the ranger's legs. Sam saw the bay stallion take a longer start. This next lunge would be a bad one, Sam knew.

"Okay, pal!" Sam said, close to Doc's bleeding ear. "Take him down, as hard as you need to."

As if knowing what the ranger was saying, Doc let out a deep, threatening stallion's roar and shot forward, his teeth bared, meeting the blood bay's attack with a wild fury like Sam had never seen.

Sam moved in closer and closer as the two big stallions battled. Irish Mike came up beside him and spoke just between the two of them.

"I brought my horse kit from the barn. I'll do the stitches your roan is going to need."

"Thanks, Mike," Sam said.

"And I want you to know," said Irish Mike, "I saw that turd Benibar Greenly a while ago rubbing a mare's fresh cloth all over his blood bay's muzzle—he got him all steamed up. Doc was the only other stallion at the rails today. Greenly started this whole damn thing."

"Much obliged, Irish Mike," said Sam.

He eyed Greenly at the edge of the crowd. The other man seemed to enjoy the bloody spectacle. Sam looked away before Greenly saw him watching.

Doc had the blood bay down on its front knees, its

muzzle twisted in the powerful grip of Doc's teeth. Doc's front right hoof rose and fell on the bay's withers mercilessly.

"Doc, come here, pal," Sam called out. "He's had enough."

Chapter 10

At the rail where he'd left Doc earlier, Sam fished out a soft length of rope from inside his saddlebags and fashioned a comfortable hackamore on Doc's wounded jaws and muzzle. Doc grumbled and jerked back a little at first, but then he settled, breathed deep and let Sam wash his wounds.

"He's your patient now," Sam said to Irish Mike, who had set up a wooden folding table at the hitch rail and laid out his instruments—long hooked needles and spools of heavy black thread.

"First, I'll numb him down good," said Irish Mike. "Steady his head for me, Sam."

Sam held Doc by his hackamore and watched Mike fill a big syringe, then reach up into Doc's mouth to slather inside his lips and gums with a cloudy gray liquid. Doc grew passive and quiet right away.

"I learned about this stuff from the Mexicans down here," Mike said. "It's made mostly from cactus pulp. But it sure does its job. I wouldn't try stitching inside a big animal's mouth without it."

Sam kept the big stallion comforted and settled as Mike plied his handiwork. All the while he stood hold-

ing Doc's head, Sam kept Benibar Greenly in his pe-
ripheral vision. Sam knew there was trouble coming
between them—he welcomed it. He was biding his
time, hoping the street crowd would thin down some
more before he let it happen—*caused* it to happen if he
was being honest.

Like any horse fighter, Greenly had gotten his big
bay stallion off the street and out of sight as soon as he
could. When he'd returned, Sam noted he'd started
moving around a lot, standing on one side of the street
for a few minutes, then the other. His big hand brushed
the butt of his gun with every step.

A gunfight? All right, Sam told himself. That would
suit him fine. He wondered if Greenly had already
known a gunfight was in the making. If he didn't know
now, he would know soon enough.

"All done," said Mike, rubbing Doc's head and ex-
amining the bands of stitches he'd sewn in here and
there.

Doc seemed to have taken it all in good tempera-
ment. His right eye was puffy, and the black stitches
stood high across the stallion's badly swollen nose.

Irish Mike rolled down his shirtsleeves and walked
toward his livery barn.

"You're a tough guy, Doc," Sam said, leading the
wounded stallion toward the barn as well. He'd loaded
his saddle on Doc's back, its sliced cinch dangling loose
down both sides. Then he hooked Doc's sliced bridle
and reins over the saddle horn. These were items Irish
Mike's hostler would repair in the next day or two. Sam
noticed Greenly watching them both from a block away,
inching closer, step by step. This thing was boiling to a
head. *Let it boil. . . .*

Sam drew his Winchester from the saddle boot and

carried it in his gloved hand, looking calm, easygoing, but ready to beat Greenly into the ground with it at the drop of a hat. As Sam and Doc walked along, Jack Swift trotted up beside him.

"There you are, Ranger!" Swift said, a little short of breath. He gave Sam a thin counterfeit smile. "My goodness, I'm glad to see you weren't hurt in that barbaric fracas back there." He gestured toward the horse blood still in the street. Children were touching their bare toes in it for further examination.

Sam only glanced at him without slowing down.

"You mean the *barbaric fracas* your man Greenly started? The one who got my stallion here a face full of stitches?"

"Okay, Ranger," said Swift, "I apologize for Greenly. He is an ass and an idiot. Everyone knows it. But I can only hope that what you and Mr. Melford and I just discussed—"

"Tell your boss, Mr. Melford, that the plans we agreed to will still be carried out . . . as expressed. Can you remember that?" Sam caught the sarcasm in his own voice. He immediately regretted it, too late.

"That's not fair, Ranger," said Swift, coming to a halt in the street. "I'm only trying to run my business. If that requires me showing an extra measure of respect to the man who pays me, then so be it!"

Sam saw that Greenly was a half block away and getting closer. *Keep coming,* Sam prompted him silently. Keeping one eye on Greenly, he said, "That was short-spoken and uncalled for. I hope you will accept my apologies. How you run your business is no business of mine."

Swift suddenly looked embarrassed; he milled awkwardly in place as if uncertain how to take the ranger's apology. Finally, he tried changing the subject to defuse any lingering bad feelings Sam might have harbored since they'd met the other day after the explosion.

"Yes, Ranger, thank you," Swift said. "I say we let bygones be bygones and forge ahead." He leaned in closer. "You know my proposition for you to join us the other day is still on the table even today. I'd hoped that was part of the reason you came here today!"

"Let's not keep repeating ourselves, Swift," Sam said, catching sight of Greenly fifteen feet back in the foot traffic along the dirt street. "What I came here to do is still *all* I came here to do—"

Sam stopped short as a stunned look came over Swift's face. From the corner of the alley leading to the livery barn, Benibar Greenly reached out and clasped a hand down on Sam's shoulder.

"Hey, Ranger!" Greenly said. Swift tried to signal Greenly away, but the burly gunman would have none of it. "I saw you put your hands on my blood bay while he was defending himself from an attack!"

Swift's thoughts raced and his eyes widened in fear at the sight of the big, hulking gunman over Sam's shoulder. When Sam did not answer, Greenly shook him.

"*Hey!* Did you hear me, Ranger?" he said.

Oh, God! Swift took a step away as Sam turned and faced Greenly.

"I heard you," Sam said quietly, his eyes slightly lowered.

Greenly was now an arm's length away. He stepped forward. "Yeah?" He grinned, a little surprised but apparently pleased with himself. "Well, don't you ever forget, if you ever lay a hand on my stallion again, I will rip your head plumb off. You hear me?" His voice grew louder as he made his threats.

"I won't put hands on your stallion again, Greenly," Sam said almost meekly. "You have my word." He handed Doc's reins over to Swift. "Take these," he said.

Swift took the reins without hesitation. Something in the ranger's voice caused Swift to move back another step, Doc right beside him. But Greenly didn't get it. He stood broad faced, grinning like a fool.

Sam moved as quick as a snake. In a two-handed grip, Sam's rifle snapped back above his shoulders and slammed forward, full force, the brass butt plate burying itself into Greenly's grinning mouth. Blood and teeth flew. Swift's eyes squeezed shut to blot out the sight. Doc jerked his wounded head sideways.

The big man staggered back, but was too big to go down easily. Sam stalked forward a step and let go another powerful blow. The brass butt plate struck the same spot.

Onlookers stared and groaned. A woman shrieked. Greenly staggered more, yet remained upright, even when the third blow jammed his face half around onto his cheek.

"See?" Sam asked him coolly, still stalking forward, readying for his next pounding rifle blow. "No hands on your stallion."

"Ranger! Stop! Don't kill him! Don't kill him!" Swift gave a nervous look up at the window in the Frenchman Hotel, not wanting Clement Melford to see the ranger chop down another one of his professional gunmen.

"Why not?" Sam said in a low, even tone.

He stared grimly at Swift as he stepped in closer to him and to the big, bloody, staggering horse fighter.

Luckily for Greenly, his legs gave out on him and dropped him to his knees just as Sam got ready to hit him again. Weaving in place, Greenly let out a bloody gasp as fresh urine circled and spread around his crotch.

"Plea— *Please*," he managed to rasp.

Sam started to shove him backward with the toe of his boot, but mercifully, Greenly fell on his own, his arms and knees on either side folded back like the twisted appendages of some ancient earth-stricken waterfowl. Now that Greenly was down and out, Swift's men started to gather in a half-circle around Sam and Jack Swift. Greenly's eyes rolled up in his head.

"Is he . . . ?" said Swift.

"I don't know," said Sam. He stepped around the badly beaten gunman and looked down at a broken hand that had caught part of a rifle blow. He picked up Greenly's bloody hat from the dirt and dropped it over his bloody broken face. "I think he'll be all right— might be a little sore."

"A little sore . . . ?" Swift looked aghast as Sam reached for Doc's reins.

"Get the hell away from Greenly!" a harsh voice demanded from among the gathering detectives.

Sam reached Doc's reins back out to Swift, who took them again. The detectives had circled in closer now that the action had simmered. Sam looked around at the half dozen armed men as he chambered a round in his blood-streaked Winchester one-handed.

"If you want him, come get him," Sam said. "I'm done here." He looked from one face to the next, all of them with their suit coats pulled back behind their holstered six-guns.

"Damn Ranger," one man cursed under his breath.

"Stick together, men," said another detective. "He won't take on all of us. Get ready."

"Everybody, wait!" said Swift, unsure what to do. His own men weren't listening to him.

Sam heard a gruff voice behind him.

"He won't take you on alone because I won't let him," said Irish Mike Tuohy. "I want some of you buzzard bait myself." His big double-barreled shotgun clicked twice as he cocked back each hammer. "Who's first?" he added. "Don't be shy. There's plenty for all."

The men stalled, seeing the ranger's big Winchester and now a double-barreled ten gauge covering them.

"Everybody, *please*!" Swift called out. His eyes slid past the hotel room where he knew Melford must have been watching. "Let's stand down here!"

"Shut up, Swift! I'll cut you in half!" said Irish Mike, swinging the shotgun toward him. "I haven't forgotten whose men brought in the dynamite that blew down my saloon. You owe me! Now pay up like you said you would." He held up a single stick of dynamite. "Or this is all for you." He bit down on a smoking cigar stub.

"Wait. Hold on, please!" said Swift. "I said I would pay you. I meant it. Look!" He jerked a stack of cash from inside his lapel.

Sam stepped over to give him room and watched him pitch the banded bills on the ground near Mike's feet.

Swift's men looked stunned. They had looked to him for guidance; they saw none. This was not the act of a man in control of a situation. It even drew a curious look from the ranger.

Jack Swift stared at the ground as if wishing the dry barren earth would swallow him whole. Under Greenly's bloody hat came a terrible gurgling sound. Sam nudged Greenly's limp shoulder with the toe of his boot.

"Get him out of here," Sam said, nodding down at Greenly, "before I beat him again."

Broken tendons stuck out the back of Greenly's crushed hand. The detectives moved forward with caution.

Sam looked back down at the gurgling Benibar Greenly. "Your gun fighting needs work, Greenly." He leaned down a little and added, "Guess what happens to you if you ever put hands on Doc again."

Watching from his window above the street in the Frenchman Hotel, Clement Melford stood back out of sight and puffed his cigar. He smiled and spoke to Dan'l Thorn, the tall, well-dressed lawman from Indian Territory who stood watching the street with him.

"You have to admit, Dan'l," he said, "he is a feisty one, our Arizona Ranger Samuel Burrack."

"I've always known him to be," said the dapper Scots-Cherokee. "Seems to have a healthy knack for crowd control too."

They both watched Sam lead Doc away toward the livery barn, Irish Mike covering the men with his ten gauge, backing away a step at a time, the brick of cash from Swift stuck down his trouser pocket.

"I still don't understand why you don't want me to kill the ranger today and be done with it," Thorn said. He swished whiskey around in his glass and tossed it back in a gulp. "I've been here over a week, and I ain't earned my keep."

"As I just explained, Dan'l," said Melford, trying to be patient, "he has my money hidden out there somewhere around this godforsaken dung bucket!" He reached for the cut glass decanter on a nearby serving table and refreshed both their drinks. "If he should die before telling you anything—and from what I've seen of him, he just might—I stand to lose more money than most men ever see in a lifetime. Have I made it all simple enough this time?" He raised his glass to Dan'l Thorn. "If so, then *salud*," he added.

Thorn gave a little chuckle and shrugged. "Sure thing, boss. Simple enough. *Salud*," Thorn repeated, his glass extended. They drank.

"Still, I have to say," said Thorn with a slight whiskey hiss, "three minutes with me, and you'll be wanting me to cut his tongue out just to shut him up." A gleaming Cherokee-crafted knife appeared in his hand as if by magic.

Melford almost reeled back from surprise. He hardened his tone of voice. "We are doing this *my way*, Dan'l. Do you understand?" He ran a crooked finger around the inside of his starched white collar. "Let's make no mistake who is in charge here." He glanced down at Jack Swift on the dusty street. "This terrible place has reduced ol' Jack Swift's grandson to some sort of babbling, jelly-minded *pédéraste*." He added quickly, "Careful it doesn't do that to either of us." He looked at the big knife in Thorn's hand. "Now, put that away."

A jelly-minded pédéraste . . . ? Thorn looked at Melford for a second, puzzling it out.

"Whatever you say, boss," he said. "I won't kill him until you tell me to." The big knife spun forward on his finger in a flash, then backward, then seemed to disappear.

Melford smiled, raised his glass to Thorn again and sipped the strong Mexican whiskey. "As for your idea, Dan'l, I'm not dismissing it out of hand. Let's first see how trading Sims and his men for the money goes." He grinned and touched his glass to Thorn's. "If all else fails, you can carve Burrack up like a holiday goose and I will cheer you on."

They both laughed.

Thorn smiled and smoothed down his mustache. He swished his whiskey again and glanced down at the street, where Sam, Doc and Irish Mike Tuohy walked out of sight in the alley toward the livery barn.

"Anything you say, boss," said Thorn. "You're in charge here."

Melford nodded. "With both hands," he said, "and don't forget it."

Thorn stretched, stifled a yawn and looked back down on the street. "If it's all the same to you, boss, I think I'll take a ride around this mountainside, familiarize myself with some of the local color."

"Watch out for Sims and his Bad River Gunmen," said Melford. "They rode south into the valley to pull a job. They might come back tonight, asking questions we don't want to answer."

"I wasn't going to mention it, but since you brought it up, how will you get Sims to settle down once you tell him the French mine money is gone?"

Melford grinned. "Simple," he said. "I won't tell him. Not yet. At least not until I see the ranger is going through with this plan. I won't be taken in. So far I have no proof he's serious. Then, and only then, will I be a part of it."

This man has no idea who he's fooling with . . . , Thorn mused silently. The ranger had been serious from the get-go, else he would not have come here with this kind of deal. He gave Melford a look. "You don't say?"

"I certainly *do* say," said Melford. The two chuckled.

"No wonder you wanted me to come here and hang around awhile, just in case," said Thorn. "You've been expecting something like this."

"Dan'l, old friend," said Melford, "I have found that the more wealth a man acquires, the less he should have to use it. I have placed a lot of my personal money in an account I set up at *my* bank. I'm shoveling money out to Sims just to keep him and his men happy. I've convinced him the money is safer in my bank than it is in the hands of his gunmen or down some varmint hole in the rocks. This will cinch what I've been telling him."

"So only you, Swift and myself know the ranger has all the mine money?" Thorn said.

"Correct," said Melford. "Until I see it's time to tell Sims about it."

Thorn considered it. "It all sounds risky as hell." He grinned. "I wouldn't miss it."

Chapter 11

After dark, Irena had taken the doctor's buggy and delivered a small bottle of medicine he'd mixed for a feverish elderly woman living on the outskirts of town. In the first purple spur of moonlight on her way back to the doctor's, she thought she heard a horse's shod hooves on the trail closing nearer behind her. She slapped the reins to the buggy horse, and as the animal sprang forward, she rocked back on the brake handle and caused the small rig to fishtail slightly, dragging its stopped wheels in the loose dirt and gravel, deliberately raising heavy dust.

"Buen caballo," Irena said to the horse under her breath.

Quickly, she released the brake handle and let the buggy straighten out forward as the dust roiled and rose. As the buggy straightened, the experienced buggy horse let its sudden surge fall back into its slow normal pace as if the incident had all been a false alarm of some sort.

Irena listened closely to the trail behind her. After a moment, she heard a horse chuff in the risen dust.

"All right, Irena, wait for me. I give up!" Antonio Villa called out with a little laugh. "You have caught me fair and square."

Irena smiled but only a little. What did that mean, she had caught him fair and square? He gave up? *Huh-uh!* She didn't like that. Why was he following her anyway, causing her to catch him fair and square? Why was she catching him, period? She was not known as a young woman given to childish games of any sort, especially with a man in whose eyes she had seen time and again the wantonness of a mountain wolf.

"I am in a hurry, Antonio. I cannot wait," Irena called back to him. Even as she spoke, she raised a small .30 caliber U.S. Navy Colt from the right pocket of her dress, laid it across her lap and smoothed her work apron down over it.

"It's all right. I will catch up to you," said Antonio, gigging his horse forward in a quick trot. Beside her, he reached down for her buggy reins, but Irena held them away from his reach.

"No. I told you, I am in a hurry. Dr. Jorgenson is concerned when I am out after dark like this."

"Aw, *sí,*" Antonio chuckled. "If you were mine, I too would be concerned if you were not near me."

He dropped his horse back and gigged it forward on the other side of the buggy. Before Irena could either stop him or speed up, Antonio stepped out of his saddle and onto the empty seat beside her. He spun his horse's reins around a brass hitching hook and relaxed, his left arm coming up around her shoulders.

"I bet you're cold out in this night air, eh?" he said. He tried to draw her closer but she shrugged him away.

"Whoa!" Antonio laughed. "A beautiful night, a moonlit sky like this. We're all alone. We can be *friends.* Who will know?"

"I will know. That's who!"

Irena raised his arm from her shoulders and laid it

over on his side. He smiled, as if taking all of this as some playful joke between a man and woman. A game he already knew he would win.

"Speaking of friends," she said, scooting away from him, "how is my good friend Sara? Where is she tonight?"

"Oh, she's waiting for me at home, I'm sure," he said. "I have been in the valley for two days taking care of some business. I told her I will be home later tonight." He smiled and wiggled his finger. "So here I come." As he spoke, he reached his wiggling fingers over and loosened the linen string up high on her bodice. "But I have time to taste your sweet neck, your bare breasts, your shoulders." He buried his face where he had loosened her blouse.

"Stop it, Antonio! Stop it!" Irena snapped at him. "I will do nothing to shame myself—or my friend." She yanked on the brake handle. The buggy stopped with a jerk. "Now, get on your horse and go! Or by the saints, I will shoot you! I mean it!" She held the Colt for him to see clearly.

"Stop it, Irena," Antonio chuckled. "Guns are pointed at me all the time. I no longer fear them." He quickly grabbed the gun from her hand and laughed.

She hurriedly tried closing her blouse, but Antonio was persistent. He shoved her hands away. Her breasts shone silkily in the moonlight. "I have seen some of you. Now I must see more."

"Easy there, ladies' man," said a voice in the darkness behind the buggy.

Antonio and Irena looked around quickly, surprised by the Gunmen Eli Denton and Chaz Campo, who were sitting on their horses midtrail, watching what was going on.

"You didn't forget about us two pards waiting back there, did you?" asked Campo.

Irena hurriedly closed her blouse again, clutching it together with one hand.

Antonio gathered himself enough to give a sheepish grin. "No, I did not forget you," he said to the two. He thought about making a grab for his gun, but realized they had theirs already drawn and cocked, lying across their laps.

"All we've heard since we left the valley," said Campo, stepping from his saddle, "is about the pretty señoritas you have up here all to yourself."

Irena dealt Antonio a look of horror, realizing he was even worse than the craven wolf she had thought him to be. "Antonio, how could you?" she said, tears welling in her terrified eyes.

"Irena, I—" He tied to speak, but Campo cut in, stopping him.

"Come out of there, ladies' man. Give me some room," Campo said.

Irena tried to keep a clear head, knowing she would fight for her life if it came to that. She secretly crossed herself and thought of the small paring knife from the kitchen that she carried sheathed in her apron pocket.

Two miles farther back on the same dusty switchback, Dan'l Thorn called out to darkness ahead of him, "Hello, the trail." He waited and listened until the ranger called out in reply only twenty yards ahead of him.

"Hello, Dan'l Thorn," said an unsurprised Sam without turning in his saddle. "Come on up. I've been waiting for you."

"Waiting for me?" Thorn gigged his dapple gray forward. "That's a hell of a thing to say to a man who's been following you the past three miles on the sly." He slowed his dapple gray beside the ranger, who was riding one of Irish Mike's stable horses, a wiry little mudbank desert barb. Thorn saw Sam's big Colt slip back into its holster. Nodding at the Colt, he said, "So you weren't too certain it was me after all?" When Sam neither confirmed nor denied, Thorn said, "I suppose that soothes the Cherokee part of me some."

"I'm one of the few people who knows that you are no more Cherokee than Whistler's mother," Sam said.

"I am part Cherokee," said Thorn, "just part. That's all I ever claimed. I'm Scots-Cherokee." He paused, then added, "Anyway, you're Scots-Irish-Cherokee. So what of it?"

"Are we through talking bloodlines?" Sam asked.

"I am if you are," said Thorn. "I only played on being Cherokee back when I was tracking for a living. If you're a tracker in the high West, you're either Indian or starving, waiting for a wagon train to flounder somewhere and folks to start eating one another."

"Good to see you, Dan'l," Sam said, out of the blue, putting all else away. "I saw your face up in Melford's window at the Frenchman. How is that place?"

"I'm good staying there," said Thorn. "I suppose you're sleeping on the ground somewhere?" He looked around as if expecting to see the ranger's bedroll among the rocks and cacti.

"I will be until it gets too crowded," said Sam.

"I hear you, Ranger." Thorn nodded with a slight look of remorse. "In this world, it *could* happen."

"There go bloodlines and world affairs," said Sam. "Are you going to mention the money I'm holding—?"

"Look," said Thorn, "we both know Clement Melford is going to do whatever he has to do to get the money back from you—or else Sims will kill him or they will kill each other."

So Melford had already mentioned their private deal to Dan'l Thorn. Sam wasn't surprised.

"You mean Melford can't keep putting his own money in the game?" he cut in.

"Not if there's no end in sight," said Thorn. "If you were to cut out with all that money, Melford might have to feed himself a bullet." He gave Sam a serious stare. "So instead of thinking of me as being here to kill you, remind yourself I might be here to try to keep you alive—for Melford's sake. Hell, for Bad River's sake far as that goes. If Melford falls, so does the whole damn town."

"I'll keep that in mind," Sam said. "How much is he offering you to kill me?"

"I don't work like that for him anymore," Thorn said. "I do a small job here or there, and he gives me a big chunk of money. Between jobs, I drink as much Tennessee sipping whiskey as I can stand."

"I suppose I'm honored just being part of all that," the ranger said.

"You should be," said Thorn. "He's got me standing by right now, says *if* he wants you dead, he'll let me know and I can carve you like a goose for all he cares." He gave Sam a sidelong glance and found a dark, curious look on the other man's shadowed face. "His words, Sam, not *mine*," Thorn added.

"Wait a minute, Dan'l," Sam said, stopping the desert barb suddenly on the trail. "Did you hear something just now?"

"I might've," said Thorn. "Prob'ly a coyote."

"No, not a coyote," said Sam. He looked at Thorn as if wondering if this might be a trick. "I hear voices."

* * *

"We can beat on you all night, pretty señorita. It does not hurt us a bit," Chaz Campo said loudly into Irena's swollen face. "If you're smart, you'll get with our plan here!" He took a drink from the bottle of whiskey Denton handed him, then handed it back.

Outside the buggy, Antonio paced back and forth in short steps like a scared child. "Stop it!" he said. "This is not why I brought you here with me!"

"Oh, really, Badman Villa!" said Denton, only half joking, wagging the whiskey bottle. "Why *did* you bring us with you? All the way up from the valley floor, we had to listen to your boasting, your big stories about the men you killed at the bank and the two beautiful women you have waiting here for you."

"But to beat them is not right!" said Antonio. "Let's go to town. There are more women there than you can count."

"No!" shouted Campo, standing over Irena, his shirt open, his gun belt on the ground with Antonio's. "First this one, then the other one." He gave a whiskey grin. "You know, the one waiting in the little hacienda farther up the road? Might interest you to know, the Barret brothers are already headed there to keep the pot warm, so to speak."

Antonio saw fury in Irena's swollen eyes as she glared at him. "I lied to you, amigos!" he said. "There is no other woman waiting!"

All he could see now was Sara, there alone in the little adobe two miles up the road, a small fire in the *chimenea* to guide him in the dark. *¡Santa Madre!* Just the way he had described the scene to these two killers, these Bad

River Gunmen pals of his. Holy Mother of God! What had he done?

Antonio saw no way to reach his gun belt on the ground. But he saw his horse standing where he'd hitched him to the brass hook on the seat frame. The reins were easily loosened, he told himself. Then without another thought, he leaped up the side of the buggy and into his saddle. He yanked the reins from the hook and was on his way. His horse streaked away up the dark rocky trail as bullets flew past his head.

A stupefied silence fell over the buggy, its inhabitants and the space it occupied on the trail. Campo stood in the buggy, naked from the waist down, his shirt open. He stared in the direction of the fleeing horse. His gun hung smoking in his hand. "I'll be galldanged and gone to hell!" he said drunkenly.

Their horses, unreined, had been spooked by the outbreak of gunfire and bolted away.

"Could you have done something, anything at all, to keep our horses from running off? You know, maybe tied their reins?"

"Don't go giving me what-fors, Chaz," Denton warned him. "I'm dog-killing drunk and—"

While the two bickered, Irena watched for her chance. When Campo looked away, she sprang up enough to throw the buggy brake handle forward, grab the reins and deal the buggy horse a sharp slap on the rump. Beaten and half-naked in the buggy seat, Irena realized Antonio had left her there to fend for herself or die. She didn't plan on dying, nor would she allow these men to have their way with her! She knew Sara's condition; she did not blame Antonio for going to her, but she had no forgiveness for him.

The buggy jerked forward. Campo staggered a step. Irena stabbed him down low in his back with her paring knife. Campo screamed, grabbed for the knife. As he did, Irena planted a bare foot on his off-balance butt and gave him a hard shove out of the moving buggy.

"What the hell?" Denton shouted, seeing dust roil as the buggy rolled out of sight.

In his surprised drunkenness, he fired two shots at Campo on the ground, missing both times.

"Don't shoot, Eli! It's me, damn it to hell!" Campo screamed. "Help me up from here. I can't get up! She's ruined me!" His hand was bloody from reaching around to the knife handle.

From midtrail, Sam and Dan'l Thorn looked at the two gunmen, one naked on his knees, and the other behind him, his hands under the first man's arms, trying hard to lift him to his feet. Thorn glanced away, shaking his bowed head; then he looked back at the two drunks. He cleared his throat, just loud enough to be noticed.

"Are we interrupting anything here?" he asked quietly.

"Uh, no," said Eli Denton. "That is, a woman stabbed my pard here." He gestured down at Campo. "We've drunk some whiskey, so . . ." He let his words go unfinished as if the remark explained everything satisfactorily.

Sam sat and watched, knowing that Thorn was an old hand at dealing with these types of hard cases.

"You there in the dirt, hero!" Thorn said to Chaz Campo. "You look familiar. Where're your trousers?"

"I should look familiar, Thorn," said Campo. "I rode down a bounty with you and some of your pals last year."

Thorn looked closer and said in recognition, "Chaz

Campo. Yes, so you did. Get your trousers on, hero. Or do you just prefer going around bare-assed in public?"

"Look, Mr. Thorn," said Campo, "nobody calls me hero or any other name but my own. I don't like it. And I don't tolerate bad-mouthing of any sort from anybody, even you—"

"Get your trousers on," Thorn said. "Then you can tell us how tough you are." He stared coldly at Campo until the gunman started pulling on his trousers.

"A while ago, we thought we heard a woman's voice," said Sam. "Was that woman with you two?"

"Not wanting to lie to you," said Campo, "I'm thinking, yes, she might have been. She took off that way in a buggy right before you fellas came along."

"What was her hurry?" Thorn asked. "You two weren't being rude, were you?" He gave a friendly little knowing grin.

Campo returned the grin. "Well, you know how it is," he said. "We mighta got a little rowdy . . . maybe?"

"That's what I thought," said Thorn. He drew his long six-gun and looked it over as he spoke. "Didn't you hear me last summer when I said how bad I hate a man who mistreats women?"

"Wait a minute," Campo said, getting nervous. "I might have heard you mention it last summer. But I don't see what that's got to do with any of this. We ain't mistreated anybody out here! Not to any great extent." He absently rubbed blood from across his knuckles.

Thorn gave the ranger a flat I-could-have-told-you-so look.

Eli Denton started to step away toward the edge of the trail.

"Where are *you* going, sidekick?" Thorn asked bluntly.

Denton pointed off toward the darkness. "Our horses,"

he said. "They took off in all the noise. We'll need to gather them."

Thorn shook his head slowly. "No, you don't," he said in a calm, resolved tone.

"Now just a damn minute," said Campo. "Let's stop yanking one another's reins. You know who we're riding for. We know who you're riding for. Hell, we're purt near on the same side! I say whatever's got you aggravated, we shut it down—ride away from here and all four of us keep our mouths shut. You don't have to worry about us saying a word to anybody ever!"

"I'm not worried," Thorn said with finality. He smiled and let out a breath. "I'll tell you what. I find this woman in her buggy up the trail and she tells me there was no harm done here, I'll be remorseful as hell that I killed you both." He gave the ranger a cool gaze. "Ain't that right, Sam?"

Sam didn't answer but gestured toward the trail ahead. "I'm going on to check on the woman."

"This ain't right, damn it to hell!" said Campo. "Accusing me of mistreating a woman, which maybe we did some. But tell me this! If a man can't mistreat women some, who the hell can he mistreat anymore?"

Sam heard Campo's voice stop suddenly.

"Stupid bastard," Thorn said under his breath. When Sam looked back, he saw Thorn step down from his saddle, walk forward and pull his big knife blade from Campo's throat.

"All right, I understand about the woman!" said Denton, his eyes wide as Campo sank to the ground, hands gripping the slit in his throat. "You two lawdogs didn't want to be seen out here. I won't talk—"

"Start running," said Thorn.

"What?" said Denton, shaking all over. "I told you, I understand your situation!"

"You heard me," Thorn said softly. "Start running."

"Just a damn minute here!" shouted Denton. "I'm a noted fast gun, just like Campo. You are not going to shoot me in the back."

"Not if you keep standing there running your mouth," said Thorn. He checked his big Colt, recocked it and held it up close to his face as if posing for a tintype, his finger on the trigger.

Denton looked at the ranger. "You ain't letting him do this, are you?"

Before Sam could respond, Thorn cut in with a mocking half-smile. "Allow me, Sam." To Denton he said, "You see, hero, the ranger is here in Old Mexico working under what's called the Matamoros Agreement to take three *Americanos* back to face trial. He has nothing to do with enforcing Mexican law, or in any way—"

"That's enough, Dan'l," Sam said quietly. "We need to go on and see about this buggy. I've got a feeling it belongs to the town doctor." He pointed at the buggy tracks in the trail dust. "There's a woman who works for him."

"*Dan'l?*" said Denton, coming apart in drunken fear and rage. "He calls you Dan'l like you two are pards?"

"I gave you a chance to run," Thorn said to Denton.

"This is all rigged! Every damned bit of it! *Rigged!*" Denton turned, running as he spoke. "You sonsabitches!"

"One thousand . . . two thousand . . . three thousand . . . four thousand," Thorn said quietly.

The big Colt bucked in his hand in a loud belch of blue-orange flame. Denton's head popped and spilled like an overripe melon.

Without a word, Sam turned the barb to follow the moonlit buggy tracks.

"I had to shoot him, Sam," Thorn said, "else by morning everybody in Bad River would've known we'd met out here."

"I understand," Sam said, although he knew they could have played it off some way—two lawmen meeting by chance on a well-used trail into town.

"I felt like you would," said Thorn with his thin smile. He replaced his spent round with a fresh one and spun the chamber.

Ahead, in the near distance, two rifle shots resounded. A second later, a pistol shot followed.

"This is a lively place," he said. As he turned his dapple gray, he nodded toward Denton's body and said, "Anything you want to say for this one before the coyotes move in?"

Sam looked down at Denton as they rode past his body. "Adios, Eli Denton," he said.

Across the rocky mountainside, waiting red eyes cut back and forth in the darkness.

Chapter 12

Sara, frightened and alone, pulled a feather mattress from the bed to wrap it around herself as best she could after hearing the gunshots in the hillside yard. She'd heard shots earlier, but these latest ones were much closer, more threatening. From a window, she had cautiously peeped out minutes after the first shots. At eye level above the windowsill, she'd searched the dim moonlit path leading down to the shadowy trail.

Across the yard at the edge of a greater darkness, she saw a figure move into the pale moonlight, then out of it again. The figure of a woman? *Yes!* She believed it was. She watched, straining her eyes against the unyielding darkness. Where was Antonio? Her only prayer—not for herself or even for the tiny baby growing inside her—was for Antonio, a prayer that nothing bad had happened to him.

Another silhouette moved from the yard and into the greater darkness. *A woman?* This time she could not tell.

She had taken an old cap-and-ball Colt six-shooter from a drawer and, kneeling beneath the windowsill, held it against her bosom. She'd seen the brass caps on each of the six chamber nipples. They were turning dull and dark with age, but she hoped that even if the caps would not fire, at least seeing the big gun might scare away whoever was out there.

Voices sounded in the dark yard and she listened intently, both hands gripping the big gun. She still needed to cock the difficult old cap-and-ball Colt, but she would wait, knowing that if it was too much for her, she might have to let the hammer go and set off a round that would give away her hiding place. She waited, breathless and shaken.

Out near the trail, Irena had run away from the buggy, barefoot, her clothing torn, leaving the rig, horse and all hidden from sight among a wide leafy hedge. On her way across the yard, she picked up a fist-sized stone and carried it at her side, ready to bash someone's head if need be. Hearing a sound in the shrubs beside her, she stopped suddenly.

"Irena, thank God it's you! And you are alive!" Antonio whispered excitedly. He rose up only slightly and held out his arms as if a hug would be welcomed.

But Irena backed away, her stone weapon in hand. "Alive, no thanks to you." She eyed him in the darkness. "So you got away," she said coldly. "Where is Sara?"

"*Shh*, keep your voice down!" Antonio said. There are two Bad River Gunmen here."

"I thought you were also a Bad River Gunman," she said, "and that they are all your friends."

"They *are* my friends, but they have been drinking, and I am unarmed. They could kill me. They could kill us both!"

Irena shook her head in the darkness.

"Where is Sara?" she demanded. "I heard those other two pigs say more men had come here while you beat on me!"

"I didn't beat on you, Irena," he said. "I tried to make them turn you loose!"

"You *ran away*, Antonio!" she shouted. "How could you be such a coward and a fool? Did you give Sara to them?"

Before he could answer, Irena swung her stone furiously and felt the impact of it jar his head. Irena heard voices and running boots coming toward them.

"Get a clear shot," a voice called out.

"I will, damn it!" a second voice replied. "If you don't like it, do it yourself!"

"Yeah?" said the other voice. "I'll burn the place to the ground in about two more minutes!" He raised his voice toward the adobe as Irena ran closer to the partially hidden front door. "You hear me in there? I'll burn you down. I don't give a damn. I'll take what I've come here for!"

Irena raced away across the front yard, zigzagging toward the firelight in the window of the little adobe.

"Let me in, Sara!" she called out in a guarded voice. She pounded on the thick front door, trying to make herself heard, yet at the same time trying to avoid the two men stalking forward across the yard behind her.

Sara pulled back the big iron latch on the inside of the door and stepped back, the big gun bobbing in her small trembling hands.

Irena saw the gun. She turned and relatched the door behind them. "You poor thing!" she said. Then, almost sobbing, she said, "Thank God you have a gun!" Dropping the stone on a table, she hugged Sara to her and took the gun.

"Antonio is out there. I heard him," said Sara. "He will save us!"

Irena didn't bother answering. She led Sara to a dark corner away from the firelight and pressed her down against the stone wall. "You must stay here until I come back for you," she said. "Don't move!" She looked at the dull brass firing caps on the gun. "Will this gun fire?" she asked. Then she answered herself, saying, "It will shoot. It must shoot!"

"You won't know until you pull the trigger," Sara managed to say through her fear and trembling. "You can't risk it. Antonio will come for us!"

Irena cupped her cheek and said, "Listen to me, Sara. Antonio sent them here. He is one of them."

Sara only stared at her, shocked, speechless.

"Latch the door behind me," Irena said gently. "Let no one in except me."

"But won't they burn the house down?" Sara said.

"They will have to kill me first," Irena said, heading for the front door. "And I will not die so easily."

At the edge of the hacienda's hilly front yard, Sam and Thorn stopped their horses and sat for a moment, gazing at the dark silhouette of the buggy and its horse half-hidden in the leafy hedge. They saw the dark figures of the two gunmen on foot, cursing, talking crudely, laughing drunkenly as they passed the hedges and came into view on their way to the dimly lit house.

"Look, Sam," said Thorn. He raised his right hand in the shape of a gun and said in a hushed tone, "Pow-pow." He blew on the tip of his finger and smiled. "That's how easy it would be from here."

"Come on," said Sam in the same lowered tone. "We've

got the women to think about." He stepped the barb forward, staying on the edge of the shadow.

Thorn said in mock surprise, "Well, thank you, Ranger. I had plumb forgot all about the women. Boy, oh, boy, do I feel foolish." He followed close beside Sam along the line of shadows.

In a downward roll of the rocky hill, the two men disappeared out of sight, still headed for the hacienda.

"Brother Hugh," said Jake Barret, "I'm out of whiskey, and I wasn't too keen on chasing women all night anyway."

"Me neither, Jake," said Hugh Barret. "So what is it we're doing here?"

"Lover boy Antonio shot his mouth off so much, talking about his two beautiful señoritas, I reckon I just wanted to call his bluff—see for myself."

Hugh stopped in his tracks.

"Then what in the blue blazes are we waiting for? We look like a couple of wild ganders watching for thunder," he said.

"I don't know why we're waiting," said Jake. He gave a tired little laugh. "Hell, we've both got money in our pockets. Let's get to Bad River. If we need some feisty filly to yank our boots off, we'll find plenty there—"

"*Hola, hombres,*" said Irena in a come-hither tone, appearing beside them as if out of nowhere. "I bet you come looking for me, eh?" She held up one side of her full skirt to reveal a long, shapely leg. "Do I have something you both want?"

The Barret brothers stared, their eyes wide and their smiling mouths agape. Their waning desires snapped back, full force, never mind Irena's haggard look or her tangled, uncombed hair. Once again, the prospect of sex overwhelmed them.

"Why, mercy yes, señora," said Jake Barret. "You sweet-looking little peach, you." The Barret brothers took a short step forward. "Is that a bottle of hootch you're holding behind you? We're dying for a drink."

"How did you know?" Irena said sweetly. She stood rocking back and forth on her bare feet, her blouse shredded and revealing.

"Okay, stop fooling around," said Jake. "Give it up, little darling."

"*Sí,*" said Irena, "here it is, all of it for you!"

She had cocked the big cap-and-ball on her way from the hacienda. Raising it as quick as she did, the weight of it caused her almost to stumble, but her mission was clear, and this was a matter of life or death for her and her friend Sara.

The Barret brothers' expressions were horrified in the fiery orange-and-blue flashes of sudden fire. Her first shot hit Jake full in his face, emptying much of his brain matter on the grass behind him.

Hugh, caught off guard, saw the hammer of the big gun draw back under both of her small thumbs. His instincts were torn between running and going for his holstered Colt. As it turned out, his Colt was half-drawn and his body half-turned as Irena's second bullet tore through his neck and left him lying dead at his brother's feet.

When she saw a dark figure spring from the shrubbery and run toward her, she recocked the gun for the third time and held it up with both hands.

"Irena, don't shoot. It's me, Antonio!" He slipped and almost fell in the blood and gore slathering the ground around the Barret brothers. "Whoa!" he said, catching himself. He spread his hands toward the bodies. "I was going insane, thinking about them coming here, and you and Sara alone! Thank God you got here and stopped them, Irena—thank God we both got here!"

"Yes, thank God, and all of his saints in heaven," Irena said. The big gun bucked in her hand. Antonio fell dead, a bullet having punched its way through his heart.

She saw two horses coming across the yard and started to cock the big gun again. Each time she had pulled the trigger, she had said a short, silent prayer to the Holy Mother that the gun would not fail her. The Holy Mother had answered her prayer each time. The gun, with its dingy caps and rusting patina, had killed the men and protected Sara and the baby inside her. Had the Holy Mother not meant it to be so, the gun would not have fired. These men, Antonio included, would have killed Irena and Sara and the baby. Irena and the Holy Mother had spent some strange and sacred moments together. She knew that. And that was as much as she would make of it now and forever.

She crossed herself and lowered the big gun as she recognized Sam's voice calling out to her, "Don't shoot. It's Ranger Burrack and Dan'l Thorn." The two rode up close, stopped their horses and looked down at the dead men on the sloping hillside. Sam dismounted and took the heavy gun from Irena's hand.

"You're okay. We're here with you," he said gently.

"I shot Antonio," she whispered, casting an eye toward the dimly lit hacienda. "It is so dark. I was so frightened. He was with those men—"

Sam leveled his face close to hers. "Look at me, Irena," he said.

She raised her eyes from the dead men on the ground to the ranger's face so close to hers. She felt safe now, warmer inside with him here.

"You did right," he said, almost in a whisper between them.

At Sara's insistence—and in Sam's case, out of respect for Father Lawrence—Sam and Thorn found two shovels and a breaking pick for the rocky ground and buried Antonio in a strip of woods behind the hacienda, which, as it turned out, had belonged to the church since long before anyone could remember.

"You know," said Thorn as they neared finishing their grave digging and the dawning sun crept up on the distant horizon, "I bet lots of people would stop killing if they knew they would have to bury the idiot they killed."

"Prison hasn't stopped the killing," Sam put in. "Hanging hasn't stopped it." He looked at Thorn, who shrugged.

"All right, forget it," Thorn said. He drew on a short, thin cigar. "I thought I had something there, but I guess I didn't." He nodded toward the hacienda. "I'm glad that one has stopped her wailing over this worthless bastard." He spit on the fresh-turned earth blanketing Antonio Villa.

"I hope the priest isn't going to want to see him," said Sam.

"If he does," said Thorn, "he'd better bring his shovel and get to digging. I'm through with this one. Come on," he added, walking toward the woods a few yards away. "I'm going to water the landscape."

* * *

Through the window, Irena and Sara watched the two men disappear over the edge of the hillside. Even though she knew it was going to hurt her friend, Irena told Sara about Antonio. She hoped the knowledge of what sort of man Antonio had really been might help Sara find peace.

"I am sorry to tell you this, but all the while he was going to marry you, he kept trying to bend me to his will."

Sara stared out the window toward Antonio's grave as tears ran down her cheeks.

"I must tell you, Irena," she said at length, "there was a time a few days ago that I wondered what it would be like to give myself to the ranger. This I wondered even as Antonio's baby's tiny heart beat in my belly."

Irena gaped in shock.

"It is true," said Sara. "I tell you this so you will understand that none of us are perfect. I must confess this to Father Lawrence so he can grant me forgiveness—"

"Stop it, Sara. Stop it!" said Irena. "You must not tell Father any of this. Make this your own secret to take with you to the grave if need be. Yes, Father is a priest, but he is retired. And even so, it would break his heart to know any of this. Antonio is dead and in the ground. Let him rest in peace. And you, rest in the peace that comes from knowing you did nothing wrong. You only considered tasting a forbidden fruit. You did not taste it." She was amazed by what Sara had told her and didn't know what else to say. Finally, she said, "Go now. Pack enough clothes in travel bags to carry on horseback, and come with me."

"On horseback?" said Sara. "What about the doctor's buggy?"

"Dr. Jorgenson will get his buggy back." Irena pointed out the window at the two dead outlaws' horses tied to a hitch rail. "A buggy cannot take us where we will travel, but these horses can. I know paths and trails down the mountain that no one else knows. I will give the lawmen the buggy to follow." She smiled. "I know the buggy horse. He will take the lawmen to the doctor's cottage." She cupped Sara's cheek. "And I will take us places far from here where you can have your baby and put all of this behind you. Have your child, and I will help you raise the *niño* as if it were my own."

Sara stared at her for a long moment, considering what Irena had told her when she said she had shot Antonio—that shooting Antonio was an accident and that she had been a frightened woman with a loaded gun. Sara thought about it and realized in her deepest heart of hearts she didn't care. She was glad Antonio was dead. She could admit it. Had he lived many years with her and their child, it would have been year upon year of his trifling, dishonest ways.

But now that he was dead, she felt a lightness she had never felt before. She turned slowly to her dear friend.

"Go with you, Irena?" she said in an almost dreamlike state. "Yes, I want to go with you. Let us go quickly though, before I change my mind."

"Poor Father Lawrence will be destroyed when he hears Antonio is dead," said Irena.

"Ay, *sí*, poor Father Lawrence," Sara said cuttingly.

"But he raised you, Sara—you and Antonio both!" Irena said.

Sara gave her a tight, concealing stare. "*Sí*, he raised

us," she said. "And I will say nothing about *how* he raised us or why."

The stare continued until Irena broke it by looking away. She had spent time in Father Lawrence's rectory as well as the doctor's house. She had seen plenty of things she would never mention. Neither man was honest or pure.

"All right, what are we waiting for, my dear friend?" she said.

She had tied a faded red curtain sash around her waist. Now she placed the big cap-and-ball Colt down behind the sash.

"¡Vamos! ¡Vamos!" she said, offering the best smile she could conjure, given the gravity of the situation. "Let us leave while these lawmen are not watching."

Chapter 13

———◆———

Earlier in the night, James Radlear Claypool had woken up and discovered his head and entire body were now hairless—even his eyebrows were gone—and half of one ear was missing. He'd realized he was in a bed in the Frenchman Hotel, a bed that smelled of burned hair, urine and charcoal. He'd pulled on one of his boots, which rested on the floor, but the other would not go on his foot. He would light a lantern and see about it.

No sooner had he considered it than he walked out the length of chain around his ankle and fell just close enough to the door to strike his forehead and raise a painful welt. He clasped both hands to his head and struggled to hold back a cry and a curse. He writhed for a moment on the floor, then dragged himself onto the bed and looked at the iron shackle on his right foot.

What the hell . . . ? Am I under arrest? No! He thought about it as he stared at the chain. The shackle on his ankle required a key to open it. *So . . .* He looked around the shadowy room. There wasn't a key in sight. Then he looked down at the floor and saw that the other end of the chain was simply hooked around a leg of the bed.

Well, that's crazy. . . .

He held his head and shook it slowly. After a moment, it came back to him. He had told Irish Mike Tuohy that he had a habit of walking in his sleep under certain conditions. Mike, under his instructions, had shackled him to the bed for his own safety.

"All well and good," he'd told himself, raising the leg of the bedstead and freeing the other shackle.

But now he was feeling better. It was time to get his fingers back in the pie. He had watched the streets and not seen Sims, Jack Swift or any of their men. He intended to find out why.

His first stop would be the doctor's house. The doctor's housekeeper, Irena, always heard things Claypool might find helpful. Next stop, Father Lawrence's rectory. Nothing happened in Bad River that the doctor and the retired priest didn't know about. He congratulated himself on his good thinking and felt around on the chairs and furniture for his newly clean clothes. Mike Tuohy had sent them out to be washed, beaten, rinsed and hung outdoors to dry in the sunshine. The process should have gotten rid of the revolting odors left from the outhouse overflow, the dynamite blast and the smell of burned hair. Holding his nose close to his singed gray shirt, he realized the odors were still there, only a bit milder.

He had been knocked down and out for . . . what? Three days? Four? Okay, he wasn't sure, but for a man who made his way through the world by gathering and sharing important information, he'd been left flat on his back too long. It was time to gird up and get busy. He stepped into his trousers, pulled them up and tried to button them. He couldn't.

Damn it, had he gained so much weight his clothes

didn't fit? He struggled and pulled and wiggled until he got his trousers up over his hips. Than it dawned on him that his clothes had shrunk.

Damn it!

Just to make sure, he picked up his swallowtail dress coat and put it on. It was tight all over. The back seam felt as if it would split at any second. The sleeves reached a quarter of the way up his forearms.

Not to be deterred, he dressed in the darkness, hung his ankle chain over his shoulder and carried his boot under his arm. At least he knew where to get himself a horse.

When he'd slipped quietly downstairs and pulled the door to the Frenchman Hotel closed behind him, Claypool felt around for his glasses and realized he no longer had them. In fact, he couldn't remember having them since the explosion. He'd have to make do. This would all get better now that he was dealing himself back into the game.

He slipped along in the shadows until he found the livery barn door and eased inside. He saw only stalls with horses in them. He walked up to the first and recognized the stallion even without his glasses. It was Doc, the ranger's big roan, contemplating him as he crunched on hay.

"Hey there, Doc." Claypool reached a hand out over the stall rail, but instead of Doc sticking his nose forward, he pulled back a little. Seeing the stitches on Doc's tender-looking nose, Claypool lowered his hand.

"All right, I heard you had a fight with Greenly's blood bay. I wish you would have killed him—doing something like this to you. I'm glad to see you're taking a little healing time for yourself. That's good. You can't go with me tonight, but I'll look in on you later." He walked to the other horse in the barn. *Uh-oh!* The chestnut bay stood looking at him from over the stall railing.

Claypool considered it. The facts were, the last time he'd borrowed the chestnut bay, he had barely, by way of wit and wile, avoided a beating from the horse's owner.

All was well that ended well, he reflected. He opened the stall gate and walked inside. *So here goes.* He reached for the horse's bridle hanging on a stall peg.

"Let's try this one more time, ol' buddy," he said, rubbing a hand down the bay's long jaw.

The chestnut bay sniffed him, his rank odor, then gave what sounded like a disgusted puff of breath and looked away.

"We'll get used to each other all over again," Claypool whispered.

Keeping an eye on the front door for the bay's huge owner and his ax handle, Claypool led the bay out the rear door, mounted it bareback and eased along, past the doctor's office sitting dark and closed. He rode onto the mountainside trail, heading toward the doctor's hillside adobe-and-frame cottage out of town on its secluded hectares of rugged land.

His heavy chain cast over his shoulder, his unusable boot up under his arm, Claypool let the big bay run, following the rocky up-reaching trail. For over an hour, he raced along in his tight, shrunken suit, his swallowtails flapping on the night wind behind him. The bay seemed to enjoy the good strong run in the pale moonlight, and even without his glasses, Claypool managed to negotiate the twisting switchback trail with ease.

He kept an eye on the dark ground for any tracks or signs that might be helpful in guiding him in the direction of the doctor's home. He knew his way there in the daylight, but in a dark night without his glasses? He wasn't so sure. He slowed for a few minutes to consider some buggy tracks and the prints of three sets of hooves.

All right. It didn't take a master tracker to see that two sets of hooves were layered atop a set that stayed dead center between a buggy's front wheels. *The buggy horse.* And another set that rode along on the driver's side. Once his eyes adjusted to the tracks and their riding order, he smiled to himself. *Pretty damned good at this,* he thought.

When he'd remounted and started to tap the bay forward, he heard the hushed sound of men's voices on the trail close behind him.

"Easy, big boy," he whispered to the bay, sliding down from its back and keeping it settled as he led it off the trail and down behind a broken boulder half-buried in the rocky ground. He heard the men coming closer, two riders, talking openly about Antonio Villa by name. He could hear whiskey having its way with their slurred voices. They talked about Villa riding close ahead and about a woman he intended to catch up with.

See? he thought. He'd known he needed to be out here tonight, getting his hand back in the game. He'd just known it!

Claypool dropped back a few yards into darkness on the narrow trail. He kept the chestnut bay walking on the gravelly trail's edge, close to a thin downhill game path. On either side of the path was a steep drop at least a hundred feet deep, hidden by the swallowing black darkness. But Claypool knew if the riders heard or saw him following, he could skip over the edge and get down out of sight fast. After all, he thought, who in their right mind would choose such a place to hide?

He rode silently and listened intently. When he saw Antonio and the doctor's housekeeper wrestling in the doctor's buggy in the pale moonlight, he stared, absorbed in the scene before him. But it turned out there was more to see. He stayed back and took it all in, following, ducking out of sight, keeping the big chestnut quiet. By dawn, he had seen it all, more than he could have ever hoped for. The last thing he saw was the women riding away on the dead outlaws' horses.

Traveling light, he figured.

They were slipping away from the two lawmen and everything that had held them to Bad River most of their lives.

Good for them, he told himself.

For nearly an hour before daylight, he and the bay combed the jagged hillside, back and forth between two lengths of switchback, before he could finally admit to himself the two women had made a clean, smooth getaway from right under his nose.

That's okay, he told himself. He'd seen plenty; he'd seen the idiot Antonio shot by the housekeeper, Chaz Campo killed by Dan'l Thorn. And he'd seem much more. For example, the ranger and Thorn riding the switchbacks together. He smiled to himself. Oh, yes, he had a lot to tell. . . .

Good information? He thought about it for moment. *Good for what, for who?*

He reached up and thumped his palm on his bandaged half-ear. Maybe he was still in a bit of a fog and not thinking straight. But regardless, he'd seen what he'd seen throughout the night. He hadn't imagined it.

When he got the chance, he would sit down and go over everything in the order he'd seen it.

Put the pieces together, he told himself. There was value here; he was sure of it.

His clients would be Melford, Cree Sims, Jack Swift or anyone else who needed to know and was willing to pay well for good information. He had been out of touch for a few days, but damn it, he was back now, back in high spades!

He let the chestnut step a little quicker down to the main trail. Along the way, he had paid no attention to quiet sounds he'd heard; but he drew up tight on the chestnut's reins as they walked onto the less slanted trail and saw seven mounted gunmen close up around them.

At the center of the trail, Cree Sims and the Russian Assassin sat staring at him with hard, cold eyes. On the other side of Kura sat Dupree. Next to Sims sat Tillis, a rifle sticking up from his thigh. Three more gunmen sat watching.

"Good God, Claypool! Is that you?" Sims said with a dark chuckle. "You look like you jumped off a grill and got fell upon by wild hounds!" His circle of men moved forward with him, offering a compulsory laugh. "I know Swift's men blowed you up, but damn, son!"

In the spirit of the gibe, Dupree looked at Claypool's bare foot with the chain around his ankle and at the boot up under his arm.

"Couldn't find your other foot?" he joked as he and Tillis sidled their horses up to Claypool.

"Yeah," said Tillis before Claypool could answer. "But he ain't going to let it get away again." He reached over and jiggled the chain that hung from Claypool's shoulder.

Claypool looked at them with spite, his eyes slightly cocked without his glasses.

"Har-har," he said. "You fellas are as funny as ever. Go ahead and laugh like a bunch of baboons. You won't be giving me what for when you hear what I've done all night."

The men fell silent at Claypool's serious bearing and turned to Sims for guidance.

"Bunch of baboons, huh?" said Sims, stepping his horse up close to the big chestnut bay.

"I only said that, my friend, because I know you will appreciate everything I've found out, and you're not going to want to be put off from hearing it!" Claypool's voice got a little more confident as he spoke.

Sims gave him a close and serious look up and down, noting his tight, too short swallowtail coat, his bare foot, his face the color of an over fried egg, the bloodstained bandage on his left ear.

"Did you lose an ear?" Sims asked.

"I lost *half* an ear," said Claypool. "Dr. Jorgenson sewed up the other half while I was knocked out cold."

"Why?" Sims studied the bandage, only half the size it should have been.

"I don't know why," said Claypool. "I meant to ask him myself."

"He didn't do you no favor saving it," Sims said, inspecting, gauging the overall size of the maimed ear through the unwholesome-looking bandage.

"You might be right," said Claypool. He reached up and touched the bloodstained bandage with his smoke-stained fingertips. "But that's not at all what I'm wanting to tell you about this morning. I've got more important news you'll be glad to know about."

"All right," said Sims. He looked around at his men,

who had started talking quietly among themselves. "All of yas, shut up now. I want to hear what JR has to say."

The Gunmen fell silent. Sims nodded at Claypool. But before Claypool started speaking, Sims raised a hand and sniffed the air. "Hold on a minute. What's that smell?"

"I don't know," Claypool said. "I don't really smell anything." His head bowed slightly.

"Damn, I do," said Sims. He looked all around, at the chestnut bay, at Claypool, his tight clothes, his shrunken trousers. "What the hell is it?"

"I'll tell you what it is," said Earl Dupree with authority. "It's cat spray."

"I never smelled cat spray this bad," said Sims.

Dupree chuckled. "You're smelling it now. Certain times of year, cat squirt smells as bad as a skunk's."

Damn it! Make these fools listen, Claypool told himself.

"Go ahead, JR," said Sims. "You were out riding the switchbacks last night and you saw what?"

"Okay," said Claypool. "One thing I saw was the young woman who works for the doctor blow a hole through your new gunman, Antonio Villa." He waited for a response from Sims, but the outlaw only gave him an unconcerned look.

"I'll be damned," Sims said. "Anything else?"

"Yes, plenty! I saw Dan'l Thorn kill a couple of your men and leave them lying off the side of the trail—" He stopped abruptly when he noticed a two-horse mine wagon come up around a blind curve in the trail. Irena and Sara sat in the driver's seat, looking defeated. The dead outlaws' horses were behind the wagon, their reins tied to the tailgate.

"What the hell?" said Claypool, a strange look on his singed, hairless face.

"Oh, yeah, I meant to tell you, JR. We found these two crossing the switchback this morning on our way back from the Mexico Valley."

"Which way were they headed on the switchback, up or down?" Claypool asked.

Sims gave him a dubious look.

"What the hell difference does it make?" he asked. "They'd just stepped onto it." He chuckled. "Next time, I'll be sure to ask."

Claypool looked all around and lowered his eyes.

Sims said, "I think they're going to be our prisoners for a while anyway."

"But why?" Claypool asked, a puzzled look on his face.

"We'll talk about that later." He gave Claypool a wide grin and a slap on his back. He looked around and called out to a new man who rode up quickly.

"JR, meet Dallas Curio," he said. "Dallas here just got cut loose from Yuma Prison. He's riding with us Bad River Gunmen now."

The young gunman tipped his hat up enough to see Claypool's face. He touched the brim of his hat and nodded as he chewed a jaw full of tobacco behind a thick, drooping black mustache.

"Dallas here is going to do you a big favor," Sims said.

"What's that?" Claypool asked.

"I'm going to give you some things to do—things that pay well, JR," he said. "But you can't do them if your head is beaten in from an ax handle. So Dallas here, who has a way of talking to folks, is taking this chestnut bay to town and explaining to the owner how he found him out here running wild and brought him home." He grinned.

"But how will he know where to take the bay?" Claypool asked.

"That's the sort of thing that Dallas is good at," Sims said. "Now give him the bay and go get one of our horses behind the wagon. Let's roll. Daylight is burning all around us."

Chapter 14

The ranger and Dan'l Thorn sat their horses atop a high ridge overlooking the next levels of the lower switchback trail. In the early sunlight, the clear blue sky appeared to go on forever. A large mountain eagle circled and prowled, then dropped close to the sides of the rugged terrain. The next level down, the doctor's empty buggy traveled easily along the well-known trail.

"What do you think, Sam?" Thorn asked. "Were they just throwing us off their track?"

"Maybe," Sam said, "but I don't see why they wanted to run away from us. We saw what happened. I never accused them of anything. Did you?"

With a short pocketknife, Thorn carved slices of a sweet-smelling apple and ate it as he spoke. "Naw," he replied, "you heard everything I said to both of them. Maybe it's not us they wanted to throw off their back trail."

"Yes, I'm wondering about that," said Sam.

Thorn added, "Sometimes, it's just the fact that you're wearing a badge or ever wore one." He gave a slight grin. "It gives some folks gooseflesh up their arms."

"I have found that to be the case many times," Sam said.

He glanced all around. The rugged land showed no sign of apples, apple trees or any other thriving fruit on the barren mountainside. *Nothing.*

Seeing Sam's curiosity, Thorn carved a couple of slices of apple and handed them over.

"Obliged," Sam said.

He took a slice and ate it in one bite, surprised at how moist and fresh it tasted. He folded the other slice into a pocket kerchief and put it away as their attention went to the rider who suddenly charged out onto the trail below and brought the buggy to a rough halt. The buggy horse neighed and almost reared, but its tack held it down until it settled.

"All right," said Thorn, his voice lowered. "Whatever else you might call Bad River, it is *not* a boring place."

"I've found that to be so," Sam agreed.

He looked off in the direction of the doctor's mountainside cottage, then back down to the single rider, who had jumped down from his saddle and stood rummaging through items under the driver's seat and in the space behind it. He wore a red Cowboy sash around his waist and, cursing loudly, threw something on the rocky ground.

"Whatever he's not finding sure ain't making him happy, is it?" Thorn said. He laid a hand on the rifle butt sticking up from his saddle boot.

Sam saw him drumming his fingertips on the polished brass plate.

"Think how bad it would upset him if I stuck a bullet through his leg—say, right above his kneecap."

He gave a dark little laugh. "I bet it would ruin his whole day."

Sam ignored him.

"Or if he leads that wagon on up toward the doctor's place, we can ride down and meet him," Thorn said.

At this point the rider mounted his horse and led the wagon on up the switchback.

"So I take it you don't want me to shoot him?" Thorn said. "It's no trouble," he added.

"No need," Sam said. "Now that we see where he's headed, we can ride ahead from here and be waiting for him on the doctor's front porch when he gets there."

"Yeah," Thorn said grudgingly, "we can do that too, I reckon." He took his hand away from the rifle butt and turned the dapple gray to the up-slanted trail.

When the single rider led the doctor's buggy into the front yard and up close to the frame-and-adobe hacienda, the first thing Sam noted was that the man's red sash was no longer around his waist. At the other end of the house, Thorn stood out of sight, his rifle poised, ready in case any more Cowboy or Bad River Gunmen appeared out of nowhere, as both groups were known for doing.

"Roman Lee Ellison," Sam called out loudly, recognizing the gunman. "What are you doing out of the Colorado penitentiary?"

Roman stiffened at the sound of his name and the harsh voice saying it. Then, seeing the ranger, he breathed a little easier—a little, not a lot.

"Surprised you, did I?" Sam said, stepping off the porch toward him.

Roman Lee Ellison noted the ranger's big cocked Colt hanging in his right hand—the same Colt he'd seen hanging in front of him before he went to prison, a bullet wound healing in his shattered chest.

"Surprised me?" said Ellison. "Maybe a little, I guess. But I think I can recover and get on with my day." He reminded himself to watch his mouth and not turn a simple roadside conversation into a full-blown gun battle like he'd managed to do four years ago. "I try to avoid surprises," he added calmly.

"So do I," Sam said matter-of-factly.

Standing there looking at Sam's big Colt hanging in his hand, Ellison found himself wondering the same thing he'd wondered the day Sam's bullet had bored through him and nearly killed him. When, and how the hell, had Sam managed to pull the Colt and cock it without Roman noticing him do it?

Ellison forced himself to put the matter away, feeling that same deep pain that often accompanied such memories creep into his chest.

Still, Ellison had to wonder now, as he had countless times before, if he could do the same thing, raise his gun casually and cock it, without anyone noticing. As he wondered, he eased his fingertips down slowly to his big black-handled Colt.

"Ranger," he said coolly, calmly, "maybe we've both had enough surprises in this life to keep us—"

"Take your hand away from that Colt," Sam said, equally cool and calm, "or I will forty-five you right there in the same spot I did before."

Dan'l Thorn stepped out from the front corner of the cottage hacienda. He held his rifle, poised and cocked. "And I'll stick one in the back of your empty head, Roman Lee Ellison," he said. "Just for the hell of it."

Damn! Ellison's hand rose up away from the gun butt and covered the spot Sam's bullet had left on his chest those four years earlier.

"All right, you jakes," said Ellison affably, "I've got no bark on at nobody. You can see."

He kept both hands raised, even wiggled his fingers a little as he turned and faced Sam.

Thorn came walking in from the edge of the hacienda as Sam slipped Ellison's black-handled Colt from its holster, looked at it and shoved it down behind his gun belt.

"Roman Lee, how're you doing?" Thorn asked, his rifle still pointed.

"Tolerable, Thorn," Ellison said, lowering his hands a little. "If you're wondering why I'm bringing this buggy home—"

"Where's your Cowboy sash?" Thorn cut in, opening Ellison's leather vest with the tip of his rifle barrel for a better look.

"I mostly wear it when we're all riding together," Ellison said. He looked at Sam. "I expect if you were watching the trail, you saw me wearing it, then take it off?"

Sam didn't answer and Ellison started talking faster and faster. "Anyway, no more Cowboy Gang for me. I'm changing over to the Bad River Gunmen. So there's that. I won't need to wear a sash every time I go to—"

"Stop lying," Sam cut in.

"Lying about what?" said Ellison.

"Everything but the truth," said Thorn, also cutting in. He raised his rifle butt. "Sam, I'm going to bat his head around some, see if it helps him tell the truth—"

"Okay, hold it!" said Ellison, knowing Thorn's genuine penchant for batting an outlaw's head around some with anything he had at hand. "I'm not really lying," said Ellison. "I'm just not . . . you know . . . telling the truth." He gave a slight shrug.

"Oh," Sam said, "we understand, now that you put it that way. Right, Dan'l?"

"One good head batting coming up," Thorn said. He gave a dark little grin and adjusted his rifle in his hands.

"All right, all right!" said Ellison. He raised a hand to stop the rifle butt. "Ask me anything! I'll tell you the truth!"

Sam nodded at Thorn, who took a step back.

"There's a young Mexican-Irish woman who delivers medicine in that buggy," he said. "Last night, she and another young woman were riding in the buggy, and then somewhere they switched over to horseback." He nodded at the empty buggy. "Where are they now?"

Roman Lee Ellison took a deep breath.

"Here it is, the best I can tell you," he said. "The woman who works for Dr. Ruuz Jorgenson, she delivers medicine that he makes here in his outdoor *cocina*. But I have no idea where she is."

"His outdoor kitchen is for medicine?" said Thorn. He and Sam looked at each other, then toward the backyard of the hacienda where a *chimenea* was built into a rugged natural stone wall.

"If the medicine he makes needs to be cooked, he cooks it outdoors," Ellison confirmed. "Feels like it might start a fire otherwise, I suppose."

"Let me guess," Sam said. "Dr. Ruuz Jorgenson produces morphine mixed with alcohol?"

"Why, yes, he does," said Ellison, amazed by Sam's offhand summary. "But how did you guess that?"

"The ranger here has a gift for prophecy," Thorn joked.

"It's all legal, I'm told," Ellison added quickly.

Thorn gave Sam a narrowed gaze. "What does your Matamoros Agreement say about all that?" he asked.

"I've got nothing to say about it," Sam replied. "I understand it is legal. I'm supposed to stick with what I'm doing here. Is that clear enough?"

"Oh, I'm more than clear on that," said Thorn with a little laugh.

"See there?" Roman Ellison put in with a slight smile, "I knew I wasn't breaking no law by picking up a load of medicine from the woman and taking it into Bad River."

"How long have you been picking up medicine from the doctor's housekeeper and taking it into town?" Sam asked.

"Honest truth," said Ellison, "this is my first time, and I've no idea what's happened. Don't know what's happened to the woman, the doctor or the stuff the doctor cooked up. I was supposed to pick some up, but there was none in the buggy. I searched high, wide and to hell and gone. There's none there! So I came here."

Sam finally slipped his big Colt back down into its holster. Thorn uncocked his rifle and laid it in the crook of his arm. Ellison looked relieved.

"Why don't we search this place and see what we find?" Sam said.

After an hour-long search of the doctor's hacienda and a large empty goat barn built against the stone wall behind it, Sam and Roman Lee Ellison closed the barn doors and stood for a moment, looking around for Thorn.

"Here he comes," Ellison said.

Thorn walked toward them from the outdoor *cocina* with its ten-foot-high chimney standing atop a wide iron grill. So far the only sign of anything secretive going on was a cellar-type trapdoor in the bedroom plank-and-tile floor. The space beneath the trapdoor contained nothing but a few clear empty bottles and a handful of corks scattered on the dirt around them.

"We're burning daylight here," Thorn said, his rifle still hanging in his hand. "Remind me again why we should give a single shuck if this place was stacked to the ceiling with morphine and mescal." He looked from Sam to Roman Ellison and added pointedly, "Both things being legal."

"As much as I appreciate your company, Dan'l," the ranger said, "you can cut out if you've got something more important that needs attending to."

"Naw, I'm good, Sam," Thorn said. "All I need to attend to is an empty belly."

"We're getting ready to fix that," Sam said. "On our way to Bad River, we'll stop by Father Lawrence's rectory. I'm thinking he's feeling awfully low right now if he found out that Antonio's dead."

"Why wouldn't he have?" Thorn asked.

"I don't know," said Sam. "That's why I say we stop by and see him. Start tying some pieces of this thing together. If the doctor is selling doped-up mescal, I'm betting the old priest will know something about it."

"Good," said Thorn, "and while he's telling you all what he knows, I can work on filling my gullet with some beans and goat shank."

He looked at Ellison's black-handled Colt sticking

up from behind Sam's gun belt. "I bet you've been itching all afternoon to make a grab for that gun of yours, haven't you, Roman Lee?"

Ellison looked surprised. "No, I haven't," he said. "I figure if I'm not under arrest, I'm free to go." He looked from Thorn to Sam. "Am I right, Ranger?"

"Yeah, you're right in a way, Roman Lee," Sam said, turning to the horses.

"In a way?" said Ellison. "I don't understand that at all."

"That's because you have no deeper knowledge of the workings of the law," Thorn put in.

Ellison almost laughed, but Thorn appeared to be dead serious, so he stopped himself.

Sam started toward the horses, glancing back at Ellison over his shoulder. "Come on, Roman Lee," he said. "Take a ride with us."

"A ride?" Ellison said, keeping an eye on Thorn and his rifle. "Why do I want to take a ride with two lawmen? Hell, I don't even have my gun!"

"Because we like you," Thorn said with a straight face as Sam swung up in the saddle.

"There, Roman Lee," said Sam. "We like you. Come on, take a ride with us. It'll do you good to see how this side of the law operates."

"Damn! I feel like I've already spent a week here with you two—" Ellison thought better of what he might have said next and grumbled under his breath, "And what about my gun?"

Almost before he'd finished his words, the ranger pitched his black-handled Colt to him. Stunned by Sam's gesture, Ellison caught the gun and turned it in his hand.

"Obliged, Ranger," he said quietly, almost in disbelief.

Sam nodded and adjusted his sombrero atop his head.

"Hell, it's not loaded!" Ellison groused, and took the reins Thorn reached out and handed to him.

"One thing at a time, Roman Lee," said Thorn. "Now that we like you, don't go doing something foolish to make us change our minds."

Chapter 15

At the side yard of the church rectory, the ranger, Dan'l Thorn and Roman Lee Ellison sat partially hidden from view under the cover of a large ancient live oak. For a full two minutes, they watched three horsemen load items into a one-horse freight wagon sitting at the rectory's back door. Two of them carried items from inside the sandstone building and handed them up to the man in the wagon bed. The three had leaned their rifles against a short stone hitch wall while they worked.

"You know these men?" Sam asked Ellison, seeing Cowboy's red sashes wrapped around the horsemens' waists.

"Can't say that I do, Ranger," Ellison replied, watching the three men closely. "I'm guessing they came down from Arizona, just got to Bad River. It takes three or four days before anybody slips off their sash—you know, to discourage anyone from shooting them in case this is some kind of setup."

Sam thought about what Ellison had said, looking first at Thorn, then at Ellison, then back toward the three men.

"Makes sense to me," Sam said.

"Me too," said Thorn.

"That's a rented wagon from the livery barn," Sam observed. He reached a hand over to Ellison and gave him the five bullets he'd taken from his black-handled Colt.

"You might want to fill your safety chamber, Roman Lee," Thorn advised.

"I'm there," Ellison said quietly, lifting a sixth round from his gun belt.

"Both of you circle and come in from behind," Sam said. "I'll ride straight in and get closer to their rifles."

"What about their sidearms?" Ellison asked.

When Sam and Thorn shot him a look, Ellison gave an embarrassed half-shrug. "Sidearms too—got it," he said.

Moments later, one of the men by the wagon gave the man nearer to him a nudge and brought his attention to the single rider moving in steadily, his Winchester across his lap, his horse angling closer to the three rifles with every step. Sam's Winchester rose a little along his right arm as one of the men started to take a step in his direction.

"*¡Hola!*" Sam called out. He put his horse quarter-wise to the rifles and stopped. "Might you jakes tell a man where to find himself some loaded mescal?"

The men gave a smug little laugh at the lone rider's boldness.

"We're not jakes," said a tall man wearing a tied-down Colt. He also wore a slightly smaller-caliber Colt in a cross-draw position shoved down behind his red sash. "You've got no cause to ride in like you know us. Get on out of here." He jutted his chin toward the trail out front.

Sam gave a half-smile. "I mean no harm," he said. "Being a stranger, I thought it might be better riding in friendly-like, instead of jumping right in and shooting the hell out of yas."

He sat staring as if waiting for his words to sink in. As he'd spoken, he'd slipped his Colt from its holster and held it cocked on his thigh. His rifle covered the taller man; his Colt lay ready to throw down on the other two.

Thorn and Ellison had circled behind the three men while Sam held their attention. Seeing how slickly the ranger had drawn and cocked the big Colt, as if it was no big deal, Thorn reached down and raised his side-arm too. The three men looked jolted by the move, but saw little they could do about it.

What the hell? Roman Lee Ellison decided to try out the ranger's technique himself and couldn't believe how easy it was. His Colt came up, not fast, not slow, yet cocked and lowered at his side, pointed casually in the direction of the three men.

"You all lawmen or bounty hunters?" the tall man asked nervously as he took in the three rifles and pistols covering them.

"Pick either one," said Thorn. "While you're figuring it out, pinch your guns up from the holster with two fingers and drop them on the ground."

"Wait just a damn minute, Ned!" said one man to the taller one. "I know there's paper out on me. If we're going to die here, I want to go down with a fight—"

Two shots rang out from Thorn's pistol before the man got the rest of the words out of his mouth. He sank to his knees, then pitched forward onto his face. The other two stood frozen, staring at the guns pointed at them. Finally, the taller one made a move.

"Damn this to hell!" he shouted, going for his holstered Smith & Wesson.

Roman Lee Ellison's black-handled Colt tipped upward and knocked him backward dead with one hard, roaring shot. Ellison looked at his Colt as if surprised by how easy that had been, his gun already out, up and cocked. This was the only way to do it! He'd remember the ranger's technique. . . .

"Wait! Wait! Don't shoot!" the youngest of the three shouted, his hands up protecting his face, his short-barreled Colt already on the ground. "I didn't kill nobody! I swear I didn't! None of us did! They were dead when we got here!"

The three looked at one another.

"Didn't kill who?" Sam asked.

The young man straightened up some and gestured toward the rear of the rectory.

Sam picked up the young man's gun and pushed it down behind his gun belt as he looked around.

"Back there!" the young man said. "They were dead when we got here. I swear they were!"

Sam looked inside the wagon bed and saw a canvas bag of women's clothes, a pair of small women's red-and-gold riding boots beside it. A small footstool sat with the other items. A thin feather mattress lay rolled up and tied on the floor. Sam realized it might have been the same one that had been on his bed while he'd stayed here. It came to him whom they might be talking about as dead. But he didn't mention the two women's names yet.

"Come on, show us," Sam said.

Motioning the man toward the rear of the stone building, Sam walked two feet behind him. Thorn and Ellison gathered the horses and followed.

At the half-open door of a small grain silo, Sam gestured for the young gunman to open the door wider and step inside.

"What have we got in there, Ranger?" Thorn called out, standing behind Ellison and the young gunman.

Sam gazed upon the face of the old priest, gray and frozen in death. He was sitting on a bench at a stone table, slumped forward.

On another stone bench on the opposite side of the ancient stone table, Dr. Jorgenson was also slumped forward, his face a foot away from the priest's.

"Father Lawrence and the doctor . . . dead," Sam replied over his shoulder.

"Shot?" Thorn asked, at the same time giving the gunman a hard stare.

Before answering, Sam looked all around in the slanted sunlight and encircling darkness.

No blood, no signs of violence . . .

"I don't think so," Sam called back.

The young gunman looked relieved. He told Thorn his name was Tom Heely, but Thorn didn't believe that was his real name. He'd seen the young gunman somewhere before, but he couldn't recall where. He smiled affably.

"Hear that, Heely?" he said. "It appears you've told us the truth. I'm not going to have to waste a bullet on you after all."

The gunman looked even more relieved.

Thorn glanced at Ellison. "Where's the rifle you picked up earlier from the dead outlaw?" he asked gruffly.

"I stuck in in my saddle boot," Ellison replied. He patted his holstered Colt. "I figure ol' Blackie here can handle anything that pops up."

Thorn shook his head at the man's foolishness.

Inside the small stone silo, Sam had struck a match and lit a candle in its reflector stand. A soft glow of light encircled the inside of the silo and shone stark and flat on the two dead faces. A fat barn mouse raced across the stone floor, wiggled down through a wide crack and disappeared.

The holy man and the man of science lay opposite each other, their cheeks on the cool stone table, their right hands only inches apart as if they had just shaken hands on a final secret deal or had been about to when death caught them short. In the center of the stone table lay a large hypodermic syringe and an empty morphine bottle. A two-foot-long strip of rawhide lay where it had fallen from the old priest's upper arm.

"What say you in there, Ranger?" Thorn called out. "If they're dead, they'll stay that way until somebody comes by and buries them. I hope you're not going to say we need to—"

"No," Sam said, stepping out into the daylight, having snuffed out the candle. "We'll let the nearest neighbors know about them. These old men were both highly respected and thought well of by the folks around here. They'll want to plan a turnout for them."

Sam closed the heavy oaken door to the silo. The click of an iron lockset fell in place, making the silo safe enough for the two dead men. He tested it anyway to make sure it could stand the possible threat of coyotes.

"All right, everybody, let's ride," said Thorn.

"What about me?" Heely said. "I told you the truth about the dead men."

"I think we're going to let you go," said Sam, "unless you want to ride in with us and make Sims wonder what you might have been telling us all the way to town?"

"I might be new, Ranger," the young man said, "but Sims already knows I don't sell out my own kind."

Thorn smiled a little and looked at Sam, who made no offer of reply.

"Is that a fact, Tom Heely?" Thorn said, pushing the point of his rifle barrel closer to the young man's back.

"Yes, it is a fact," the young gunman said confidently. "We might be outlaws and some no-good sumbitches, but us Red Sash Cowboys and Bad River Gunmen are all alike when it comes to one thing. We live by a code to always look out for one another."

"Well, I'll be shucked," said Thorn in mock surprise. "I never knew that." He looked at Sam. "Did you ever hear about any of that, Ranger?"

"A time or two maybe," Sam said in a flat, quiet tone, never one to go along with razzing a man, especially one held at gunpoint.

"I know you lawmen jakes are only making fun," said the young man, his empty holster tied low to his thigh, just right for him to hook his thumb in as he walked, getting closer to the horses and to the dead man's rifle sticking up from Ellison's saddle boot. With his head tilted down only slightly, the gunman had a good view of the shadow of Thorn's rifle barrel, the tip of which he could feel brushed against his shirt now and then.

"But the truth is," the gunman went on, "one day you might regret ever making your wise-off remarks with a mouthful of blood spilling from your lips!"

As sudden as the strike of a snake, he spun full circle, knocking Thorn's rifle away from his back, throwing its aim off and skyward.

"Run, pard, run!" he shouted at Ellison as he ran hard himself, racing zigzag to Ellison's horse standing hitched among the rest of the horses and the freight wagon. But instead of running with him, Roman Lee Ellison stopped dead in his tracks and raised his hands. Sam looked at Thorn, who stood with his rifle still pointed away, watching the gunman snatch up the dead man's rifle from Ellison's saddle boot, cock it and throw it to his shoulder.

Thorn saw Sam give him a stern look, his Colt out and cocked and hanging down his thigh, as if waiting to see what Thorn was going to do.

"I've got him, Sam," Thorn said in a quiet, offhand manner, raising his rifle and taking aim only loosely.

"And when might that be?" Sam inquired in a cool, steady tone.

"Any second now," Thorn said.

"You're dead, you son of a—!" Tom Heely shouted. But he shut up as he pulled the trigger on the dead man's rifle and heard only the dreadful metal-on-metal click of an empty chamber.

"Oops!" Thorn said. He gave a dark little laugh, watching the gunman hurriedly racking the lever on the rifle again, once, twice, three more times. . . . Still nothing but the dull thud of metal on metal.

"Throw down the rifle, idiot!" Thorn called out.

The gunman threw the empty rifle and immediately started digging through Ellison's saddlebags like a squirrel searching for nuts.

"Look at him go!" Thorn said with another dark laugh.

Sam didn't like it. He raised his big Colt and asked Ellison over his shoulder, "Have you got any guns in there?"

"I can't say for sure, Ranger."

No sooner had he said it than the young gunman swung around with a small pocket gun and started shooting wildly. Thorn was about to pull the trigger on his rifle, but Sam's Colt fired first, a single shot that resounded with a bearing of finality. The echo of the blast rolled away across the mountainous land.

"Damn it, Sam," said Thorn as the gunman hit the ground, causing the horses to stir. "I told you I had him! What was your hurry?"

Sam gave him a cold look, then nodded toward Ellison, who was struggling in vain to pull himself up by the horse's stirrup. "Take your hands down, Roman Lee," said Sam.

"All right," said Ellison. "You shot me once before. You can't blame me for being a little gun-shy."

"Good point," Sam said, "but, since I haven't shot you yet today, it's not likely I'm going to." Sam walked over to Heely and squatted beside him.

"What made you do something like that?" Sam asked. "I told you we were turning you loose." He saw dark blood spewing hard from the young man's chest.

"I—I didn't believe you the way that one kept baiting me on and on." His eyes rolled up to Thorn, who had caught up and stood beside the ranger. "Satisfied, you lawdog bastard?" Heely said to Thorn, his voice getting weaker. "I'm . . . bleeding out."

Sam stuck a thumb against the edge of the wound, and the blood flow slowed down a little. But when he lessened the pressure of his thumb, the wide, gaping bullet hole started bleeding heavily again.

Thorn loosened the bandanna from his neck and handed it down to the ranger. Heely had started to look more and more like he was dying. Ellison offered him a canteen.

"Obliged, Roman Lee," Thorn said, taking a drink and passing the canteen down to the ranger. "Why did you just wound him, Sam? I mean, he asked for it, turning rabbit the way he did. But two inches farther down, and you would have blown his heart out."

Sam looked up, frowning at the question. The ranger was still pressing the bandanna to the wound, but it was doing little to stem the bleeding. "I didn't appreciate how you baited him."

Thorn gave his dark laugh. "I never baited you *too* much, Tom Heely or whoever the hell you are. I held up a nice rifle as bait. You jumped for it like a wildcat and tried to cut out fast."

"That's enough, Thorn," said the ranger. "He's dead."

Thorn shut up. He shoved his hat farther back atop his head.

Sam stood up, the bandanna hanging from his hand and dripping blood.

Ellison picked up the unloaded rifle. He held it for a moment, then leaned it against the low stone wall.

"I will say this," Ellison said. "Because he's young and new at outlawry, it would have gone over better for him in the Bad River Gunmen's eyes if he'd killed one or two of you and made a clean getaway. That would have been a reputation builder for him."

"And there you have it, Sam," said Thorn. "I gave the man a choice, and he chose wrong. It got him killed. Be glad it's our nameless friend and not one or more of us lying dead there, building him a reputation." He spit on the ground near the dead man. "Good riddance!" he added. "All right, I did bait him a little. But it's better he made a move that I baited him into than to have made a surprise move on his own."

Sam nodded. He poured water over his hands, washed them and shook them dry. With no more to say on the matter, he told Thorn, "Make room for him in the silo with the others. These folks up here will take care of him. We can't leave a dead man lying in the church-yard."

Thorn and Ellison nodded. Sam looked at the wagon and its contents—the rolled-up feather mattress, the women's riding boots, the bag of women's clothing.

"I've got better than a halfway feeling these things belong to the women who were in the doctor's buggy," Sam said, glancing again at the rolled-up mattress.

"If we take it all with us, we'll find out soon enough," said Thorn.

"We'll do Irish Mike a favor," Sam said, seeing the small green shamrock painted on the back of the wagon seat, "and take his wagon to him, else he might not get it back right away."

To Ellison he said, "Are you riding into Bad River with us?"

Ellison looked back and forth between them.

"I ride with whoever I want to," he said petulantly. "Melford or Sims—neither one tells me what to do."

"Just think about it on the way, Roman Lee," Thorn said. "If you want to go your own way, you're free to go. We've got nothing to say about it."

"I know that," Ellison snapped.

Sam capped the canteen and handed it back to him.

"Ranger," said Thorn, "maybe you haven't noticed, but our Roman Lee here doesn't like answering ques-tions from lawmen like you and me."

Without responding, Sam touched the desert barb's reins and turned the horse toward the trail. "Let's get on into town," he said. "I need to turn this horse in at Irish Mike Tuohy's and see how Doc's doing."

Part 3

Chapter 16

The ranger, Roman Lee Ellison and Dan'l Thorn stopped at Bad River's town limits. Sam drove the rented one-horse freight wagon. The other two rode their horses at a walk and stopped on either side of him. Broken afternoon shadows stretched long across an endless plain of upturned slabs of stone and fields of piled boulders. Short, spiky ground-cover cacti and rugged, low-standing succulents stood against views of Bad River drifting at the farthest edge of sight.

Sam's rented desert barb stood reined beside the freight wagon, close to the driver's seat. As a half dozen horsemen came up on the trail and stepped their dusty horses over and wide around them, Thorn and Ellison touched their hat brims to the riders, while keeping their faces partially hidden. In the wagon seat, the ranger had raised the edge of a serape up on his neck and lowered his sombrero as the men first came up around the trail. He lowered the serape as the men rode on. The smell of rye and beer set in and lingered above the trail. Ellison saw a tall whiskey bottle pass among a few hands, then go out of sight.

"Must be some of the new men from Arizona I told

you about," Ellison said, nodding at a couple of red sashes hanging from saddle horns as the men disappeared over a rise in the trail.

In the near distance, the sounds of guitars and horns resounded along Bad River's main street. Laughter spilled across the stony land in rolling waves.

"Pards, we have returned!" one of the riders said to the others, gesturing toward town.

"I think I'm going to like this place," another man called out, laughing.

"Sounds like Irish Mike's saloon is still running full force," Thorn said quietly. "Wonder what it takes to kill a saloon in a place like this. Sounds like getting blown up hasn't made a dent in business."

"If we're done out here," said Ellison, "I'm going to ride in, see how tall they can pour a beer without spilling it."

"Don't forget the rye," Thorn said.

"I'm not about to," Ellison said.

Thorn gave him a look of pleased estimation and touched his hat brim. "Happy we didn't have to shoot each other down, Roman Lee," he said.

Ellison nodded and touched his hat brim in return. "Same here, Dan'l Thorn," he said, then turned his horse and rode off behind the other riders.

As Ellison loped out of sight around the turn, Thorn wiped his palm across his brow and gave a private chuckle under his breath. "Sounds like you gave that one some good forty-five-caliber rehabilitation," he said.

"I don't tell it to many people, Dan'l, but I meant full well to kill him." He kept a cool gaze leveled on Thorn for a moment.

Thorn nodded without reply and looked off in the

direction of Bad River for a few seconds. He shook his head, like he was considering something, and let out a breath.

"I have to tell you, Ranger," he said, "this day has been like the good old days to me."

"Hmph," Sam said, looking off again. "Had I known your good old days were *this* bad, I'd have sent you home early this morning."

They laughed.

"Okay, then," Thorn said at length, straightening in his saddle. "I think I'll mosey on in, see if I can't drink a bunch of Melford's good Tennessee whiskey before he realizes drinking his whiskey is all I'm doing here."

"Good luck on that," Sam said. "I'll turn off the trail here, circle around the back of town and take Irish Mike's wagon to him—hear what's gone on around town today."

"Want to know what I'll tell Melford if he asks me anything about today?"

"Not right now. Tomorrow maybe," said Sam a little crisply.

He gave Thorn a look that told him to keep quiet. Thorn shut up, not knowing what Sam's sudden change meant, but knowing it meant something.

"I'll see you tomorrow, then," said Thorn.

Sam sat watching as the tall Cherokee lawman rode off into town. After a few minutes, he touched the wagon's reins to the horse's back and turned it off the main trail onto a thinner, less trafficked dirt path, his rented desert barb right beside him.

At a clump of tall cacti beside the path, he looked all around from beneath the brim of his sombrero and eased the wagon over, half off the path at an unusual angle. Taking his time, he drew his big Colt out of its holster and cocked it beneath the faded serape. Watching the surroundings from the dark shade beneath his sombrero, he picked up a heavy iron bar from a side panel of road tools in the wagon bed.

Hefting the tool, judging the weight of it in his hand, he walked off the path, deep into the clump of tall cacti and prickly pear ground cover. He looked around, found a partially hidden stone covered by spindly cactus shade, out of the hot Mexican sun. He'd heard someone on his trail earlier. This was a good place to see who it was.

A half hour passed before the ranger heard any sound coming from the dirt path or the direction of the wagon twenty yards away. But finally, there it was, a muffled sound of metal clanking up the trail. When it reached the wagon, he heard the tool panel closing quietly, someone clearly trying to keep the noise down.

When the sound stopped, Sam crept into the clump of cacti, and stooping down, he saw a long brown trail duster walking toward him, hidden in dark circling shade beneath a broad straw sombrero. A small-caliber pistol was held at arm level as the man came closer and stepped into the clump of cacti.

Nobody with sense carries a handgun stuck out that way, Sam thought as he watched the gun stretched out in front as if leading the man on a leash.

Sam stood as still as stone and waited until the gun cleared the cacti and proceeded forward. At just the right moment, he tossed the iron bar over into the brush and rocks a few feet behind the man. Startled, the man turned quickly with his gun aimed. Seeing no one behind him, he turned forward again fast, just in time for the barrel of the ranger's big Colt to slam down on his exposed wrist.

The man screamed in pain and the small gun flew from his hand. His sombrero flew off his head as he crouched, holding his injured wrist.

"No! Don't, *please!*" shouted James Radlear Claypool, seeing the big Colt ready to knock him senseless.

Sam hesitated while the battered gambler moved around in a huddled circling crouch, holding his throbbing wrist. He looked for a place to hit Claypool, but couldn't find one that wasn't already swollen or broken or badly singed. A soiled bandage hung loose from a half-missing ear.

Instead of hitting the man, Sam grabbed him by his duster collar, swung him around and seated him roughly down on the wide shaded stone. As Claypool squeezed his stricken wrist, Sam stepped back, picked up the small pistol and shoved it behind his belt.

"I'm—I'm JR Claypool! Remember me? The one who got blown up by the dynamite?"

"Why are you following me with a gun, JR?"

"Right, yes, I will tell you," said Claypool most obligingly. He tapped the chest of his duster. "I have a card here I'll present if I may," he said.

Sam stepped in and moved Claypool's hand away with the barrel of his big Colt.

"Allow me," Sam said harshly. He reached in the lapel pocket and pulled out one of Jack Swift's business cards. "Now you're Jack Swift?" Sam asked, already knowing better.

"No, I'm not," said Claypool. "But that's Jack Swift's business card—"

"But you're carrying it. So you work for Swift?" Sam asked quickly, not giving him time to gather a good lie.

"Well, not exactly—"

"I see," said Sam. "You just go around giving out his business cards?"

"No," said Claypool, "I'm an investigator like Swift, only I don't have cards like he does. Not right now anyway."

Sam looked at him dubiously.

"For your information, I have some cards being made right now in Mexico City," Claypool said, feigning an arrogance that did not quite dovetail with his appearance. "I investigate and gather information for clients, the same as Swift and his detectives do. Do you understand all that?"

"I see. Only, you sneak up on people with a gun?" Sam said. He paused as if giving the situation thought, then said, "Here's how we're going to do this, Detective Claypool. Every time I ask you something and you lie, I'll find a spot where nobody has hit you yet, and I'll hit you there." He wagged his big Colt. "Do *you* understand all that?"

Sam took another step forward, Colt in hand, and jiggled the chain hanging from Claypool's shoulder. "What the heck is this?"

Claypool glanced down and shrugged at the dangling chain. "That's just something I use of a night—I call it a sleep aid. But I was looking for something I could use to cut it off—"

Sam raised an eyebrow, then got back to the matter at hand. "Why are you following me?"

"Well, see, I followed you and your friend Thorn last night, and I gained a lot of information along the way, which I think you'll want to buy from me." He offered a weak smile. "I know you need to hear it!"

"So you needed a gun to bring me information?" Sam added.

"I admit bringing a gun along was a mistake, for which I apologize," Claypool said. "But there are violent people around here. I didn't want to take a chance."

"What's the information you have and how much will it cost me?" Sam said.

Claypool managed a sly little grin. "Like I said, I was on the switchback last night. I saw young Antonio Villa and two other drunken gunmen trying to have their way with the doctor's housekeeper, Irena. When they couldn't, I saw Antonio manage to get to his horse and ride away." He grinned. "And guess who I saw come along and kill those two gunmen."

Claypool was there, no question about it, Sam thought. *Damn it.* He didn't want to hear that Claypool had seen Thorn kill anybody.

"What else did you see?" he asked to shift the subject forward away from Thorn.

"A few things," Claypool said guardedly. "But here's the main thing you're going to want to hear. I followed the two women after they got away. Eventually I saw them switch from the buggy to the two horses that belonged to the dead gunmen."

"Followed them where?" Sam asked.

Claypool didn't answer directly. "They sent the doctor's buggy on up the switchback," he said. "I figure they knew the doctor's buggy horse would go home. They cut down off the switchbacks and took some game paths down the mountains."

"Go on," said Sam. "Where did the women go then?"

Claypool paused, then confessed, "They got away from me before daylight." He looked embarrassed.

"And that's it?" Sam asked. "That's your important information?"

Claypool smiled. "It would have been," he said. "But I ran into Sims and some of his Bad River Gunmen and guess who they had caught getting off the switchback onto a level trail."

"The women," Sam said flatly.

"Good guess." Claypool lowered his voice as if someone might be listening and said, "Sims sent me on to Bad River today to tell Melford he's going to hold the two women hostage for some mighty big ransom money."

"Hostage?" Sam asked. "Who would pay ransom money for a couple of Bad River women?"

Claypool's voice got even quieter. "Maybe that's something you and I need to talk about, Ranger Sam Burrack." He gave a thin, tight smile and sat waiting, his bearing growing more confident right before Sam's eyes. "See, I'm way ahead of you, Ranger. Now you have to either pay up or fold your hand and push your chair back."

Gambler talk . . . Sam thought for a minute. Claypool had spied all around, and he knew some things. But Sam couldn't waste time on him.

"I don't like this smug attitude you're giving me," he said, "and I don't like guessing games." He took a worn pocket kerchief from inside his duster, shook it out and laid it smoothly across his knee. "If you've anything else to say, get it said."

"I can take you to the women if you're interested," Claypool said bluntly. "We're going to play this the way *I* say, and there's nothing you can do about it. Now I'll ask the questions, and you'll give the answers."

Sam shrugged as if in submission and said, "Maybe you're right."

"You're damn right I'm right," said the ragged, battered gambler. "If I say we—"

He didn't finish. Sam's left hand came out, snatched him by his duster collar and yanked him forward. His right hand balled into a fist and smashed the hapless Claypool's nose into his face. Gristle cracked. Cartilage mashed sideways. Blood flew. Claypool swooned backward on the rock, his eyes slightly crossed, but Sam held him, steadied him in place and shook him a little.

"Don't you pass out on me, Claypool!" he said. "It sounds like you've got lots to tell me." He handed him the kerchief from across his knee.

Claypool held it to his gushing nose. "I think it's broke," he said with a gurgling sound, his head tipped back, blood dripping down his throat.

"People always think that at first," Sam said, "but you're going to be all right." He didn't want to shame the man by telling him he'd hit him only half-strength. "Let me trim everything down to size for you," Sam snapped.

"*Huh?*"

"You heard me," said Sam. "You're going to tell me everything you know about anything going on around here. Call it your civic duty. And stop stalling. If those two women are in danger, I want to know about it right now!"

But Claypool wasn't ready to accept the quick turn of authority. "Wait just a damn minute, Ranger!" he said. "*I'm* the one in charge here, not you!"

"Make me ask you one more time, Claypool," Sam said in a dead-serious tone, "and I'll start clipping your toes off right to left." His big Colt came up cocked and aimed.

"Okay! Wait," said Claypool. He raised a bloody

hand to protect his face. "I can't say the women are in danger right now. Their hands weren't tied last I saw them."

"See?" Sam said. "That's some good information you can get for me right away. Find out where they are and where they're going and get back to me."

"But—but I provide my services for pay, Ranger!" he stammered.

"You'll be paid for information when you have some worth selling me, not before," said Sam.

"But what is Sims going to say when he finds out I'm working for you?"

"Don't let him find out," Sam said. His big Colt tipped back down toward their feet. "Think about your toes."

Chapter 17

Night had fallen when Sam, atop the desert barb, led the wagon to the rear door of the darkened livery barn. Claypool sat in the wagon's driver seat, sound asleep, his head slumped forward onto his chest. Looking up in the darkness, Sam gave a touch to his sombrero and saw Irish Mike's silhouette step away from an upper window of the Frenchman Hotel.

Claypool stirred a little as music and revelry resounded along the street from the charred empty lot where the Bad River Saloon used to be. He slumped back down in the seat as Irish Mike headed through the barn and opened the rear door for the freight wagon.

"Where'd you find this one?" Mike asked quietly, tilting his head at Claypool in the wagon.

"We met on the trail a couple of hours ago," Sam said, handing the wagon reins down to Irish Mike as the wagon stopped inside the barn.

"The poor sod," said Irish Mike, seeing Claypool's swollen nose, dried blood on both cheeks, two black eyes. "Every time I see him, he looks worse than the time before! Look at his ear! His nose!"

"I hit him in the nose, Mike," Sam said. "The rest of it, he'll have to tell you about. I don't think the doctor was very serious about fixing his ear."

"I'll say he wasn't." Irish Mike winced at the sight of the half-ear behind the loose bandage. "Sometimes it seems like Dr. Jorgenson has his mind on other matters."

Sam nodded, thinking about the morphine, the hypodermic syringe.

"I have to tell you, Mike, Dr. Jorgenson is dead. So is Father Lawrence."

"Oh, my! Both dead?" said Mike. "That's terrible news. Those are the two most respected members of the community here. Did someone kill them?"

"No," Sam said, "I don't think so. It looked like a suicide frankly." He paused, then said, "Has there been much morphine-laced alcohol around Bad River?"

"Yes, there has," said Mike, "but not as bad as it was. They were making it down around Mexico City and shipping it all around. For a while it was cutting into my saloon sales, but it went away. People didn't give up their beer and whiskey for it."

Sam wasn't going to say much more about the morphine mescal unless he was pressed for it. "We found them both in a silo behind the rectory . . . along with the bodies of three Bad River Gunmen."

"Sims's men?" said Mike.

Sam nodded. "They were everywhere last night along the switchback," he said. He pointed at the sleeping gambler. "Claypool claims he was out there too."

"If he said he was there, he likely was," said Mike. "He goes everywhere, trying to find out what's going on. He says he does it for the money, but I don't think that's true. I never see him with any money from it. I think he's just trying to be part of what goes on around here."

"What's all this?" Sam pointed at the length of chain reaching up from the gambler's ankle and draped over his shoulder.

"He had me lock it on him," said Irish Mike. "Says it helps keep him from walking in his sleep. Being upstairs, I expect he didn't want to take any chances and stagger out the window some night."

"Does it work?" Sam asked.

"Look at him," Mike said with a chuckle. "He's asleep. He's not walking."

"Good point," Sam said. He nodded in the direction of the music and laughter in the street. "Sounds like you're having a good night out there."

"A lot happens in a day, Sam," Mike said. "The unusually large crowd tonight is not only my saloon drinkers. I took over the German Ale and Whiskey House this morning. I now own the only two drinking establishments in Bad River!" He gave a wide grin and spread his hands.

Sam smiled and shook his hand.

"Congratulations, Irish Mike Tuohy," he said. "Now that you own them both, maybe you'll sponsor Claypool running a card game for you?"

"I will indeed," said Mike. "It would keep him out of trouble and start making him a living, instead of this craziness of snooping around all the time."

"Good luck," Sam said. "Has anything else gone on here today?"

"In fact, yes," Mike said with a sad look. "Townsman Clement Melford found our sheriff, Showdown Art Forbes, sitting dead at his desk—he had a stack of

Wanted posters in front of him. He was going through them, I expect."

"I'm sorry to hear that," Sam said quietly. He idly lifted his sombrero and held it at his chest. "I remember hearing the name Showdown Forbes when I was no more than a boy. I wish I had gone by to see him when I got here."

"He wouldn't have seen you, Sam," said Mike, "so don't feel bad. Showdown was not a social man near the end. He once locked up a drunk and forgot about him for over a week. Nearly starved the poor man to death, then threw him out in the street, wanted to accuse him of vagrancy."

They both shook their heads and fell silent for a moment.

"Does Showdown have any family left?" Sam asked.

"No, hasn't had any family for many years," said Mike. "Like I said, he wasn't sociable, not by a long shot." He paused, then said, "I'm handling the funeral arrangements." He gave Sam a questioning look and added, "It might be hard rustling up six pallbearers."

Sam caught the look. "Put me on the list as a standby," he said. "If you can't find six, I'll do it."

"Obliged, Ranger," Mike said. "I know Showdown would be obliged too. I mean, if he hadn't gotten so blasted old and mean-hearted like he did." He considered something for a moment and said, "With Father Lawrence being deceased, I don't suppose you know any funeral prayers or—"

"Let's not push it," Sam said, cutting him off. "I said I can be a standby pallbearer, that's all."

Down the row of stalls, Sam heard Doc neigh at the sound of his voice.

"I know who that is," he said, turning toward the

sound. He reached into his pocket and took out the slice of apple that Dan'l Thorn had given him earlier.

"He'll be glad to see you, Ranger," Mike said, walking along the stalls with a lantern raised for light. "Especially when he sees you brought him some sliced apple."

Sam nodded. "By the way, Mike," he said, "Claypool is working for me now, gathering information like he does."

"That's good, Ranger," said Mike. "He's been needing somebody to give him some direction—maybe shake a little sense into him. He was a good man. A gambler but good at his profession. That is, till his wife died three years back. He's been walking half-sideways ever since. Nothing seems to go right for him. Some men get that way when they've lost a good woman. It makes things go wrong in their head."

"That's too bad," Sam said. "But it's good to know his circumstances."

"Oh," said Irish Mike, "you mean it might save him some wear and tear on his nose?"

"It could," Sam said. "I'm obliged if you'll unlock the chain and get rid of it. I hate seeing a man turn himself into an animal."

"Will do," Mike said. "What about him walking out the window in his sleep?"

"He'll have to be careful, just like the rest of us," Sam said. "I expect if he wakes up a time or two lying in the dirt down by the hitch rail, he'll smarten up."

Mike gave a chuckle and said, "Yes, you would think so."

"If I want to know who rules the roost around here above Clement Melford, where do I look?"

"Easy enough," said Irish Mike. "You'd look up at the

Fitzhugh Mountainside Rancho, right atop the switch-back. Dolan Fitzhugh has the biggest gold purses this side of the Valley of Mexico." He paused and looked curiously at the ranger. "Why do you want to see Fitzhugh? He keeps his nose out of everything that goes on in Bad River—thinks the town is bad luck, I hear. But he owns a lot of property, a string of banks across Sonora, cattle, timber. Lord knows what all else. Why?" he asked again.

"Just curious," Sam said.

Clement Melford had never mentioned the name Dolan Fitzhugh, Sam noted. *Understandable among the big dogs,* he reminded himself.

"Do the French mines do any business with him?" he asked.

"Probably, but he'd never let it be known," said Mike. "I heard that Melford went to him a couple of times for some short-term financial assistance. You know, to get him across the hump in a couple of tricky situations."

"I hear you." Sam nodded. "At the top of the switch-back, you say?"

"You'll know the place when you see it," Mike said. "I don't know if ol' Fitz will talk to you though. I hear he's a hard man to see. Like Melford, he keeps lots of hired hands around him." He gave Sam a shrewd look and asked again, "What's your interest in Dolan Fitzhugh?"

Instead of answering, Sam asked, "Has there ever been anything between him and Irena?"

Irish Mike looked taken aback. "How'd you know that?"

"Just a hunch," the ranger said. "Tell me about them."

"Not much to tell," Mike said. "Irena worked for the Fitzhughs until a couple of years ago. She more or less managed the rancho. Her and Loris Fitzhugh were good friends."

"Were?" Sam asked.

"Loris caught the fever and died," he said. He looked uncomfortable but continued. "I don't like to repeat what might be just gossip. But I heard that Irena and Fitz had been more than friendly for a while before Loris's death. Being uncomfortable with the situation, Irena left and came to work here for Dr. Jorgenson. In my opinion, her and Dolan Fitzhugh have been pining for each other ever since."

"I see." Sam nodded. "Can I get another horse from you?"

"Sure can," said Mike. "You want one waiting first thing in the morning?"

"How about in a couple of hours?" Sam asked. "A fresh horse, some dried beef, a biscuit and a canteen of strong, hot coffee."

After visiting Doc, giving him his slice of apple and making a careful inspection of his stitches and bruises, Sam had loaded Claypool over his shoulder, carried him across the street and up to his room in the Frenchman Hotel. He'd set Claypool down on the side of his bed and unlocked the shackle from his ankle with a key Mike had given him.

Partially awake and bleary-eyed, the ragged, battered, one-booted gambler gazed all around and down at his dirty bare ankle. "What will I do now?" he asked the ranger.

Sam could tell the weary man wasn't just talking about what to do tonight. "Do like the rest of us," Sam said, pitching the chain over in a corner. "Deal with it."

Claypool looked out at the starlit darkness, at blue-orange stems of light shining in from flickering torches along the main street. "What about this window here? Can I trust myself?" he asked.

"We all gotta watch our step, don't we?"

The gambler cast his swollen eyes to the floor in misery.

"Look at me, Claypool," Sam demanded loudly, standing over him. "You get some more sleep, rest up. In the morning, you're going to find out where the women are. Get that information and get it to me. Then we'll talk about what you can do next."

"I—I'll do my best—" Claypool stammered.

"No, Claypool," said Sam, "*I'll do my best* is an excuse you're already coming up with in case you fail. I don't want to hear it. When I see you tomorrow, I want to know you've been on the job. Have you got that?" Sam wasn't expecting anything but wanted to keep Claypool occupied and out of the way.

Claypool looked troubled. He almost repeated himself, but the look in the ranger's eyes wouldn't let him. Resolve came over his face.

"I've got it," he said.

Sam looked at the short boot the gambler had carried under his arm all day. He'd kept it against his side wherever he'd been, in the wagon, in his horse's saddle, sitting on the stone in the cactus shade, getting his nose busted. He'd dropped the boot to the floor only when he'd been plopped onto the bed. Now his eyes had fallen shut again.

You'll do all right, Claypool, Sam said to himself. *We've just got to keep you busy.* With a slight shove from the ranger, Claypool fell backward on the hard, lumpy bed.

Sam backed out of the room, closed the door quietly and walked up to Clement Melford's office on the third floor. He knocked.

Inside the office, Melford looked up at a mirror that had been installed that day up on the hallway ceiling. Inconspicuous, the mirror in the hall ceiling hung at an angle in line with the clear transom glass pane above the door, revealing in the dim hall light the mirrored image of anyone standing there waiting.

Ingenious, Melford congratulated himself. He motioned his new personal bodyguard, Waco Bird Wheeler, into an anteroom and waited until the door closed behind him.

He fanned his hand against the odor of a slim Black Briar cigar that Waco Bird had left in an ashtray. The damned thing smelled of licorice, sweat and vomit. He'd have to talk to Bird about the Black Briars. Nothing smelled worse.

"Come in, Ranger Burrack," he said loud enough to be heard. He saw the top of Sam's head turn back and forth, looking both ways in the empty hallway.

Like magic, isn't it, Ranger? Melford drank the last sip from his glass and set it on a tray of sparkling crystal on a bar near his desk.

Sam stepped inside the office and closed the door behind him. He caught the odor of the slim twisted cigars right away, but showed no sign of it.

"What can I do for you, Ranger?" Melford said, gesturing him to a chair that sat with its back turned almost entirely to the anteroom door. "May I offer you a drink?"

"Much obliged, but I'll stand," Sam said, his sombrero off, hanging in front of his chest. "I've sat in a saddle most all day out on the trails."

"Oh, indeed?" said Melford with feigned interest since he already knew where Sam had spent his day, along with the Cherokee lawman who'd ridden up the dusty street not more than an hour ago. All Thorn had given Melford was a touch of his hat brim. That was all right, he assured himself. Thorn was on his side.

The ranger was a different story. Melford had not spoken to Sam since watching the two stallions fighting it out down there, right below his office. All he knew was what Jack Swift had told him afterward. The deal with the ranger for Sims, Tillis, Dupree and the Russian was still on.

"I haven't heard from you, Ranger," he said now. "I understand we still have a deal—you know, the invitation to a gunfight?" He grinned.

"Yes, our deal is still good," Sam said. He wasn't carrying his rifle, but his big Colt stood holstered inside his reach-through duster pocket. "I heard about Sheriff Forbes dying. I'm sorry for Bad River's loss."

As he spoke, he held his sombrero to his chest. It covered his Colt from view, along with his badge and the upper lapel of his range duster. Without Melford noticing, Sam had inched around until he stood covering the door to the anteroom, behind which, based on the rancid smell alone, he was pretty sure Waco Bird Wheeler stood waiting, watching.

Looking for an edge? Sure he was. Men like Wheeler, Thorn—and yes, men like himself, he admitted—were always looking for an edge.

"On behalf of the town of Bad River, we appreciate your words of respect, Ranger," Melford said.

"I know this is not the best time to bring it up," Sam said, "but I need to use Sheriff Forbes's office for a few days."

Melford looked surprised. "Why?"

"Why?" Now it was Sam's turn to look surprised. "Because I need a place to hold my prisoners when I start rounding them up. If any of them decides to come along peacefully, that is," he added. "If they don't come along peacefully, I'll stack them in a barn somewhere." He looked at Melford, waiting for an answer. When none came, he finally said, "Well, can I use the jail?"

"Oh, yes! I mean, our jail building is never locked, so use it . . . yes, of course," Melford said. He opened a desk drawer, took out two large keys on a brass ring and pitched them to the ranger. "Those are cell keys," he said. "They fit all four cells. Sheriff Forbes started leaving them with me after an unfortunate incident occurred—"

"I heard about it," Sam said. He stuck the keys behind his gun belt.

"You know, I haven't heard anything about the women. The money. Not from Sims, not from anyone." Melford offered a shrug. "Are we sure this is a good time to let Sims know what's going on?"

"I figure Sims already knows. Everybody seems to know everything around here almost as it happens. I think he's just waiting to hear about it from you, instead of Swift or one of his detectives. Or even from one of your men." He gave Melford a pointed look. "Let's be honest. Are you afraid of Sims? Afraid to tell him about our deal?"

"All right, Ranger, let's get this straight!" Melford said, his voice growing stronger. He stepped from behind his desk, slamming the drawer closed on his way.

His hand was poised on the butt of his engraved Colt. "I'm afraid of neither man nor beast. But this is not a good time to engage Sims. Have you seen the number of Red Sash Cowboys arriving here day after day?"

"I have," said the ranger. "Do you think they will stop showing up next week? Two weeks from now? If you think so, I'll wait. I'll wait to arrest my wanted outlaws, and you can wait on me giving you the money—if I don't decide to leave first or if somebody doesn't stop my clock."

"All right! I get your point." It was all sinking in. Melford's right hand fell away from his gun butt. "You caught me by surprise is all, Ranger," he said, stepping back around behind his desk. He offered a slight smile. "Caught me unprepared, I should say."

"Get prepared," Sam said forcefully. "Don't worry about the Cowboys showing up. I've got them covered."

Melford gave him a somewhat disbelieving look. "All right. What happens next?"

"You lay the deal out to Sims. I've got the money close by, and I'm ready to bring in the women."

"You have already found the missing women too?" Melford asked.

"I've stayed on the job," the ranger replied. He let Melford see his eyes move across the closed door to the anteroom as if he knew someone was there. "I'm leaving no room for any tricks or last-minute surprises." He looked at the anteroom door again, making sure Melford understood his implication.

Melford understood.

Chapter 18

On a high ridge overlooking the cattle and rail-siding town of Vista Hermosa, Kura Stabitz set his horse beside Cree Sims. Each of them wore bandanna masks hanging readily below their chins. The Russian Assassin carried a short double-barreled shotgun standing from his thigh, his right hand wrapped around the small of the stock near the hammers.

Sims carried a pair of French military binoculars hanging by a strip of rawhide around his neck.

"Here they come," he said quietly as if the enlarged figures in the circular lens might hear him.

Four men were walking purposefully from the railway office to a waiting train. Three of the men were Sims's Bad River Gunmen, the fourth a young Mexican *federale* soldier, *sargento* Alverez. They had brought him out of the rail office at gunpoint to open a big safe aboard the security car. The three outlaws had weapons covering the other man from beneath their dusters.

"Open that safe for us, *sargento*, and we likely won't kill you," one of the three men told him.

On the ridge, Sims smiled a little, watching the sergeant cut a tin seal from the door of the security railcar that was standing in a line of other freight cars bound for Mexico City.

"If this work gets any easier, I'll be embarrassed telling my kinfolk I'm an outlaw," Sims said to the Russian.

His English not being the best, Kura Stabitz only nodded and gave an uncertain smile.

But his smile turned into a grimace as he squinted with his naked eyes and spotted a column of a dozen or more mounted *federales* moving their animals along at a walk. They had emerged into full sight as a cattle train pulled away, leaving them exposed across the wide freight yard.

"Oh, hell no!" Sims shouted, seeing the soldiers advance along the rails in the direction of the express security car where the Bad River Gunmen stood, the shape of their guns visible under their long dusters, their masks now up across their noses.

The Russian started to gig his horse toward a thin path down the ridge and into the rail yard. Sims grabbed the horse by its bridle, stopping it.

"Where the hell are you going?" Sims said.

"To help out our pal-ez," Stabitz said. "Are we not?" *Help out our pal-ez? This stupid flat head!*

Sims was tempted to put a bullet in the Russian's head, until he saw the hammers already cocked back on the double-barreled shotgun now lying across Stabitz's lap, loosely pointed in Sims's direction.

Sims yelled, "Yes! Of course we are! But wait! Let's see how this goes. The soldiers might ride on by or turn away before they get there!"

He gestured down at the rails, noting the twenty or so cars lined up between the security-car robbery in progress and the slowly advancing *federales*.

"We've been in tight spots before!" he said, slipping down from his saddle. "Stay calm!"

He motioned the Russian down from his saddle. Crouching behind the cover of their horses, the two of them watched.

The three outlaws had already yanked down their masks and shoved the young *sargento* up into the freight car. The three men scrambled up into the car behind him, guns aimed and cocked.

"Not a word, *sargento*," said Dupree, "or you will die here in the dirt. *¿Comprende?*"

"*Sí, entiendo.*" The young sergeant nodded, his hands held chest high.

"Keep an eye on him," Tillis said to Dallas Curio, who was making his first raid with them. "If he turns rabbit on us, kill him."

"Got it," Curio said, giving the young sergeant a dark half-grin.

Come on! Come on! You slow sonsabitches! Sims silently coaxed his men as he watched the column of *federales* make its way along the line of railcars.

Sims took heart as he saw one of his men slip under the car and head to the other side, the sergeant's seal snippers in hand.

All right, that's better. He felt somewhat relieved. This was what he had expected them to do, get all set up to make their way out of there.

The door of the security car slid slowly closed. He knew that his men would be getting ready to use the door on the other side, where the second seal had been clipped and the door pulled open so they could spill out, guns ablaze, to go racing to their horses, currently being held three sets of rails deeper inside the rail yard by a former Red Sash Cowboy named Virgil Settles.

Any second, Settles would race forward with the horses and see that the Gunmen got mounted and on their way. Sims raised his binoculars again. *So far, so good . . .*

"Keep watch for the express bag," he said sidelong to Kura Stabitz. "If shooting starts, cover the man carrying it."

The Russian nodded, watching the mounted *federales* moving right along, slowly and steadily, dust rising and wafting easily in their wake.

The mounted soldiers filed past the security car, where the robbers would be watching through a crack in the heavy wooden doors. On the ridge, Sims rose up enough to pull his rifle from his saddle boot and lever a round into the chamber just in case. Crouching back down, he saw a rider near the back of the *federales* swing his horse around, circle back and look down at something in the dirt.

Uh-oh! Sims and the Russian both saw the soldier dismount and pick up something too small to be seen from atop the ridge, even with binoculars. *Easy now,* Sims thought to himself.

Yet in a second, the column stopped and the man ran forward on foot. He handed the small object up to the officer in charge. Beside the officer, the sergeant in charge of the column shouted and brought the men to a halt. Sims held his breath, his hand ready on the rifle.

"Open that door!" the officer shouted in Spanish. "The seal is broken!" He held up a piece of the door seal that the other soldier had picked up from the dirt.

Damn it! Here we go . . . ! Sims dropped to one knee, taking aim.

Seeing Sims maneuver his rifle, the Russian did the

same. He drew his rifle and shoved his short-range shotgun into the saddle boot.

As the big door to the railcar opened, the soldiers saw sunlight beaming in through the open door on the other side. The fleeing outlaws had left the door open as they jumped out and raced straight toward their horses. Virgil Settles was already riding forward, hard, bringing their getaway horses to meet them.

"They robbed the safe!" *Sargento* Alverez shouted, waving his arms in the railcar doorway.

From atop the ridge, Sims and Stabitz watched the outlaws grab their horses, mount and ride away at a full run across the rail yard.

Almost before the young sergeant finished his words, a rifle shot rang out from the other side of the car and a bullet hit him squarely in his lower back, knocking him onto the ground.

Six men in the *federale* column had dropped from their saddles and hurried into the empty railcar, rifles in hand. The officer in charge, Lieutenant Geraldo Mazemo, directed the other six men to cross over the tracks.

"Is that sergeant dead?" he shouted, looking at the wounded man lying on the ground.

Hearing the officer's question, the young soldier pushed onto a knee in spite of his pain.

"I am not dead, Lieutenant," he said. "I am Sergeant Alfiano Alverez. And I am *alive* . . . and fit for duty!" He lost his balance and fell from his knee, but managed to push himself back up.

"He is *fit*?" Mazemo asked as he stepped from his saddle onto the railcar. The soldier who had helped the wounded sergeant onto his knee shook his head and touched a finger to his temple. "Lieutenant, I think he fell hard and has lost much of his senses."

"No," the wounded sergeant butted in, "I can fight. Get me on a horse! I will kill all of these bandits!"

Suddenly, gunfire exploded back and forth across the rail yard. Remaining calm, Lieutenant Mazemo watched the soldiers bring his men's horses around to the door on the other side. Before stepping out of the doorway and down into his saddle, he shouted to anyone who could hear him, "Attend to this man at once and then send him to me!"

From the ridge, Sims and Stabitz sent out a few rifle rounds, none of which struck any of the soldiers or sent them running for cover. As Tillis and the others rode out of sight, the soldiers firing wildly at them, Sims gestured for the Russian to stop shooting at the railcar below.

"We're wasting bullets," he said. "Let's get off this ridge and catch up with the money bag. The *federales* will stop chasing us in less than two miles, especially once we shoot a few of them out of their saddles."

In a second, the two were up, mounted and on their way, leaving only a fresh rise of dust in their wake.

In the silvery dawn, Dolan Fitzhugh answered a familiar quiet knock on his rear office door. As a security precaution, he turned a brass peephole cover to the side and looked out at the face of his personal bodyguard, Crayton Stivers.

"Morning, sir," the former U.S. cavalry sergeant said in an officious tone. "We have a visitor at the front entrance."

He stepped a little to the side, affording Fitzhugh a

fog-streaked look along the side of the large hacienda. Across a hilly two-acre front yard, at a board fence that ran along the front edge of the well-kept property, a single mounted horseman sat looking back at them from beneath a wide sombrero. Lingering wisps of fog swirled around him.

"Arizona Ranger Sam Burrack, I'm going to guess," Dolan Fitzhugh said.

"Yes, sir, that is the name he gave me," said Stivers. "He asked for you, and he mentioned the two women."

"Did he indeed?" Fitzhugh said.

He studied the ranger as best he could from a distance. He saw a rifle butt standing from a saddle boot. The ranger's long riding duster covered him from his calves to his neck, a large round button closed at the collar against the early-morning dampness. Under his duster, no doubt his big Colt lay across his lap, cocked and ready, the ranger having no idea what he might find here.

"Should I bring him to you, sir?"

"No," said Fitzhugh. "I'll get a coat. We'll meet him out there."

He looked over into a nearby corral where two of his men were working with a young saddle horse. With a lift of his hand, he signaled both men to join him. They picked up the rifles that they had leaned outside the corral gate and the four of them walked out to meet the ranger, stopping a few feet from him.

"Ranger Sam Burrack," Fitzhugh said.

Sam nodded and took off his sombrero. "Mr. Dolan Fitzhugh," he replied.

"What brings you up here, Ranger?" Fitzhugh asked.

Sam noted that Fitzhugh made no gesture of hospitality. He didn't invite Sam to come in or offer water for himself or his horse after the long uphill ride.

All right, Sam thought. *Straight to the point.*

"I'm searching for a couple of missing women from down in Bad River." As Sam spoke, his eyes made a close search around the yard, the corral, the large hacienda. "Did they come by here over the past couple of days? Might have been some riders with them." He paused, then said, "Or close behind."

"Haven't seen anyone come by," said Fitzhugh almost too quickly. No questions, no curiosity. He looked at his three men. "What about it, men? Two women traveling by? Maybe some riders with them?"

The three men only shook their heads as one. Sam cast each of them a steady gaze for a few seconds, long enough to know not to believe them.

Seeing the ranger wasn't having any of it, Fitzhugh spoke again. "The thing is, Ranger, we're the last hacienda up here on the switchback. Anybody going past us makes us all wonder why."

Sam stared at him as his hand closed around the big Colt beneath his riding duster. *Here goes . . .*

"I hate calling a man a liar in his own yard, Fitzhugh, but I've tracked shoe marks of the same two horses for the past twelve miles. They came right in here toward that barn." He nodded at a barn that sat thirty yards away. He looked at the three men, then at Fitzhugh. "You're all lying."

One of the men with a rifle started to raise the barrel at Sam. Without exposing the big Colt, the ranger barely tipped the barrel from under the duster's edge.

"That'll be the worst mistake you'll ever make," Sam said in a quiet but deadly serious voice.

"Stand down, Thomas!" Fitzhugh said to the man. "All of you, stand down!" He glared at Sam. "Whatever you might think is going on here, Ranger, you're wrong!"

A woman's voice called out from the front door of the hacienda, cutting Fitzhugh off and drawing Sam's attention. "Ranger? Ranger Burrack, is that you?"

Sam recognized Irena's voice. Only she sounded weak. Without taking his eyes off the men, he called out to her, "Yes, it's me, Irena. I've been looking for you and Sara. Are you all right?"

"Lower your rifles, men," Fitzhugh said.

Sam saw the barrels point down at the ground. He raised the Colt from under his duster. He let them see him ease the hammer down but keep the gun in his hand.

He looked over at Irena, who was walking toward him, limping slightly. Her face was battered, and she held an arm to her side as if protecting a wound there.

"You shouldn't be out here, Irena," Fitzhugh said. "You should stay in bed."

When Irena ignored him, Sam swung down from his saddle and met her as she crossed the yard.

"I thought you and Sara had been taken by Cree Sims and his men. What did they do to you and Sara?" He looked around. "Where is Sara?"

"Sara is here, Sam. She's here with me, and she's all right. She says she will name the baby after you—if it's a boy, that is." She smiled stiffly.

Sam didn't like the way she was rambling. Was she feverish?

"She says she will name him Samuel and call him Paco. It is the name Father Lawrence told her is the name of her blood father. Or was it Poncho?" She took a breath. "Anyway, we are both fine, Sara and I." She gestured a hand at her bruised face. "*Sí*, I took a beating. But I will soon get over it. And I will teach little Samuel to ride." Suddenly her legs started to fold.

Sam reached for her, but Fitzhugh was instantly at her side, his arm supporting her around her waist. "She shouldn't be out here, Ranger. She needs rest. Can't you see the shape she's in?"

Before Sam could answer, Irena said, "I killed another one of them, Sam, maybe two!" Her voice was growing weaker. "I drew one's gun from his holster hanging on the wall . . . and I shot him through his forehead! Then the gun misfired. But I dropped it and grabbed a long wheat scythe! I got both hands in place—"

"Irena, darling," Fitzhugh cut in, "don't talk about it. Try to forget it ever happened." He looked at Sam. "Isn't that right, Ranger? Tell her. Maybe she'll listen to you—"

"Thank God, Ranger!" Sara cried out loudly from the open front door. "You have come to me—to *us*!" She clasped a hand to her flat stomach and ran to him, throwing herself into his arms. She kissed Sam's face, his cheek, his mouth.

"*Hola*, Sara," he said, holding her back with both hands. "I'm happy to see you both. I heard stories you two were kidnapped after I last saw you."

"We were, we were!" she cried. "But we escaped as you can see!" She twirled in place and started to throw her arms around him again.

But Fitzhugh saw the reluctant expression on the ranger's face. "Sara," he said, "please go prepare a fresh pot of coffee. I'm sure the ranger can use a cup after such a long ride uphill."

"Many thanks," said Sam, feeling the atmosphere sweeten now that guns had lowered and threats and cautions had been put aside. He pointed at the trough near the barn. "With your permission, I'd be obliged to water my horse?"

"Of course. Allow me, Ranger," Fitzhugh said. He turned to one of his men and said, "Thomas, take the ranger's horse and water it. Grain it too," he added as an afterthought. To Sam he said, "I owe you an apology. But you see, I had no idea what legal implications your coming here might have meant."

Sam realized Fitzhugh was still testing the waters, seeing if Sam might consider Irena to have broken any laws in defending herself and Sara. Not wanting to explain the Matamoros Agreement once again, he took a peaceful breath and relaxed.

"I understand," he said. "Everything's good as far as I'm concerned. Had the women not fought back, the men would have killed them like as not. Citizens have the right to defend their lives." *Okay, shut up now,* he reminded himself. He had no business interpreting the laws of Mexico.

"Yes, I'm certain you're right, Ranger," Fitzhugh said as the ranger fell silent.

Satisfied that the ranger was not there for any reason other than concern for Irena and Sara, he excused himself with a nod and walked away toward his office.

"Sara is working for Dolan and me," Irena said to Sam, "at least until I get better or until she has her baby . . . or maybe longer. We'll wait and see."

"I understand," Sam said. They were both aware that Sara was taking on the position Irena herself had held here at the Fitzhugh Mountainside Rancho, that of housekeeper and best friend to the lady of the house.

"Well," she said without Sam offering another word on the subject, "we should always do our best to help our friends and always trust them. Don't you agree, Ranger?"

"Yes, of course," Sam said. He looked over at the barn, where his rented horse stood with its muzzle down in the water trough.

Sam looked at the house. "Coffee sounds good right about now," he said. Offering his arm, he helped Irena back toward the door. "I'm just happy to see you're both alive."

Chapter 19

"Damn this all to hell! These bastards have never followed us this long or this far!" Cree Sims fumed. His men, each from their own position behind the cover of rock, fired a long, hard barrage of bullets at the well-covered soldiers.

"Something ain't right with none of this!" Earl Dupree said under his breath to Giles Tillis. "It's gone wrong since the get-go! How come they never followed us this hard before?"

"I don't know," Tillis said. He fired two shots and chambered a third, his rifle barrel smoking. "If I ever get the chance, I'm damned sure going to ask them!"

"Don't poke fun at me, damn it!" Dupree shouted above the gunfire. "How come we left backup men to join us along the trail out of the yards, and damned if they hadn't done the same!"

"I don't know," said Tillis, "but that's another thing I'll ask them first chance!" He fired a round, levered up another and looked at Dupree, who sat cursing under the heavy blanket of gunfire.

"Are you going to shoot anybody, Earl, or just holler *how comes* at them all day?"

"We should have cut out from this bunch of jakes back when we first talked about it! Now look at us!"

Blood ran down Dupree's shirtsleeve from a ricochet wound in his shoulder. Tillis and he lay hunkered down together behind the same rock, the same fallen mesquite tree. Their new horseman, Virgil Settles, lay stretched out, dead or close to it, behind the rock next to them. His eyes stared off vacantly, an open canteen in his bloody hands.

Leaning out from behind the rock he shared with Cree Sims, Dallas Curio and Roman Lee Ellison, Stabitz methodically, carefully took aim at a *federale* and squeezed the trigger. He shouted something in Russian as the man melted out of sight in a blossoming red spray.

"Good shot, Kura!" Sims shouted, levering a round into his rifle chamber. "Do that a few dozen more times and we can all go home!"

Son of a bitch! Roman Lee Ellison looked along the trail behind the *federales* chasing them.

A column of more *federales* rode forward at a gallop in a hurry to draw blood from these bloodthirsty gringo outlaws who had plagued their lives for so long. Roman Lee was about to tell Sims about the onrush of more soldiers, but decided that if Sims hadn't seen them yet, he would soon enough. Why should he be the messenger?

"The hell is that behind the soldiers?" he asked Dallas Curio, looking past the mounted riders along the trail with his naked eyes.

Curio, who lay stretched out on his belly, was looking down at the long trail through a battered French telescope.

"That, my curious amigo," Curio said without lowering the telescope, "is a team of mules pulling an eight-pound French field cannon."

"Oh, *hell*! No, it's not!" said Roman Lee.

"If you don't want to know, don't ask," Curio said.

"Who the hell do these jakes think they're fighting up here, Napoléon?"

Dallas Curio gave a little grin, still scanning the trail, the oncoming *federales*, the cannon, the big black-and-tan mules.

"Don't worry," he said. "The eight pounder looks tough as hell, but it's only accurate at about twelve to fifteen hundred yards."

Hearing Curio, Sims gave a little gallows laugh. Those close enough to hear him gave the same dark laugh as they fought on round after round.

"What are we here, around two hundred yards give or take?" Ellison said.

"Yep," said Curio, "and they're closing in quick. Fastest damned mules I've ever seen."

"They've been feeding them racehorse oats," Tillis interjected.

"Good God *almighty*!" said Roman Lee, making a dark joke of it now himself. "Sims! Tell me to get the hell out of here!"

Sims, having just fired his rifle, levered a fresh round, spit and said, "Roman Lee, get the hell out of here! You're starting to scare everybody!" His quip brought more dark laughter.

"Right away, boss!" said Roman Lee. He started scooting back toward the horses, which stood behind the cover of a large boulder.

"What the hell about the rest of us?" Earl Dupree shouted at Sims through the rifle fire.

"Everybody! Follow Roman Lee! Fire hard and fall

back to the horses," Sims shouted, looking all around. "Get out of here before that damn cannon starts in on us!"

How many men had he lost on this job?

How many men had he lost in this simple railcar robbery?

Too damned many. Settles and another new man lay dead on the ground. Counting the backup men who'd joined them on the trail from the rail yard, there had been . . . what, a dozen of them only a few minutes ago? Now there were six of them left, maybe a few more backup men? Sims gazed back along the trail to the rail yard. A couple of men could have gotten through, taken another way around. But he wasn't counting on it.

"Stay together if you can!" he shouted. "If not, we'll meet in Bad River!" He looked over at the Russian, who nodded discreetly and patted the bulging canvas money bag he held against his chest. A bullet zipped past Sims's head.

"Damn it, let's get out of here." He couldn't resist looking over at Earl Dupree. "If that's okay with you and Roman Lee!"

"I'm good with it," Roman Lee said, ready to cut toward the horses.

"Smart-mouthed turd," Dupree growled at Sims under his breath.

"Come on, Earl!" said Tillis. "You've been wanting to get out of here, let's go!"

Crouched, firing wildly, the men made their way to the horses, mounted and in a moment were gone. Virgil Settles's blank eyes were turned to the thin path as if watching their retreat. His canteen, now capped, was hanging from Dupree's saddle horn. His horse—a fast, sleek, headstrong prairie mustang—ran alongside Sims. A bullet had grazed its rump and left a bloody streak, but it didn't slow the animal down.

When they had descended the path from the hilltop they had occupied moments ago, they started up the next one in this seemingly endless world of rock and gravel, of sharp hillsides and deep, ridged valleys.

A deep whistle made every man look back, and they saw the first round from the cannon shatter the huge boulder where just a few minutes ago their horses had stood shielded from the gunfire. The blast shook the ground as the upper half of the boulder disappeared in a skyward spray of dirt, rock and broken scrub juniper.

"There went our horses, had we stayed," shouted Dupree, the blast giving his horse all the motivation it needed to keep galloping along the dusty trail.

Before Sam had left the Fitzhugh Mountainside Rancho, Irena told him where to find the body of the outlaw she'd dropped with a bullet through his brain, the contents of his head splattered on the white lime-washed wall behind him.

The other outlaw? Well, she was sure he couldn't have gone far. She had grabbed a two-handed wheat scythe, swung it hard, using all of her strength, and sent its sharp three-foot-long curved blade through his chest. The man had lost four fingers trying to stop it. Sam agreed the man could not have gone far after that.

At midmorning, Sam turned off the switchback onto an overgrown path leading to a lower clearing. There he found a crumbling abandoned coach station and a rickety old stock barn that stood leaning so far over, it wouldn't stand much longer. Seeing an old iron hitch

ring on a slanted post out front of the station, Sam
stepped down from his saddle, led the rental horse
there and hitched it.

A fast rustle of brush drew his attention to the wide-
open station doors and he saw four young coyotes
darting out across a stretch of rocky ground. They
seemed to vanish into a crevice in the stone wall bor-
dering the rear of the place.

Sam looked around, drew his rifle from its boot and
walked inside the open main room of the station, out
of the sunlight.

Inside, he saw what had held the coyotes' attention
even as he'd walked his horse to the hitch ring. The
body of the outlaw Irena had shot lay sprawled on its
bloodstained back. Most of the man's face had been
eaten to the bone, leaving his grimacing skull staring
up at a thick-beamed ceiling. The body's right boot was
missing, as was most of the right leg.

As Sam stood looking around, a heavy sound of batting wings filled the room. Now that the coyotes were
gone, a huge bird of prey swooped down and stood on
the man's open belly, where other scavengers had clearly
been before.

Sam had seen enough. He stepped into an adjoin-
ing room. There, the outlaw skewered by the big two-
handed scythe lay on his side in an awkward-looking
position. Sam stepped forward and pulled the man's
gun from its holster to take it with him, lest it should fall
into the wrong hands. He thought about the Mexican
kids he'd found playing on the dangerous old wagon in
front of the mine. As he straightened and shoved the
Remington behind his gun belt, he heard footsteps.

"Yoo-hoo in there. Ranger? It's me, JR," Sam heard

Claypool's voice say. "Please don't shoot! I'm on your side now, remember?"

Yoo-hooo? Yes, that was JR Claypool.

Sam let out a breath and eased down, but he kept a poised hold on his Winchester all the same. "Come on in, Claypool, easy-like," he said.

Cautiously, Claypool stepped into the room, his hands held chest high. "I saw your horse out front." He glanced at the dead outlaw, at the black blood that had seeped out around the scythe blade.

"My goodness, Ranger, I know this man," he said. "He's Andy Nichols—Dirty Andy, some folks called him. Another Arizona Cowboy, if that's him."

"It's him," Sam said. "I've had him on my list for a long time. I'd started thinking maybe he was dead."

"So is there still a bounty on Dirty Andy, Ranger?" Claypool asked hesitantly. "Because if there is and if you don't want it—"

"I don't collect bounty," Sam said. "I can't under the Matamoros Agreement."

"I see," said Claypool. "I don't suppose . . . ?" He let his words trail off.

"You can collect the bounty," he said. "Last I checked it was three hundred and fifty dollars. Not a lot, but not bad either."

Claypool looked happy. "Do I have to take in his head and his hand?"

"In this case, no," said Sam. "Being a ranger, I can sign a form for you saying it is Andy Nichols and that you're claiming the bounty."

"That's great!" said Claypool. "*Really* great!" Then he quickly added, "What about the other one lying out there?"

"Do you recognize him?" Sam asked.

Claypool considered lying but changed his mind, apparently deciding it might ruin a good thing. "No, I can't honestly say I do."

"Neither do I. That's good, Claypool," Sam said. "If you can't attest to it, let it go. You can't get them all."

Claypool got the idea that he'd just passed the ranger's test somehow. "I'll keep it honest, Ranger. I truly will," Claypool said.

"Okay," Sam said, "Dirty Andy is the good news. Now I've got to tell you this. I've already been up to the Fitzhugh Rancho. The two women are there and doing well, so I won't need you to ride up there."

Claypool thought about it. "That's all right," he said. "You gave me Andy Nichols. That's more than I would have made searching for the women anyway, right?"

"Now you get it, Claypool," Sam said. "Information is worth something, but never as much as a posted bounty."

"All right," said Claypool, feeling good about making some honest money. "Are we going to bury these two before we go?" he asked.

"I'm not," Sam said.

They exited to the wet sounds of smacking, clacking beaks and the pulling and tearing of flesh. The big bird of prey and several friends had circled around the dead man, while outside the four coyote pups sat on a stone portico, seeming to be waiting their turn for dinner.

"I feel bad leaving those two to the hostile elements this way," Claypool said. He glanced back at the crumbling trail station as they rode on.

"Are you a religious man, Claypool?"

Unprepared for such a question, Claypool stalled for a moment before answering. "Well," he said finally, "I am certainly a believer. I was raised in the holy church. I like to think I have kept those beliefs I grew up with."

Sam shot him a look. "Yes or no?" he asked, trying to trim Claypool's response down. He should have known it was going to be a long roundabout answer.

"In that case, yes." Claypool said. "I like to think that, overall, I have a certain affinity for the rudiments of religion, if perhaps not for religion itself per se."

Sam shook his head, knowing it was his own fault for asking. Before Claypool could continue, as Sam was sure he would, he asked another question. "Would you agree that once a man is dead, he has given up all kinship to the elements around him?" Before Claypool could reply, Sam said, "You needn't answer right away. It's just something to think about."

"Oh, you mean, something to ponder silently along the trail?" a smiling Claypool said.

"Yes, something like that," Sam said, just wanting out of the conversation.

He had buried many outlaws in his years as a ranger, and he had left many to the elements. In both cases, he had followed the dictates of his conscience in the moment. Over his years, he had found no other way to do this work.

Amen, Sam said to himself, the two of them riding on.

Twenty silent minutes later, as they followed a thin stream of running water, Sam's horse perked up its ears at a lone distant sound of thunder. Sam rubbed the horse's withers, keeping it settled.

"Hear that?" he said to Claypool, who was riding behind him.

The words echoed through the hilltops west of them, but Claypool gave no reply.

Sam looked up and all around the sky. "Looks clear enough though," he said.

When he still received no answer from Claypool, he stopped his horse and looked behind him. Claypool's horse, riderless, kept walking forward, its reins dangling to the ground.

What is this? Sam picked up the horse's reins and checked the animal to a halt, looking back and all around for JR Claypool.

"Claypool," Sam said at a medium volume. He disliked calling out in hilly country like this, announcing his location to anyone listening. He heard his echo drift away. "Claypool," he said a little louder. Still nothing as he listened to his fading echo.

He stepped down from his saddle and led both horses back along the thin stream of spring water. Ten yards up, around a short cliff line in the rocks, he saw the back of Claypool's swallowtail coat. Claypool was lying facedown in what appeared to be less than an inch of water. He wasn't moving. Sam dropped the horses' reins and hurried forward, the horses following behind him.

"JR! Wake up!" Sam shouted. He grabbed Claypool by his shoulders and flopped him over, out of the water. "Look at me. Look at me!"

But while Claypool's eyes were open, they were staring blankly, off up the hillside. Water ran from his partly open mouth, from his nose, his half ear, which had lost its bandage and dangled loosely.

The ranger quickly turned Claypool over and tried pushing down on his back. No water or air came out of Claypool's open mouth. After a few tries, Sam flipped him back over and tried the same thing on his chest. Still, there was no change. Sam stood up, stepped back and looked down at Claypool.

Drowned? In a trickle of water—a stream less than an

inch deep? What are the chances of that happening? Sam thought. *But there it is.*

The improbability of Claypool's death in such a fashion lay wet and cold and dead on the ground before Sam. Claypool was as dead as the men they'd left lying in the coach station.

Sam stooped and picked up his sombrero from where it had fallen on the wet ground. He shook water from it and placed it atop his head.

"Dead? From such a small stream of water?"

Chapter 20

———

Cree Sims knew there was nothing like dragging and wrestling more than two thousand pounds of cannon, ammunition and supplies through sweltering swampland to take much of the fight out of man and beast. Instead of staying on the lower hill trails, which were brutal and difficult to negotiate, he decided to cut across a bottom corner of the Valley of Mexico with blazing cannon fire licking at their backs. As Sims and his men fought their way across the swamps, he measured in his mind the fierceness of the mounted attacks as well as the frequency of cannon fire.

By the time the outlaws reached the first level of switchbacks up off the hill lines and onto the mountains, the cannon shots had fallen away to almost nothing. Rifle fire was not as heavy, or near as close, or as eager and accurate as it had been.

Because I'm so damn good at this, Sims told himself.

He looked down on the lower switchbacks, seeing that many of the *federales* had turned back. The ones left wouldn't be hanging on much longer. He was certain of it.

"Where the hell have you drug us to, Sims?" Dallas Curio asked, stirring a stick around in a low fire.

Sims pointed his rifle barrel at a small town sitting, as if clinging, to a steep hillside.

"Right over there is Pico Alto," Sims said.

"Speak American," Curio insisted. "I told you I don't like Mexican spoke at me. Can't understand it." He let his hand rest on the butt of his holstered Colt.

Roman Lee Ellison cut in. "Pico Alto means *high peak*, you broad-footed clod," he said. "How do you plan on living down here if you don't even try to speak the language?"

Ellison had grown edgy from spending the day dodging fire from an eight-pound French cannon. Not to mention the mounted *federales* softening everybody up for it.

Curio gave him a long, cold stare, his hand closing around the butt of his gun. "I expect they'll just have to talk the same way I do or stop speaking at all. Do you get my meaning?" His stare continued after his words had stopped.

Roman Lee was ready for this. He returned Curio's stare with a look of his own, one that gave nothing away.

"I get your meaning," he said, calmly, easily. As he spoke, he reached down unconcernedly, eased his black-handled Colt up and looked at it closely as if inspecting it. "But if that's a threat intended for me, you're calling out the wrong dog." He cocked his Colt slowly and laid it along his thigh.

Curio looked surprised—not greatly, but enough that instead of pushing Ellison, he eased back some. He withdrew his hand from the holstered Colt and gestured slowly with it, taking in the rugged land around them. "I come out of Yuma hell to rob, pillage and hat dance in the high life, not for all this kind of dung dabbling."

Seeing the fight about to break out between the two, Sims said to Curio, "You mean, you didn't come here to be shot at by cannon? Pinned down by Mexican cavalry? What the hell kind of desperado outlaw are you anyway?"

Curio gave a faint begrudging smile. "All right, I can live with all this," he said to Sims and anybody listening. "But it's time we whooped it up some too, don't everybody think?"

He looked from face to face. Each haggard face nodded agreement. When he looked at Ellison, instead of keeping his bark on, Ellison gave a little nod too.

"Whooping it up sounds, sure enough, good to me," he said, letting all the heated air out of the near argument.

"In case nobody here noticed," said Sims, "we dragged this bunch across the wetlands down there before we pulled them onto these high switchbacks and broke them in half."

Dupree wiped a hand across his dirty face. "Maybe *you* didn't notice," he said to Sims, "but when you led them through those wetland swamps, that was *us* in front of them getting our butts shot at by that hell-blasted French cannon!"

"How long since you've heard from that hell-blasted cannon, Earl?" Tillis asked.

Dupree shut up. It had been over an hour since the last cannon round exploded on the high trail behind them.

Sims chuckled and said, "Hell, no need to thank me. All I did was get us here by wearing their men and mules down to a frazzle. Once the cannon and mules couldn't go no farther, the soldiers wanted to go on home and play with their kids' mamas."

Sims took a canteen that was passed to him. He drank from it and passed it to the next pair of hands. He wiped a shirtsleeve across his mouth.

"If we have really gotten rid of the *federales* and that damned cannon, I'm all for riding into Pico Alto when darkness falls, and I will make sure they welcome us with open arms." He grinned, looking around him among the rocks at the dirty, haggard faces.

"What if they don't make us welcome?" Dupree asked with expectation.

"Then, by Lucille, we'll shoot the living hell out of them and welcome ourselves," said Sims.

The men offered a laugh. But Sims raised a hand and cut them off with a strange look on his face.

"Hold it, men!" he said in a cautious voice. "I just saw somebody move around over there." He pointed toward a large boulder.

"Coyote, ya think?" said Dupree, standing with his gun drawn, looking all around. "Ha," Dupree answered himself. "As food poor as we are, a coyote is risking his life coming around here."

Sims, crouched now, gun in hand, motioned all around the area. "Everybody, up and spread out," he said. "Somebody's out there. I saw them moving around at the bottom of the rock."

The men stood and spread out, crouched low.

"If you see anybody move"—Sims's voice got louder—"shoot the hell out of them!"

"Whoa, don't start shooting now," a voice called out. "We're with you, Sims! We came looking for you."

"If you're with me, you'll need to have a name and a damn good reason you're here."

"I told you, we come looking for you! All the way from Arizona! Brayton Lowe sent us! We had to fight through *federales* to get up here to you!"

"So far you haven't said squat," Sims said. "Brayton Lowe is dead as hell. I'm going to count to one and we're going to lay into you!"

"If Brayton Lowe is dead, somebody had better tell him," the man said. "He sent us, and he warned us you might say something like that."

Sims gave a little chuckle. "All right, he ain't dead, but he smells like it," Sims replied with the agreed-upon code words.

He motioned for his men to lower their guns. Their numbers were down to six now: Sims, Dupree, Tillis, Stabitz, and the two new men, Dallas Curio and Roman Lee Ellison.

"I'm Bud Fowler," the man said. "My *segundo* here is Bob Summit." He pointed at a tall man near him whose chest was crossed with bandoliers of ammunition. To the men standing around him among the rocks and juniper, Fowler said, "Tip the barrels down, men. These are all our Red Sash Cowboy brothers here."

Sims's men stood up. Fowler's men all stepped forward, nine of them counting Fowler.

Taking a quick count of Sims's men, Fowler let out a breath of disappointment. "Man, oh, man, Sims," he said, "I could tell by them *federales* shooting a cannon at you, you'd done something to aggravate them." He looked Sims up and down. "Couldn't you have tried talking it out?"

"Once they get their hands on a cannon, there's no talking it out," Sims said.

"Ain't that the truth though," Fowler said. He looked at the dirt-smeared faces in the thin moonlight and shook his head. "Still, six men? How many did you start with?"

"Five hundred," Sims snapped at him, barely controlling a flare of anger. "Let it go, Fowler," he said. "What brings you here anyway in the middle of a running gun battle?"

Fowler gestured his rifle barrel around. "Easy living, we heard. Was I misinformed?"

Sims laughed. "Misinformed? No," he said, "you were flat out lied to."

"What do we have to shoot to get something to eat here?" Fowler asked.

"Coyote," Sims said. "How hungry are you?"

"We can wait a while," Fowler said. "We slipped past a town over that way." He pointed toward a glow of light on the hillside. "It was crawling with *federales*—looking for you, no doubt. But they were plumb worn out. They've gone home by now, I'll wager. We saw the mules headed downhill, pulling the cannon."

"We just talked about going over there, spit a goat or something. What do you think?" asked Sims.

"Goat meat beats coyote any day," Fowler said. He pointed toward the thin path they came in on. "I've got two trail guards out there. Let's not mistake them for somebody we don't like."

"We'll do our best," Sims said. He turned and said, "Men, let's go eat. Keep a lookout for two trail guards. They're with us."

It was dark when the last of the *federales* left the Gato Rojo Cantina. Inside the cantina, the only patrons left were two women and a Texas teamster named Henri Spooner. Spooner stood at the small bar tossing back shots of local mescal and sucking salt and a juicy lime behind it.

Spooner grinned and hissed with his teeth clenched. He set his empty wooden cup down, licked his lips and jerked his head toward the open front door.

"I know you gals always like to see that bunch arrive, but for me, unless there's a serious rooster fight about to start, I'm just as happy to see them leave."

"They spend money here, Henri," said Lopez, the cantina owner standing behind the bar.

"Yeah? What do you call this, cabbage palm?" Spooner said.

He pulled a thick fold of American dollars from his shirt pocket and slapped it on the bar. The women on either side of him fell upon the money like gators on red meat. Spooner swatted them back.

"Easy, gals!" he cautioned them. "I'm just making a point here. I spend more money coming through here once a week than half them soldiers combined."

"It is true, what Henri says," Lopez said.

He huffed a damp breath on a drinking glass in his hand and wiped it with a greasy bar rag. As they talked, a musician wearing soiled peasant clothes and a bright red bandanna around his neck slipped inside from the street and raised a cracked violin up under his chin.

"Oh, no, not tonight," Spooner said at the first long screech from the violin.

"*Sí*, tonight," said Lopez. "People come here because they enjoy the *música*. Do you think they come here to listen to you brag about Tejas?"

"Careful where you tread, *mi amigo*," Spooner warned. As he spoke, he poured three more shots for himself and the two women standing close to him. "I'll bite the head off a bull rattler for saying something bad about my beloved stomping grounds."

"*Sí*," said Lopez, "I know. We all love Tejas. I was born there. My wife and her whole family were born there." He shrugged. "Still, I love the place."

Another musician slipped in and stood beside the violin player. This one held a small drum and a single drumstick.

"This one too?" Spooner said sourly. He tossed back the mescal and gave another hiss. "I might ought to get on out of here. It'll soon be you can't hear yourself think for all the caterwauling going on." He looked at the woman on his right, a large Oklahoman redhead known as Little Ol' Betsy for reasons no one ever knew.

"You want to take care of me before I cut out, Little Ol'?" he asked.

He started to bounce one of her large, unsupported breasts on his open palm. Little Ol' Betsy caught his hand, stopping him, and pulled him toward the open front door.

"What's wrong with upstairs?" Spooner asked, following her all the same.

"It needs tidying," said Betsy. "Anyway, the alley is bigger!"

They'd started through the front door when Cree Sims and Bud Fowler walked in, all their men bunched up behind them. They stopped, and so did Little Ol' Betsy and Henri Spooner.

"Well, well, look here," said Sims. He started to bounce her breast on his hand too, but Betsy eased it away from him.

"Later, cowboy." She smiled across two gold front teeth. "We're just stepping out for a breath. Be right back with you though."

Sims continued as if he hadn't heard her.

"Look at this big pretty woman standing here, full rigging, red hair and all!" he said. "We come here to eat! If we lay you on the bar, we could eat you all night long—"

"Hey, hey!" said Spooner. "The lady is with me. I've got no time to dally! Get out of the way!"

Sims laughed. The men laughed with him, seeing the hurry the teamster was in.

"Hear that, pals?" Sims said to the men, stepping aside to let them rush into the cantina. "Let these randy folks out, lest we be slipping all over this floor all night!"

The men laughed as they filed in and over to the bar.

"Let's go, Henri." Betsy pulled on Spooner's hand.

"Little Ol' Betsy is with me, mister," he said to Sims, "and I don't like your mouth."

Sims gave Fowler a curious look, thinking what to do to the teamster.

"I'm awfully hungry," Fowler said. "We all are."

"I hear you." Sims stepped back from the door and motioned the couple out with his hand.

"You folks, excuse us, please," he said cordially.

Spooner looked back over his shoulder as if expecting a trick.

"All right, everybody!" Sims called out from inside the doors. "Drinks are on me!" He shouted at Lopez, "What's the best thing to eat here, lamb or goat?"

"They are both delicious, señor," Lopez called back to him above the noise of the musicians' zippy Mexican tune.

"Okay!" shouted Sims, taking out a handful of U.S. greenbacks and flipping them up to flutter in the air. "Stick us a young goat and a lamb both on a spit! Bring out whatever you've got here to drink! Keep every glass and cup full."

Seeing all the money fanning around, the other woman at the bar walked over to Sims and jiggled his crotch. "I'm Constance." She smiled. "When you're ready for me, I'll be right there at the bar, hotter than a blue hen!"

"Well, all right," Sims said. He pulled out a shiny twenty-dollar gold piece and shoved it down into the low-cut bosom of her dress. "Keep this warm in there until we're finished talking."

"I can do that," Constance said in a low, sexy tone. "I can do that sure enough."

Chapter 21

—◆—

In the middle of the half-moon night, mariachi music blasted the sharp limestone cliffs and overhangs surrounding Pico Alto and the rocky little towns clinging to the sharp mountainsides above the Valley of Mexico. Trumpets and glittering horns of all sizes and tones screamed and echoed in every direction. Guitar, bass and fiddle vied to dominate the trembling cantina rafters. An accordion jumped and danced in its player's hands.

Long after the *federale* cavalry and its cannon crew with its exhausted black-and-tan mules had left the rugged switchbacks, buggies and open coaches arrived packed tight with partygoers. Colorfully dressed women twirled frivolous parasols both bright and dingy in a cloudless night and spilled laughter to the brushing beat of steel drums and the clack of castanets.

"I love a good time," Sims said to Bud Fowler, a drunken slur creeping into his voice. "All the shooting, the robbing, the killing and violence and so forth, it's all right, I guess." He shrugged and took a bite of juicy, hot goat meat. He grinned, his mouth circled with grease. "But this right here is what I love best of all. Just having a good time!"

He wiped a sleeve across his lips and flung some goat meat and bone to a hound that sat drooling expectantly at him. The hound caught the flop of meat and shot out the open back door. Sims rubbed his hands up and down his trouser legs.

"You're sort of known as a good-time boy," said Bud Fowler. He gazed at Sims through a mescal glow. "Brayton Lowe told me that about you," he said, sounding as though he might have had a bone to pick with Sims over some issue, either real or imagined. "Fact is, he told me lots about you."

Sims felt his grin stiffen, turning sour. "Did he, then?" he said. "He never said nothing to me about you, Bud." He leaned forward and took on an intense gaze. "Why do you suppose that is?"

Bud Fowler sat up straighter.

Getting down to business? thought Sims.

"Look here," Fowler said. "Me and my men didn't just show up here on a lark. Brayton Lowe sent us—sent me, that is."

"Oh, really?" said Sims.

"Yeah, really," said Fowler—no more humor in his attitude, Sims noted. All business. "A lot of our Arizona Cowboy Gunmen come down here to ride with you boys in Bad River and they never come back."

"Meaning?" said Sims.

"Meaning we're tired of losing men." Fowler nodded at the trail. "Just like tonight. You lost gunmen—you don't even know how many."

"What do you think we are now, President Johnson's U.S. Army?" Sims asked. He offered a slight smile, hoping to loosen the tension. "This is a tough place down here. Some of the people we kill here kill us back."

"I know that," said Fowler. "Lowe knows it too. But he thinks, and I agree, that I can do better here." He paused ever so slightly. "He sent me down to take over." He stopped, letting his words sink in. "I don't mean take over for good. Just for a while. Get you and your men back on the right path. Then I'll go on back, leave you to it." He gave a short, crisp smile. "How does this all sound?"

The right path . . . Sims took a breath, thinking. "Sounds to me like I'm getting no say-so in the matter," he said. "What if I tell you and Lowe both—"

"Hold on, Sims," said Fowler. "I'm trying to be big about this. I could have come down here acting like the top dog, just took over and left you lying in the dirt. But I didn't do that, did I?" He shook his head. "No, I came down here wanting to straighten this out the right way. Brothers to the bone!"

Sims raised a hand, stopping him. "I see what you mean." He took a deep breath and let it out. "I'm an Arizona Cowboy through and through, and now I'm a Bad River Gunman too. If this is what Lowe and the rest of you Arizona Cowboys have decided, I'm good with it." He looked Fowler in the eye and nodded. "Brothers to the bone!"

"I'm glad to hear you feel that way," Fowler said. "And by the way, I haven't mentioned to my men why we're here. I figured it would be better if I tell everybody at once." He grinned. "Of course, it might not make any difference to your men, you've lost so many of 'em, but it's how I operate."

Sims nodded again. He looked away and ordered another bottle of mescal. A young boy ran it over to the table, opened it and set it down between two wooden cups.

Sims filled the two cups and pushed one over to Fowler.

"*Salud*," he said, lifting his cup.

"*Salud*," Fowler repeated. "Glad there're no hard feelings between us two Cowboys."

"There never are," Sims said quietly.

The two of them drank from their wooden cups and set them down.

"We'll need to go over how I plan to run things," Fowler said.

There was a smugness to his voice and expression that Sims had not noticed before.

"Give me just a minute," Sims said. He rocked his cup back and forth. "This stuff goes right through me." He stood up. "I'll be right back." He walked through the drinkers and out the back door to the long privy ditch slanting away from the cantina.

"I might as well go too," Fowler said aloud to himself under the blare of music and laughter. He got up and walked outside to where Sims stood alone relieving himself.

"Thought I'd join you," said Fowler.

"Help yourself," Sims replied. He finished his business, closed and buttoned his trousers and stepped back to admire the half-moon standing high in the purple starlit night.

"*Una noche hermosa en México*," he said. He smiled up at the sky.

"It is all that and more," Fowler agreed.

"I'll fill us another cup," Sims said. He gave Fowler a hearty slap on the back as he passed behind him to reach the rear door.

"*Gracias*—" said Fowler, but only a split second before Sims's big Colt sent a blast of bullet and flame through his unsuspecting head. He toppled forward into the ditch, slid down around a turn of rock and driftwood and slipped away in the night.

Run that, *stupid bastard*, Sims said to himself.

The big hound lay with his goat-meat bone pinned beneath his paws, chewing vigorously, and barely gave Sims a sideways look as he passed. Music blared out in a cloud of smoke as Sims opened the door and stepped back inside. He searched for Bob Summit, Fowler's second in charge, and walked up to the bar beside him.

"Where's Fowler? I've got *really* good news for him—for all of us," Sims said.

"Last I saw, he was sitting with you over there," Summit said, a woman kissing the side of his face, her hand up under his shirt, crawling around on his chest like some pet ferret.

"I know, but he went to relieve himself and didn't come back," said Sims. He nodded at the hand under the man's shirt. "You're busy. Don't worry. I'll find him, unless he fell in." He chuckled and started to move away.

"What kind of *really* good news?" Summit asked. He clasped a hand on the woman's wandering hand and held it still. "Hold on, honey pie. I got business," he whispered to her.

Sims looked all around, then said, "Maybe I'd better let him tell you himself."

Summit thumbed himself in the chest without turning loose of the woman's hand.

"I'm the *segundo* of this outfit," he said. "Telling me is no different from telling Bud Fowler himself. If he was here, he'd tell you as much."

Sims appeared to give it thought, then nodded. "You're right, Summit. I'm being overly cautious. But . . ." He motioned for Summit to get rid of the woman.

Summit pulled the woman's hand down out of his shirt and handed her a small gold coin. "Go powder your jilly or something, little darling. I ain't going nowhere without you."

"*Sí*, I will powder, powder, powder myself!" she said, wiggling in place, patting her lower belly and smiling through badly smeared lipstick. Palming the gold coin, she made her way off across the crowded floor to a tiny women's room behind a beaded curtain.

"Sweet as a little berry, that one." Summit beamed proudly, shoving his shirt back down into his trousers. He turned to Cree Sims, who was looking around the place again as if in a final effort to locate Bud Fowler.

"All right, Bob Summit, listen to me," Sims said, leaning in close to Fowler's second-in-command. "I just got word we're all getting ready to make a big raid together down here. It's a raid on a whole damned town, French silver mines and all. It's big and bold and will likely pay us more than any of us have ever made on a single job!"

"Whoa," said Summit, his brow rising. But then he looked around. "You just got word about it?" he said. "You got *word* from where?" He swept his hand around, indicating the raucous cantina.

Sims stepped even closer and grabbed the *segundo* by the front of his shirt. "Listen to me, Summit, and listen damned good!" he growled. "Has Fowler ever told you men just how big we are?"

"I can't say that he has," said Summit, not daring to look down at Sims's hand gripping his shirt.

Sims turned him loose, appearing to calm down. He brushed the front of his shirt. "All right, forget it, then. It's not your fault," said Sims. "The truth is, we've got people scattered everywhere. We hear things before there're things to hear if you get my meaning."

"I do. I sure do," said Summit. "What about this big job you mentioned?"

Sims looked all around again. "I wish to hell Fowler was here!" he said. "It's not my job telling his men what's going on. It's his!"

"Till he shows up, you can tell me anything," Summit said quietly.

"One Cowboy to another, I'm going to tell you most of the particulars," said Sims. "Ordinarily, I'd be counting on you to keep all I'm telling you to yourself. But in this case we'll need you to spread it around among your men so they don't find themselves left out in the cold on this. It's Fowler's job to do the telling, but since I can't find him, I have to expect he's hooked himself up with one of these painted-up señorita doll babies and let everything else slip plumb out of his mind."

"I've never known him to be a man who gets distracted by the ladies," Summit said, tossing another quick glance around for his boss.

"Hold on there, Bob Summit. What are you implying about the man?" Sims asked bluntly. "He's an Arizona Cowboy Gunman just like the rest of us."

"Nothing, Sims, nothing at all," Summit said. "Forget I said anything."

"All right, then," Sims said. "What I'm telling you can't be repeated to anybody except to your men, unless Fowler shows up and tells you otherwise—he's still your boss. Do you hear me, *segundo*?"

"*Sí*— I mean, yes, I hear you!" said Summit. "Talk to me about this big job. I'll work with you however I can."

Darkness had fallen with the sun behind the hill lines and mountain peaks when Sam found a small clearing off the lower trail. At the edge of a narrow creek leading down the last stretch of the switchback, Sam led the horses under a large tree canopy. He left the body of JR Claypool loosely tied over a saddle to keep it out of the reach of ground predators prowling in the undergrowth.

With the horses watered, grained and wearing hackamores, Sam hitched them to a downed mesquite tree for the night. He built a fire and cooked coffee from a bag he'd ground and set to boil. The sky was purpleshadowy dark when the coffee boiled and Sam pulled the bubbling pot off the short flames. He waited for it to cool a little before pouring himself a steaming cup full.

He looked over at the horses when he heard one of them chuff and grumble, but when it stopped, Sam looked away, picked up his hot coffee. He blew on it and took a sip.

"Can I get a cup of that coffee, Ranger?" he heard the voice of JR Claypool ask. He recognized the dead man's voice, but knowing it couldn't be him, he turned to face whoever it was, his hand going around the butt of his Colt and drawing it in the flicker of firelight.

Holy—! It *was* Claypool! A ghostly, drenched, pale Claypool standing six feet away, Sam cocked the big Colt, not knowing what to expect of a ghost with a haggard face looking grave and hollow eyed at him. What was left of Claypool's hair, which had been soaking wet, had dried now and lay plastered against his pale forehead.

"Don't move a muscle, Claypool." Sam stood slowly, his leveled Colt pulling him to his feet.

He cautiously stepped closer, looked Claypool up and down.

"You're alive," he said, sounding relieved yet doubtful.

"Yes, Sam," Claypool said. "I would not lie about a thing like that." He offered a strange smile.

"Don't try being funny with me, JR," said Sam. "This is no laughing matter. I've spent half the evening packing you down this trail. I'm not in the mood for fun."

"Sorry, Ranger," said Claypool, his weak smile gone under Sam's sharp gaze.

The ranger reached out and poked Claypool's flat stomach, not hard, just firmly enough to make sure he was real flesh and bone, while he looked on curiously.

"You really are still alive," Sam said mostly to himself.

"I told you I am," said Claypool. He pointed at the steaming cup of coffee. "I'm freezing here. Any chance I can get a cup of this before it gets cold?"

"Drink mine," Sam said. "I'll get another cup from my saddlebags."

Sam stood and backed away to his saddlebags lying on the ground beside his bedroll. When he'd come back and poured himself another hot cup of coffee, he stooped down and slid his Colt into its holster.

"Can you tell me what's been going on, Sam?" Claypool asked.

"You don't know?" Sam asked.

"I honest to God do not, Ranger," Claypool said.

"Okay." Sam took a deep breath. "You drowned— that is, I *thought* you drowned. I tried to bring you around and couldn't get you to breathe! After a while, I loaded you up to take you back to Bad River.

"Drowned, huh?" He held his damp coat sleeves out and looked at them, then at his short boots, his trousers. "That explains that," he said. He looked toward his horse. "And that's why I was all tangled up in rope?"

"I tied you across the saddle," Sam said. "The wet rope must've stretched out and let you work yourself loose." He looked inquiringly at Claypool as the bewildered gambler sipped his coffee.

"You don't recall anything that happened?" Sam asked. "Nothing about falling off your horse in a little runoff stream? Maybe you hit your head or something, knocked yourself cold?"

"Not a bit of it," Claypool said. He felt around on his head. "I don't feel any bump anywhere."

Sam looked off along the jagged line of mountains, sipping his coffee and trying to calm himself. He had to admit it had shaken him, hearing and seeing a dead man standing in his campsite and asking for a cup of coffee. He had to smile to himself. He had long ago lost count of how many guns had been drawn and fired at him by real, live man-killers who would have shot him dead without batting an eye. He'd never been scared of them, and yet he had found himself unsettled by the ghost of a poor soul like JR Claypool asking for coffee.

As if suddenly taken by a string of memories, Claypool said, "You know what, Ranger? This is part of the sleepwalking problem I've been plagued with! Dr. Jorgenson said I was blacking out for no reason, waking up and not remembering what had happened, what I'd done or anything else! I was completely blank! Last I remember I was riding a horse behind you down the path. It all goes black right there! Next thing I remember, I was tangled in rope, smelling hot coffee! What's the use in me trying? I'm what you could call born to lose in life. Everything I've ever done has failed. I finished law school in Texas and nearly starved to death trying to build a law practice."

Sam thought he saw Claypool's eyes water before he managed to look away.

"Don't torment yourself over it," Sam said. "When you get the bounty money you've got coming to you for Dirty Andy Nichols, go somewhere and talk to a doctor."

"You're right, Ranger," Claypool said. "That's what I should do. Until then all I have to worry about is walking out of open windows, blacking out and having people think I'm dead and maybe bury me alive before they see I'm not!"

Claypool shook his head, wearily. "Who am I kidding, Ranger?" he said, sounding near tears. "If I tried to tell doctors all this, they would think I've gone crazier than a jarfly! And I couldn't really blame any of them if they did."

Chapter 22

———

Early the next morning, on their way back to Bad River, the ranger and JR Claypool stopped out of sight on a cliff looking down on the main trail. They watched a group of six mounted horsemen ride slowly to the outskirts of town. Not a red sash on any of the men, nor did Sam recall seeing any of them before. Still, he waited until they were out of sight to hand Claypool a folded piece of paper.

"We're going to split up here," Sam said. "Take this signed confirmation to Melford. He'll have it telegraphed to the authorities and they will have the reward for Andy Nichols mailed to you here in Bad River."

"Melford?" said Claypool. "I can trust him to do that for me?"

"Why not?" said Sam. "He owns the bank, so he'll tell one of his clerks to do it. But it'll get done. He might be a no-good political snake, but he is still a local businessman. He'll do anything to protect his bank's image or to follow what the Mexican law dictates on something like this. Besides, I'll see him later today. I'll make sure he hurries it along for you."

"These days I suppose he's only interested in *big* money," said Claypool. He looked at the letter and put it away. "I still don't have any spectacles, but I'll do like you say and take it to Melford's bank. I want to tell you again how much obliged I am for this." He patted his lapel. "Why aren't you riding in with me, Ranger?"

"I expect things are getting ready to boil over," Sam said. "It might be better for you to ride in alone out of sight. Avoid being seen with me if you can."

"Don't worry. I'll stay out of sight. You can find me lying low at the Frenchman Hotel."

"Good. There is one very important job I'm going to need you to do later. It might be the most important job I'll ever ask of you. It'll take all the nerve and guts you've got," he cautioned Claypool.

"I—I don't think I have any. I appear to be missing everything a man should have, including courage." He shook his head sadly.

"Stop that, Claypool!" Sam demanded. "If I thought you couldn't handle the job, I would not ask you to do it! You do this, you will never again doubt your courage or anything else about yourself."

"Okay," Claypool said meekly.

"Tell me I can count on you," Sam demanded.

"You can count on me," Claypool said, if a little shakily.

"All right," said Sam. "Now, get out of here. I'll come by your hotel room to tell you more about it."

Claypool spurred his horse forward, his face ashen with anticipated responsibility.

The ranger touched the brim of his sombrero and watched him ride away.

An hour later, having given Claypool time to get into town and take his horse to Irish Mike's livery barn,

Sam swung his horse wide of the busy main streets and finished his ride on a deserted back street that led to the barn's rear doors.

"I am glad to see you back, Ranger," Mike said as Sam stepped down from his saddle. "Seems like a town goes to hell in a hurry anytime there's not a lawman around." He took the reins from Sam and held them out to a young boy who grabbed them and led the horse inside.

"What's gone on here overnight?" Sam asked. He didn't have to remind Mike that he had no authority here other than gathering wanted men and taking them across the border.

Irish Mike tipped his head toward his makeshift saloon and his newly purchased German Ale and Whiskey House.

"Aw, nothing *too* bad," said Mike. "Just some border trail hands who delivered a fair-sized herd of breeders over to Don Metaquantra's rancho. Instead of going right home, they wandered up out of the valley and stayed here drinking all night." He brushed the thought away. "They'll be all right though. Most of them are passed out now or getting close to it."

"If you want me to go say something, I will," said Sam.

"Naw, let it go," said Mike. "If they break rowdy, I'll salt them down. I took the big loads out of my ten gauge and loaded her with hill salt."

"You've got the right idea, Mike," said the ranger. "Keep your big loads ready just in case."

"You know it, Sam." Mike smiled. "I expect you're wanting to look in on Doc this morning?"

"That's my first stop," said Sam, following Mike into the barn.

"Just so you know, I'm taking the stitches out of his

nose today. They're drying up and healing real good. If I get them out now, they might not leave a scar, at least nothing real noticeable."

"That's good to hear," said Sam. He saw Doc's ears perk up at the sound of his voice coming toward the stall.

"*Hola*, pal," he said as Doc's muzzle reached out over the stall rail and nudged his chest.

Careful of the stitches in Doc's nose, Sam rubbed him under his chin. Then he took out a folded bandanna and unwrapped it, revealing sweet berries the size of grapes that he'd picked the day before along the lower trail.

"You've sure got his interest, Sam," Mike chuckled beside him.

"Here you go, pal," Sam said. He watched the berries disappear into the stallion's mouth. "That was quick," he said, folding the empty bandanna and putting it away. "All gone."

The stallion let out a chuff. He bobbed his head up and down, shook out his mane and stuck his head back out across the stall rail for a nose rub.

Sam rubbed his nose carefully on one side, away from the stitches.

"He's looking good, Mike," Sam said. "Staying here agrees with him."

"You can ride him out of here today if you've a mind to, after I take out the stitches," Mike said. "He's strong and well enough to ride."

"I'll leave him here a few days longer," Sam said, "while I get Sims and his men jailed and ready for the ride home."

"I hope it goes as easy as you make it sound, Ranger," Irish Mike said. "Anyway, I had the sheriff's office cleaned up and swept out for you. Make yourself at home. Let me know if we Bad River business folks can do anything for you."

"Obliged, Irish Mike," Sam said.

With a pat on Doc's head, he turned and left the barn. Overhead, the sky was darkening to a flat pale gray. With the keys to the jail cells, the doors and the gun case in his pocket, Sam walked through an alleyway, Winchester in hand, unlocked the rear door to the sheriff's office and went inside. Just like Irish Mike had said, the office and cells had been cleaned and swept. On the bunks in the cells, thin mattresses lay folded in half. A large yellow cat sat perched on one of the bunks in direct view of a mousehole in a lower corner. The cat turned to stare at the ranger with an almost defiant look.

"What are you in for?" Sam asked. The cat cocked its head slightly.

Stepping over to an iron security grillwork covering the front of the gun case, Sam unlocked it and set it down on the floor. He stepped back and took a moment to admire the glistening line of rifles and shotguns standing in the rack like soldiers at attention. Boxes of ammunition lay in a row across the bottom of the rack. A fully made-up bandolier of rifle ammo hung from a peg. A big bone-handled Colt .45 stood in a slim-jim holster among the long guns.

Home sweet home for a man like Showdown Art Forbes, Sam thought, liking the feel of the place, its scent of gun oil, gunpowder and stock polish. He almost relaxed for a second, but then his reason for being here moved back in and gnawed at him.

Don't get comfortable, he warned himself. He was here for only one reason. Killing was coming his way— killing he would have to accept willingly and act upon mercilessly, should the job demand it of him.

And it will, he knew.

He leaned his Winchester against the edge of the battered desk and looked all around until he found a clean coffeepot and a bag of dark whole coffee beans.

Now we're talking. . . .

In the early afternoon, in a sudden downpour of rain, two of Bud Fowler's gunmen rode into Bad River way ahead of the fourteen gunmen who'd thrown in with Cree Sims. They both still wore the red sashes of the Arizona Cowboy Gunmen. One, Harris Barnes, had wrapped his sash down around his hat and tucked it under his chin to keep his hat on. Now it hung wet around his neck. Barnes carried a long cavalry sword in a scabbard hanging down his hip, and a hand-tooled gun belt hung from his saddle horn, supporting a Spanish horse pistol standing tall in a long, sleek holster. An artful image of a rose, tooled and painted, adorned the front of the holster.

The other man—a younger, hot-tempered gunman named Doyle Shoney—rode easily beside him, eyeing the town, including the burned-out lot where the Bad River Saloon had stood only a few days earlier.

"What a pissant of a town," said Shoney, his duster collar raised against the sideways-blowing rain. He nodded toward two drinkers standing soaking wet at the plank bar, which was intermittently beneath the canvas overhead, depending on the direction of the wind and rain. The canvas flapped and slapped sheets of rain, but the drinkers put up with it.

"Shit," Doyle Shoney said, "I hope rain drinking ain't all they do here for a pastime."

"If it is," said Barnes, "I hope we see lightning strike every damn one of them."

"You mean *both* of them," said Shoney. "For all we know they might be the only two people in this pig's ass of a town."

Not hearing the outlaws, the two drinkers raised their beer glasses in salute as the newcomers rode by.

Shoney chuckled and gave a broad grin. "Best of the day to yas!" he said. Under his breath, he snarled, "That's right. Drink up, you flat-head, cripple-minded sonsabitches."

"Easy, *compañero*!" Barnes cautioned. "Let's not get thrown out of town before we get dried out and get some rye in our bellies. This is the only town around the lower switchback where we can get whiskey."

"They'd get no fight making me leave town," said Shoney. "Making me *stay* is where they might hit a wall."

"Give the place a chance, Doyle!" Barnes said, chuckling. "Look over here."

He motioned at four men coming out of the German Ale and Whiskey House. The men hiked up their coats and held their hats on as they hurried around into an alley where horses stood waiting, sheltered from the hard-blowing rain. The rain grew heavier and fell straighter as the wind waned a little.

"Right over there's the Frenchman Hotel that Cree Sims was talking about," said Barnes. "I'll order us some rye and beer if you'll get a bunch of rooms for all of us."

"How many rooms?" Shoney asked above the noise of the wind and the harder rain.

"Hell, I don't know. There's over a dozen of us," said Barnes. "So you know—figure it out."

"How many of us over a dozen?" Shoney asked skeptically.

Barnes took a deep breath. *Idiot,* he thought. "You get the rye and I'll get us all some rooms. Let's hurry before we get washed away here." He heard a loud splattering sound in the rain.

Instead of making a move, Shoney sat staring at him blankly.

"Well, go on!" said Barnes. "What's the matter with you anyway?"

"This horse is relieving himself," said Shoney. "Once the knuckleheaded fool starts, he won't quit until he's all the way done."

"Damn it! I don't believe this!" shouted Barnes, gusts of wind and rain whipping him, his wet hat flattened to the side of his head. His wet hand held it down. "I've got to get indoors! I've never seen a horse act that way!"

"I reckon he can't help it," Shoney said.

"All right, then. *Blast it all!* I'll meet you back here inside!" Barnes shouted in the downpour. "I want to get this done before Sims and the others get here— show him we've at least got sense enough to rent hotel rooms by ourselves!" He reined away angrily toward the Frenchman Hotel, mud flying up from his horse's hooves.

"I will soon as he's finished," Shoney said in a beaten voice. He sat slumped in his saddle, waiting, his horse standing spraddle-legged, peeing heavily in the mud, looking back and forth in the blowing rain.

From his office window, Clement Melford looked down through the deluge of rain. "It's finally letting up some," he said over his shoulder to Dan'l Thorn, who sat sprawled in a big leather chair, his boots propped up on the matching ottoman. His big knife lay along his thigh where he'd left it after making a show of twirling it on his finger.

Bending forward for a closer look now that the rain had slowed, Melford squinted through the wavy window glass.

"I've got one just sitting in the street in the rain," Melford said. "Looks like he don't know what's going on around him."

Thorn drained his glass and set it on a small table next to the leather chair. Picking up the big knife, he stood and walked to the window, twirling it by its brass ring on his finger. He looked down, saw the red sash.

"Yep, more Cowboy Gunmen turning Bad River Gunmen, I expect. See the sash?"

"I see it," said Melford. "I hope we don't get more Cowboy Gunmen showing up here than Jack Swift's men can handle."

"I don't know how many that would take," Thorn said. "The ranger has already maimed two of Swift's men so bad, he had to send them away. You might shoulda had me kill the ranger when this all started. We'd be done with it." He stopped twirling the big knife and examined the blade. "Never kill a man tomorrow when you've got nothing better to do today."

"Wise words. *Oops!*" Melford staggered a step at the window.

"Hey, now, don't go buckling on us."

"Well, we've drunk a whole bottle and a half of Tennessee sipping whiskey."

"The good thing about drinking all night is you needn't worry about starting too early," said Thorn.

"It's still not too late for me to kill the ranger and be done with it."

"No," said Melford. "Now that the ranger is here, I get the feeling today is the day for all things crooked to become straight."

"Yeah? What happens today?"

"If this blasted rain ever stops, I figure, this time of the week, Sims and a couple of his gang will ride in to pick up another draw for him and his men to drink on until he figures how to get back the money the ranger took."

"Which the ranger won't let him do," Thorn put in.

"No, he won't," said Melford. "He'll kill Sims and give me the money, and we'll all be happy." He smiled drunkenly.

"I have to say, Clement," said Thorn, "you've impressed the hell out of me the way you've played your cards close to the vest through all this." He grinned. "Hell, I'd smoke another cigar with you if you offered me one."

Melford motioned toward the ornate cigar box on his desk. "Get three," he said. "Take one to Waco out in the hall. He's been at his job there all night—he deserves a cigar. Careful you don't surprise him though. He might shoot you before he knows what you're doing."

Thorn gave a chuckle. Taking three cigars, he walked to the door. "If Waco Bird Wheeler ever shot me, I'd have to be sound asleep or dead already."

Chapter 23

In spite of the heavy rain, by late afternoon, the stone-tiled main streets of Bad River were baking dry in the hot sun. Wagon and horseback traffic bypassed the muddy dirt side streets. Those pedestrians who could not avoid the side streets walked on footpaths of thick boards thrown down by volunteers, connecting the town businesses, one building to the next. Inside the sheriff's office, the ranger sat drinking hot fresh Mexican coffee that he'd boiled atop a potbellied stove.

He seated himself out of sight behind a faded black window shade he'd drawn down to eye level. From this position he drank his coffee from a thick mug he'd found inside the desk drawer, and watched the street.

The end of the rain had brought out the drinkers, the gamblers, the loiterers, the skivers. Sam paid little attention to any of them until two men walked from the porch of the Frenchman Hotel up to the makeshift bar. The younger of the two he'd never seen before, but the older gunman, wearing a cavalry sword and a large holstered horse pistol slung over his shoulder, he recognized as Harris Barnes, a lifelong outlaw out from Arizona.

To make sure, Sam reached down to the floor beside his chair, picked up his telescope and adjusted it. The colorful rose painted on the holster grew larger, unmistakable.

"*Hola*, Harris Barnes," he said quietly to himself. He looked closer at the younger man, the low tied-down holster, his hand close to the butt of a big Remington .44.

Don't know this one, but I will soon, he told himself. He glanced at the desk and saw the yellow cat sitting atop it, licking its paw. He was tempted to go through the neat stack of Wanted posters someone had straightened up and laid there, but three more horsemen riding in caught his attention and drew it back to the street.

His interest was piqued when he recognized Earl Dupree among the three riders. They all rode together toward the bar, but before getting there, two of them split off toward the hotel. Dupree rode on to the nearest hitch rail and stepped from his saddle.

"All right, here we go," Sam said quietly to himself.

He realized he might not have a better opportunity than this. He stood up from his chair, picked up his Winchester and his wide sombrero and walked out through the front door. The yellow cat watched him leave, then switched to licking its other paw, letting out a rattling, satisfied purr in the empty office.

At the bar in the street, Dupree called out loudly, "All right, then!" Standing among the few drinkers at the bar, he added, "Who do I have to pistol-whip to get a beer and some whiskey in this rathole?" He pushed his hat back off his head and let it hang by its string down his back.

A large bartender named Hans walked up on the opposite side of the bar and gave Dupree a cold look.

"There are no *rats* here, and no pistol-whipping is

allowed unless it is me doing it," the bartender said. He held his hands out along the edge of the bar. "I'm Hans. What do you want?"

Earl looked up at him—*way* up.

"Hey, Hans, pal." Dupree grinned with worried eyes, "The rat comment was a joke! Just a joke!" He looked along the bar for support. "You folks understood I was joking, didn't you?"

Seeing the ranger come up quickly behind Dupree, his rifle in his right hand, barrel extended, the other drinkers took a couple of steps away. The bartender gave a faint smile. Sam reached the barrel out and tapped Dupree firmly on his shoulder. The surprised gunman looked around quickly and saw his own Colt, cocked and leveled in his face.

"What the—?" His hand slapped the empty holster, then realized he hadn't felt the gun being lifted.

"You're under arrest, Earl—"

Before he could say another word, Dupree cut him off. "Now just one damn minute here!" he said, almost shouting. "I said I was joking about the rats and the pistol-whipping. Hell, I ain't seen no rats here. Damn! You folks sure have some hard bark on you!"

Sam raised his face just enough for Dupree to see him clearly under the brim of the sombrero.

"Ah, hell, it's you!" he said. "Damn my luck to hell!"

"Yes, it's me," Sam said. "I'm here to arrest you and take you back to Nogales." He wagged Dupree's gun barrel toward the sheriff's office. "Let's go."

"Like hell I will," said Dupree. "I ain't going no damned place—"

Sam hit him with a full solid lick across the forehead with his own gun barrel. Dupree rocked back against the bar and started to fall forward, knocked out cold.

Sam shoved Dupree's gun behind his gun belt and crouched just enough to let Dupree collapse over his shoulder. He straightened up with Dupree's arms dangling down his back. Turning to a man who had stood staring drunkenly at the whole thing, Sam said, "Get the door for me."

"What door?" The man looked around, bewildered.

"Over there at the sheriff's office," Sam said, nodding across the street.

"Are you going to hit me too, Sheriff?" the man asked.

Sam turned and started walking back toward the office. But Hans, seeing a group of men hurrying from the hotel, ducked out from beneath the plank bar and caught up with Sam. He grabbed Dupree from over Sam's shoulder and slung him over his.

"I've got him, Ranger—watch out for those men coming behind you," he said.

Sam swung his rifle around with one hand, cocked and ready.

"The next man who moves gets himself a bullet!" Sam shouted loud enough for them to hear.

The six men stopped quickly, but their hands moved to their holstered guns.

"That man is one of us, mister!" one shouted. "Who the hell are you?"

"I'm the man who'll kill you right now if you don't get your hands off your guns. Starting with you," Sam said to the man asking the questions. He braced and steadied the rifle a little more, ready to peel out a shot.

The man's hand flew up off his gun butt.

"Are you a lawman?" another man asked, his hand still close to his gun.

Sam swung the rifle toward him. "Will it matter any to you once you're dead, hombre?" he asked, making sure the man took note of the big Winchester in his hands.

The man's hand came away from his gun. More hands lifted away from holstered sidearms.

Sam heard Hans open the office door behind him.

"I'm inside," Hans said. "I'll put him in a cell for you."

"That'll do," Sam said. He started walking backward slowly.

"I'll say this just one time," he said to the Gunmen. "Then, if I have to, I'll start thinning you out. I'm Arizona Ranger Sam Burrack. I've been sent here to bring this man back across the border, dead or alive. It's his choice."

"How come you can do that?" a voice asked. "This ain't Arizona."

"Ask Mexico," Sam said, tired of explaining the Matamoros Agreement.

"Why is our friend going back to the States anyway?" another voice asked from the rear of the gathering men.

"So he can attend a trial date that must've slipped his mind," Sam said. He kept walking backward carefully, one slow step at a time.

"What about this?" said another voice. "Either you turn him loose or we burn this place to the ground."

"Anybody want to answer this man and keep me from having to do it?" Sam asked.

"Yeah, I'll answer him," a voice said. He called out to the man who'd made the threat. "Charlie, shut your idiot mouth! Think about what happens to Dupree if we burn this place to the ground with him in it!"

"That ain't how I meant it," Charlie replied.

Sam backed the rest of the way inside, through the office door, shut it and locked it.

"Obliged, Hans," he said to the big bartender, realizing he could have had his hands full out there in the street moments ago.

"You are a friend of Irish Mike," Hans replied. "So am I."

Sam nodded. "We'll have to let them cool down a few minutes before you leave here."

"They won't bother me," Hans said. He smiled. "Nobody wants to make an enemy of the bartender, especially when he is the only bartender left in town. Also, it might be they know I will break their heads with my bare hands." He grinned, showing a mouthful of glittering white teeth and held up his huge powerful-looking fists.

Waco Bird Wheeler had been watching the street through the hallway window by his chair at Melford's door. He'd watched the ranger crack Dupree's pistol across his jaw and start toting him away from the bar. He'd seen gunmen run toward the bar from the hotel lobby beneath him. Heard their boots pounding across the wooden porch. That was as much as he needed to see.

He eased down the stairs, out the back door of the hotel and down the muddy alley toward the back of the livery barn.

"Bird, Bird, where are you going?" Melford said under his breath to Dan'l Thorn, who stood at the window with him. They watched Waco Bird ease along the open space between the rear of the barn and the alleyway.

Thorn drew on his cigar. "I bet I can tell you," he said. The two looked at each other.

"I have to say," Melford sighed, "this is disappointing as hell."

"I always knew him, deep down, as a runner and a no-good," Thorn said. "I'm glad you listened to me when I said to keep him close at hand."

"Okay," said Melford, "you were right, *mi amigo*. Take care of him right away."

Without another word, Thorn backed away from the window and walked out of the room.

Halfway to the livery barn, he saw Waco Bird Wheeler headed out of town on a leggy buckskin, the horse at a fast gallop along the dried tile street.

Wait until you hit that muddy switchback, Bird, Thorn said to himself. *It'll clip your feathers in a hurry.*

Humming "Sweet Betsy from Pike," Thorn wasted no time saddling his big dapple gray and getting on the trail, yet he wasn't in any big hurry either. Bird had gotten himself all drummed up nervous and taken off riding hard, the sort of thing a good smart horseman picked up on right away. These mountains and hillsides weren't designed to be handled fast and loose that way. They were meant for people on foot or in slow-moving carts. Thorn wasn't going to make the same mistake he'd seen Bird make.

As he rode the gray out of the barn, Irish Mike looked at him from just outside the doors. Thorn touched his hat brim.

Irish Mike said, "That last fella was in too big a rush for a day like today."

"I was just thinking the same thing," said Thorn. He touched his heels to the gray and kept it at a slow, easy trot out of town.

Irish Mike nodded his approval and headed back toward his livery office as Thorn rode out of sight.

"Where do you suppose those two are going after a big rain?" a tough-looking young man asked.

He was carrying a rifle and wearing a sidearm, a bandolier of cartridges across his chest and a red sash. He looked out along the start of the trail by which Thorn and Waco Bird Wheeler had left town. Eighty yards farther on, this trail ran through a canopy of shady trees, then suddenly turned barren and rocky and led right onto the first stretch of a slow uphill grade.

"When they don't say, I never ask," Irish Mike said with a friendly smile.

The young man walked inside the barn and rode out moments later on a tall paint horse. Like Waco Bird before him, he also rode too fast for the wet stretches along the trail. Within twenty minutes the agile young rider had gained on Thorn, so much so that Thorn heard the clack of the paint's hooves behind him.

Now what? More interference to deal with?

The hooves continued closing in until Thorn decided he'd had enough. He eased his gray off the trail and took cover behind a boulder to wait. With his Colt lying across his thigh, he took a bandanna from his duster, unfolded it and picked up half of an apple. His gray smelled the apple and immediately turned his head around toward Thorn.

"What are you looking at, Cochise?"

Thorn sliced the apple with a pocketknife and reached out to give the horse his portion. The rest of the apple he ate himself, taking his time, humming under his breath. Then, as the hoofbeats grew closer, he wiped and folded the pocketknife and put it away. He folded the empty bandanna, wiped his mouth and hands with it and put it inside his duster.

Holstering his Colt, he reached down and drew his

big knife from his boot, twirled it a couple of times and waited.

The young man raced around a turn in the trail, and at the last second, Thorn gigged his gray out from the rock cover and onto the trail, so close that the rider had to veer sharply fast to the side. On the wet, slick trail, the horse's hooves could find no purchase. With a long whinny, the animal went down on its side in a long slide, the rider flying from its back and his rifle flying from his hand onto the rocky hillside.

"My, my, hero," said Thorn, stepping the gray past the young man lying on the mud-slick trail, "but weren't you in a hurry there."

Hero? Did he say hero? This sumbitch! The rider looked up at Thorn, fumbled and searched himself until he laid his muddy hand on his holstered sidearm.

Seeing the paint horse rise onto its hooves, Thorn reached out and brushed a streak of mud from over the horse's eye, then turned away toward the spilled rider. The paint shook himself off and stood with his saddle twisted down onto his side.

"I wanted to warn you about this trail," said Thorn. "I didn't mean to spook your horse."

"Yes, you did, you lying old bastard," the young man shouted, his muddy gun hand coming up holding the big pistol.

Thorn's hand came up too from the edge of his duster, so fast that the young man didn't see what was shining and spinning at him. Whatever it was, he felt it slice across his trigger finger, lay open his inner arm from wrist to elbow and stick deep through his upper arm. His duster sleeve and shirtsleeve hung loose, flapping bloodily, as he caught a glimpse of his lacerated, blood-gushing arm.

"Say, that's a bad cut," said Thorn. "It needs to be looked at."

He stepped down from his saddle, laid his boot toe against the young man's gun lying on the trail and expertly kicked it up and out into the rocks, as if this was something he did every day.

"*Looked at?*" the young man screamed, sobbing, his sliced arm shaking badly. "You've kilt me!"

Thorn looked sympathetic. He stooped, took out his bandanna and held it out to the trembling young man.

"Stick it up your ass, you murdering bastard!" the man screamed.

Thorn restrained a smile. "Now, now, *hero*. That's no way to talk, so close as you are right here to hell and the devil."

"Oh, Lord!" the young man sobbed. "I'm so weak. Will you see to it my ma knows that I was thinking of her—"

"Naw, I don't do none of that stuff," said Thorn. "Where was you headed in such a hurry anyway?"

"I was headed to warn my boss, Sims—"

"Well, hell," said Thorn. "Then you're dying for nothing. Waco Bird Wheeler is ahead of you, doing the same thing."

"What a fool I've been." The young man looked up at Thorn and said, "Can I use your gun? I don't want to lie here and bleed to death."

"Why, sure, here," said Thorn. He laid his hand on his Colt, then said, "Just funning with you."

Funning with you . . . Thorn smiled to himself. He stood up and looked at the paint horse stepping around on the trail, seemingly enjoying the easy weather following the rain.

"I'll take your paint to town for you, see the coyotes don't eat him out here."

"Coyotes . . ." the young man whispered with regret. "I hadn't even thought of them. . . ."

Seems like you should have, Thorn thought. *This is where they live.*

The young man lay with his eyes half-closed, and Thorn stood waiting for him to finish dying before dragging him off the trail.

Chapter 24

Higher up on the drying switchback trail, the sucking mud tightening in the sun on the hillsides made a sound like that of locusts or other large insects that rose to the surface only every hundred years after lying dormant deep in the earth's belly. Thorn rode along easily on his gray, Cochise, leading the dead man's paint horse on a short lead rope beside him.

"Uh-oh, look here," he murmured to himself at the sight of a long, wide slide mark similar to the one he'd caused the young man and the paint horse to make. At the end of this one, he saw the large slide had gone off over the edge of the trail, plunging an unfortunate horse into treetops and boulders some two hundred feet down.

That will be Waco Bird Wheeler's buckskin, he thought. Looking on the ground, he saw a pair of boot prints headed on up the trail.

"Won't be long, Cochise," he said quietly.

A few miles later, the switchback reversed direction and turned level for a ways. He saw Waco Bird's long hair hanging from under his hat, down past his shoulders. Thorn called out as the tall gunman turned around toward him.

"*Hola* the trail, Waco Bird," he said, touching his heels to his gray's side just enough to up his pace. "I was going to surprise you."

Bird stood waiting until Thorn grew closer, then said, "Do I look like I need surprising to you, Thorn?"

Thorn chuckled. "No, you got me there, Bird. It looks like what you needed was to learn how to sit a horse after a hard rain."

Waco Bird cursed under his breath. He spit and started forward as if he would turn down any offer of a riding horse.

"Come on, Bird," said Thorn, "don't be contrary. You know if I've got two horses, you are welcome to one."

Waco stopped, looked the paint horse up and down.

"I've seen this cayuse. One of Sims's gunmen by the name of Rudy Blane rode him into town last evening."

"He won't be riding him again." Thorn held the paint's lead rope out to Waco. "Peculiar how things work." He slung a nod back over his shoulder. "This paint made it and his owner didn't. And here you are. You made it and your horse didn't."

"So?" said Waco Bird, not seeing anything of it. "Accidents can happen to anybody."

Thorn shook his head and said, "Sure, Bird, just pondering aloud."

Waco Bird took the lead rope off the paint and gathered its reins.

"What were you doing up here anyway?" Thorn asked before Waco stepped into the paint's saddle. "Word has it Sims and his men are headed into town this way with a huge mad-on at the ranger."

Waco stepped away from the paint and handed the

reins and lead rope back up to Thorn. "Here, take this horse and go straight to hell with it if there're questions attached to me riding—"

"Whoa, settle down," said Thorn, taking the paint's reins. "I'm just making conversation, you know, brotherly trail talk among friends?" He moved the paint around to his other side, tied its lead rope back onto its bridle and wrapped its reins around his saddle horn.

But Waco didn't settle down. "It happens that Cree Sims and I are friends," he snapped. "If I ride out to see him on his way to town, so what? I ain't answering a damn thing to you!"

"I'm glad to hear you feel that way," said Thorn. "You just saved us both from wasting each other's time."

He raised his Colt from under his duster as if it were a pet rattlesnake and shot Waco Bird Wheeler through the side of his head. The paint never so much as flinched as the sound of the gun blast echoed and rolled out across the rugged, mountainous terrain.

"You're one steady hoss, aren't you?" Thorn said to the paint, which was staring straight ahead. "Too damned good to be left out here and get fed to the critters."

The paint horse shook out its mane and sawed its head up and down.

"Oh, I'm glad you agree with me," Thorn said.

Sam counted the men who rode in and lined their horses along two end-to-end hitch rails standing out in front of Irish Mike's newly acquired drinking establishment. He came up with fourteen gunmen, more than he had thought there would be.

Well, Dupree was locked in a cell, so just two more

to apprehend to get this thing over with. There were no charges against Kura Stabitz, the Russian Assassin, yet from what Sam knew of the man, he would force Sam to take him down too rather than see Sims, Dupree and Tillis go down around him.

Okay, if that's his choice, Sam told himself. He was already facing big odds, even before any other Arizona Cowboys or Bad River Gunmen showed up in the area.

Brothers to the bone, these men, Sam thought. But this was the job. He'd known it coming in.

"You'd be wise to shoot yourself, Ranger," said Earl Dupree. "Save everybody else having to do it." He gave a wide, cruel grin and kicked at the yellow cat, which shot out of the cell and up onto the battered desk.

"Leave the cat alone, Dupree," Sam said. "He's kept this place from being carried off by rodents."

"Rodents don't bother me," said Dupree. "I backhand them if they get too close."

"What about snakes?" Sam asked.

"Snakes?" Dupree looked around closely at the edges and corners of the cell floor. "You can't keep a man in a cell where there's snakes. That's called incivil!"

"*In*civil?" Sam said.

"Yeah, or *un*humane or something," said Dupree. "Anyway, it's illegal."

"Not here in Mexico," Sam said. "It's legal here. A lot of things are." He walked closer to the cell. "It's legal here for me to walk out the back door and leave town if your Gunmen pals set this place on fire."

Dupree's jaw dropped. "The hell it is!"

"It is," Sam said. "But don't worry. We'll find out for sure if anybody tries it."

"The hell we will—"

A knock on the back door caused Dupree to shut up. Sam walked to the door, rifle in hand. Opening the door without allowing Dupree to see who was there, Sam saw Clement Melford sweating, wearing a worried look. Jack Swift and a half dozen of his detectives were standing six feet behind him.

"Sims left my office an hour ago," Melford said. "I don't like the way this appears to be going! Thorn isn't here! My bodyguard, Waco Bird, isn't here!"

"There're Swift's men," Sam said, nodding at the detectives.

"That's not enough," Melford said, sounding near panic. "Sims told me he still has the women! He said he will kill them! Imagine how it would look for my bank if that happens!"

"It's not going to happen," said Sam, "so settle down." He looked at Jack Swift over Melford's shoulder, and said, "If I were you, I'd get myself heavily armed."

"Why?" Swift looked wild-eyed. "What have you heard? What has Sims told you?"

"Sims is ready to blow up," Sam said. "I'm telling you what I would do. Get armed. Keep all of your men together. Find a good stone wall somewhere and get behind it."

"Does Sims— Does he have the women?" Melford asked.

Sam took a breath and let it out slowly. "Well, he says he does," he replied. "Who am I to say otherwise?"

"You said you were going to get them! What happened?"

"I went to get them. They weren't there," Sam said.

"So we don't have nothing to bargain with?"

"We've still got the money," said Sam. "And they've still got their lives."

"But, Ranger, you won't give up the money unless they turn themselves in! Sims won't do that! So we are in a deadlock!"

"Yes, there is a deadlock," Sam said. "But nothing breaks a deadlock like the fall of a gun hammer."

"Is that what you've had in mind all this time, a huge showdown?"

"No," said Sam, "but if this is where we are, this is how we've got to deal with it."

Of course it's a showdown, Sam thought. *How does a man like Clement Melford not see that?*

Melford slumped where he stood and said, "What do you want me to do, Ranger?"

"Are you still paying these detectives to stop the Bad River Gunmen?" Sam asked.

"Well, yes . . ." said Melford, "although we have a cooperative arrangement that benefits us all."

"Forget the arrangement for now." Sam motioned for Jack Swift to come closer. When Swift did, he asked, "Where is Sims right now?"

"He and his men are at the bar in the street and in the German Ale and Whiskey House," said Swift.

"Okay," Sam replied, "you and your men circle the outside bar and the German Ale and Whiskey House. I'll bring out Sims and Tillis—and Stabitz if he sticks. I've already got Dupree."

"I want to see this," said Swift.

"You will see it," Sam replied.

"And what will you charge the Russian with?" Melford asked.

Sam didn't reply, but Swift's men knew what his silence meant.

The detectives looked at one another for a moment, not knowing what to say.

Finally, it was Jack Swift himself who gave a bold grin and said, "Hell yes, we are detectives. Let's put these Bad River gunmen out of business!"

Half an hour later, Sam draped the bandolier of ammunition across his chest, hung a double-barreled shotgun by its strap on his shoulder, checked his big Colt and holstered it loosely and picked up his Winchester. He looked at Dupree in his cell and said, "The bell rope that runs to room service is broke. If you need anything, yell yourself blue in the face."

"That's real funny," said Dupree sarcastically.

Sam walked out the back door and up the alley leading to the German Ale and Whiskey House. As he passed close to the outside bar, Swift's men, who stood positioned along the way, gave him a slight nod, telling him that Sims's men—maybe even Sims himself—were inside the ale house.

Entering from the side door, Sam walked through the roar of the drinking crowd and over to a table against a sidewall. Seeing the guns and ammunition hanging on him, drinkers' eyes turned and followed him to the table. Leaning his rifle against the wall, he stepped up onto a chair and from there onto the table. Taking the shotgun sling from his shoulder, he cocked both hammers on the gun and looked all around as drinkers began thinning out in every direction.

"Any Bad River Gunmen not wanting to die, get out now while you can. Later won't do you any good."

A man at the bar struck an attitude. Sam saw the red Cowboy sash around his waist.

"You want me out? Put me out!" the man demanded.

Before he could reach for his gun, the shotgun's left

barrel exploded, sending patrons running, scrambling and crawling for their lives. The man flew out through the front door and landed on the sidewalk.

"The next shot is going to be worse," Sam shouted, breaking the shotgun open and replacing the empty shell. "And it's going to keep on getting worse every time I pull the trigger!"

A bartender's helper wearing a white apron ran up and raised his hands. "We can talk this thing over, mister!" he shouted.

"Are you a Bad River Gunman?" Sam asked.

"Well, no," the man said. "But I see there is something bothering you—"

"Get out!" the ranger shouted.

A blast hit the floor near the man's feet, and he turned and ran out the door.

Most of the crowd had left, some walking, some running, some crawling fast. Once the place was near empty, Sam stepped down and motioned the few people left out the front door. Then he walked out behind them.

Directly in front of him ten yards away stood Cree Sims. Looking around the crowded street, Sam saw lots of guns and gunmen, some outlaws, some Jack Swift detectives—enough of both to keep one another in check for the moment at least.

"I've been wanting to see you, Ranger," Sims said. He stood with his feet spread in a gunfighter's stance. "I understand you have money that belongs to me."

"I have a lot of money stashed up there," Sam said, gesturing toward the mountainside, "but it never belonged to you. It belonged to French mining companies. I've been thinking about giving it to your Bad River Gunmen. Let them split it up, decide for themselves what to do with it."

"Oh, I see," Sims said. He seemed to give the ranger's idea some thought. "Let me get this straight before we kill you," he said with a dark little chuckle. "You think my men will hand me over to you in exchange for . . . what? A few thousand dollars?"

"No," Sam said, "the total I get comes to just shy of three hundred thousand U.S. greens."

He looked around at the Gunmen, who in turn looked at one another, almost stunned by the amount he'd thrown out at them.

"Sweet holy Francis," one of them said.

"Let's not get off the subject here," Sims said. "If I don't get the money, I'm killing those two sweet little gals—"

"You're lying, Sims," said Sam. "The women are as safe from you as the money is. Everything you've tried to do, I've undone. It's time we take this crooked thing and make it straight."

Sims saw that the mention of the money had caused a restless stir among the men. "Don't listen to him, men," he said. "How do we know he's even got the money up there?" He gestured his eyes up, his gun hand resting on his holstered Colt.

Sam took note of the weapon. He looked at Giles Tillis, who stood on Sims's right. "What about you, Tillis? Do you believe there's money up there? I'm asking because you're also going back to Arizona with me."

"Like hell I am," said Tillis. "I'm going no-damn-where!"

"In your case, you're talking about only a couple of years or less, but have it your way," Sam said. He slowly reached into his duster and pulled out a stack of large-denomination bills with a bank band around it. "Here's a few thousand dollars from up there. Clean, new American greens."

"Oh, yeah?" Sims said. "Hell, I can toss out a stack of cash myself. It doesn't mean I've got three hundred thousand dollars up on the switchbacks."

Sam looked around at each man, all of them armed, all of them ready to kill at Sims's orders. "What will it take?" he said. "How much of the three hundred thousand do you need to see? Fifty thousand? A hundred? How much?"

The men looked at one another again.

Sims laughed and said, "Don't let this ranger fast talk you. He's got no more money."

"I've got it," Sam said, "right here at my fingertips. How much do you men need to see for me to take these two off your hands?"

Sims and Tillis were both ready to shoot Sam.

"Half of it," a voice said. "Show us half of it right now, or you can say hello to the devil. Right, pals?"

"Yeah," said another man, "if you're on the up-and-up, I'd like to see that much money. 'Specially if it's going to be ours."

"No," Sam said flatly, "half is too much." He held up a hand as the outlaws started to grumble. "I'll show you a third. That's one hundred thousand right here, right now. Take it or leave it."

A man laughed under his breath. "You'd sooner die than do what we tell you?"

"You'd rather kill me than see the money and know it'll be yours?" Sam countered.

The men looked at one another and agreed in silence.

"Wait," said Sims. "Don't fall for this."

Sam waved everybody back a step and let them

watch him slowly pull the double-barreled's shoulder strap from his shoulder and point the gun straight up. He fired two shots, one right after the other. A silence fell over the crowd.

"So?" said Sims. "If you were shooting at birds, you missed! Somebody shoot this fool—"

Before his words were out of his mouth, an earth-shaking blast rocked the mountains and hillsides.

"What the hell?" a man said as they all looked up at the blast still roiling out of the mouth of one of the closed-down French mines sitting on a narrow ridge overlooking the town.

Small bits of debris came raining down.

"Well, that's that," said Sims. "Looks like you've played out your string, Ranger."

"Whoa, look at this!" a man said. He held up a large-denomination U.S. bill that came floating down in the dark suety air.

"Here's another one!" a man shouted.

"Damn, it's raining money!"

"Wait, everybody!" shouted Sims.

"You *lose*, Sims," said the ranger, seeing the men mount up and ride away toward the upward trails. Overhead, out front of a gaping mine-shaft opening, a cloud of money fluttered like a large flock of birds. It seemed to hang half-suspended in the smoky air.

Obliged, Claypool, Sam thought, looking up. *I knew you could do it.*

"I haven't lost anything!" Sims shouted. "Stabitz, show him who the loser is here! Stabitz? Stabitz!"

He looked around and saw the Russian riding hard toward the trails leading up to the cloud of cash.

While Sims shouted and gestured, Sam reached down and slowly drew his Colt as if checking it. In-

stead of slipping it back down into his holster, he held
it down at his thigh.

"It's just us," Sam said, his eyes sharp and clear yet
revealing nothing. "How do you two want to go to
Arizona: in a saddle or over one?"

"You got some gall, Ranger," Sims said. "I don't
know how you did this, but I know when I've been
tricked!"

"I didn't trick you, Sims. I called you out in the street
in a way you're not used to. We made all the moves every gunfight goes through and here's what it's brought
us to. One of us is likely going to die now." He looked
from one man to the other. "I don't plan on it being me."

He heard a gun hammer click. His big Colt came up
cocked, and before Cree Sims or Giles Tillis could say
a word, a bullet bored through Sims's forehead and out
the back of his head, taking a lot of blood and matter
with it.

"No, don't!" shouted Tillis. "I don't want to die!" His
hand flew up from his gun butt.

Sam lowered his Colt but kept it cocked. When he
saw Tillis's hand drop back to his gun butt, he raised his
Colt and fired. The bullet bored through Tillis's heart.

"I've seen that move before too," he said quietly almost before Tillis settled on the ground.

Sam opened his Colt, dropped out two spent rounds
and replaced them. He looked over to his right. Now
that so many men had ridden off to grab up the money,
Sam saw Dan'l Thorn sitting his gray back behind
where the other gunmen had been only moments ago.
A ten-gauge coach gun lay across his lap. He gave a
faint smile and touched his hat brim.

Sam saw him toss a slice of apple into his mouth. He
saw him hand another slice of apple to Irish Mike

Tuohy, sitting on a horse beside him, also with a ten gauge on his knee.

Thorn handed Cochise a slice of apple when the big dapple gray reached its head around and nudged his leg.

What a day, Sam thought.

He wanted to say that all was well that ended well. But he decided to forgo declaring any such notion for now, at least until he saw JR Claypool come down from the hillside—and made sure he still had all his fingers.

Turn the page for a sneak peek
at the next Ranger Sam Burrack adventure,

A KILLING IN GOLD

Available in November 2021 from Berkley

The Valley of Mexico

Arizona Ranger Sam Burrack leaned comfortably against an ancient bare juniper tree atop a rocky rise overlooking the small town of Vista Hermosa. With his battered telescope to his eye, he watched a tall figure riding a dapple gray at an easy pace from a northerly direction out of the lower hills surrounding the wide fertile valley. The ranger recognized the tall figure as former Indian Territory lawman Dan'l Thorn.

A friend of mine? Yes, the ranger believed so. He and Thorn had somehow carved out a friendship of sorts over the years, but those four horsemen covertly fanning Thorn's trail gave him pause. He'd watched them for as long as he'd watched Thorn, as they rode in and out of sight along cleared stretches of trail between broken boulders and scrub trees and cacti.

What's wrong with Thorn? Sam had to wonder. The fact that Thorn did not seem to know the riders were there was cause enough for concern. Yet he waited and watched, making no assumptions, with his Winchester resting in the crook of his left arm. Every fifty or so yards, he reached down and adjusted the small brass dial on his raised long sight from memory.

Now that Thorn and the riders were inside his shorter range, some seventy or eighty yards, he no longer needed the long sight; he reached down with a fingertip and closed it with a quiet snap. He also closed his telescope and slipped it into his duster pocket. Through the brush and rock that lay between him and the trail below, he'd seen a thin game path that appeared to run most of the way there.

Time to go to work . . .

He made an ever-so-slight sound in his cheek that caused his dapple roan stallion, Doc, to perk up his ears just as slightly. With no fanfare whatsoever, Doc turned and walked over and stood beside him.

"*Buen caballo,*" Sam whispered.

Without slipping his rifle down into its saddle boot, he gave Doc a rub on his nose and led him by his reins over to the start of the game path and down.

Dan'l Thorn hummed a verse from a favorite song of his, "Sweet Betsy from Pike," as he stepped down from his saddle, pulled an apple from his duster and raised his big knife from his boot well. He scanned the area from under the wide brim of his black Stetson as he carved a slice of sweet Mexican Valley apple and popped it into his mouth.

He had just lowered the big knife to take another slice of apple when the four riders came suddenly around a huge boulder that formed a blind spot in the trail right behind him. With their four guns drawn and aimed at him, Thorn merely raised the slice of apple to his mouth more slowly than usual.

"Can you believe this jake?" the gunman near the center of the four said. He gave a dark chuckle. "Hell, old-timer, don't let us interrupt you eating." He was a large man with a big red face.

Old-timer? The melon-head son of a bitch, Thorn mused.

"That's all right," Thorn said. "I'm about finished." He lowered the big knife to the apple to pare off another slice.

The same man gave a dark laugh, his Colt aimed and cocked.

"You're right about that," he said. "You're finished, sure enough! Nobody with any sense stops on a trail this close around a blind turn. You're too close to see what's waiting to kill you!"

The four of them laughed.

Thorn gave a sheepish little grin. "Well, I guess I wasn't thinking straight, like I should have been," he said quietly. *Stupid melon-head son of a bitch . . .*

Except Thorn had been thinking just fine and stopped there for exactly the reason mentioned. Four men were trailing him and he'd just managed to catch all four by surprise—with a lowered opinion of him, to boot.

"Yeah, I guess not," said the man with the big red face.

One glance at the red sashes around three of their waists told Thorn that these were members of the Arizona Cowboy Gang. The one without a red sash kept his hat brim lowered. *Hiding his face? A good possibility,* Thorn thought. He'd kill him last, he decided, if this thing went the way he was confident it would.

"What can I do for you fellas?" Thorn asked and popped another slice of the apple off of the knife blade and into his mouth, talking as he chewed. He reached the knife around to scratch the back of his neck with the pointed tip.

His ease seemed to make the red-faced outlaw furious.

"When you get an itch, you've got to scratch it," Thorn said.

"Get rid of it!" the man shouted, waving his gun barrel at the big knife.

Thorn gave him a bewildered look but stopped scratching. "All right! I'll get rid of it!" Without hesitation, he raised his left hand and tossed the apple off the trail into the rocks. As the Gunmen watched, he raised his empty left hand for them to see.

"There, all gone," he said. He turned his empty hand back and forth.

Three of the Gunmen laughed a little, but not the one with the red face. His hand tightened on his cocked Colt.

"Not the apple, you damn fool!" he shouted. "The knife! Get rid of the knife!"

"Okay!" said Thorn. "See it's gone, too!" He held both of his hands up and out—both of them empty.

The men looked around as if the big knife was hidden somewhere among them.

"The hell . . . ?" one said.

"I'm killing this worthless old jake," said the red-faced gunman.

"Careful," one of the others warned him. "Ozzie said not to take this one lightly. Keep our eyes on him at all times."

"Ozzie can go straight to hell," the man with the red face said. "I'll show you how careful I'll be!"

He tried to raise his gun hand, ready to fire, but something stopped him, sudden and cold. He rocked back in his saddle before seeing the knife's bone handle jutting from the middle of his chest. All four gunmen stared at it as if having just witnessed a magician at work. Guns sagged. Eyes flashed all around. The man with his lowered hat brim stepped his horse back, and his black-handled Colt came down, uncocked.

Before the Gunmen could gather themselves, Thorn's first pistol shot rang out. One outlaw fell, his gun flying from his hand. The next was a split second faster and might have gotten the drop on Thorn. But it didn't matter. Before Thorn could fire again, a rifle shot exploded from beside the trail and sent the man flying backward out of his saddle.

Thorn spun toward the rifle shot and saw the ranger step into sight as he jacked a fresh round up into his rifle chamber.

"Ranger Sam Burrack," Thorn said, "just the man I was looking for."

"Thought I'd give you a hand, Dan'l," the ranger said, keeping an eye on the fourth gunman, who sat perfectly still in his saddle.

His Colt was back in its holster, his hands were held chest high, his eyes still shaded by the brim of his hat.

"Ha!" Thorn said to the ranger. "Don't go thinking I needed a hand against four miscreants like these!"

"Make that *three* miscreants," said the fourth man. "I pulled back before it got serious." He slowly pushed his hat brim up to give the other men a better look at his face.

"Roman Lee Ellison," said Thorn, recognizing the young gunman. "Had I known it was you up under that felt, I would have shot you just for keeping bad company." He looked Roman Lee up and down, feigning anger. "The hell are you doing following me with this coyote bait?"

Roman Lee lowered his hands and shrugged. "I was up in Happenstance drinking with some lonely women. A dozen Cowboys rode in and recognized me. I'm still one of them, you know." He gave a thin smile. "They said they were riding you down, Thorn. They invited me along. I figured you'd like seeing my smiling face if it all broke bad out here."

"Riding me down?" Thorn looked around at the three bodies in the dirt. "We see how *that* worked, don't we?"

He walked over to the jittery horse standing beside the man with the big knife in his chest. When the man had fallen from his saddle, his right foot stayed in the stirrup.

"Easy, boy," Thorn said to the grumbling animal.

He took the other man's boot out of the stirrup and pressed his own boot down on the dead man's chest, above the knife handle. He yanked the blade out and wiped it on the man's bloody shirt and slipped it into his own boot well. The horse blew out a breath, stepped away, shook itself off and stood easier.

"Well, Roman Lee," Thorn said, looking up and west, judging the evening sun mantling the horizon, "since you've managed not to shoot any of your pals here, maybe you'll help drag them off the trail. I'll gather their canteens and see if the ranger will boil us a pot of coffee."

"I will do that," said Roman Lee, stepping down from his saddle.

The ranger began searching trailside for a good place to build a fire unseen.

"While we're at it, you can tell me who Ozzie is and why he wanted these Cowboys to ride me down." Thorn replaced the bullet he'd used to kill one of the Cowboys. He tapped his Colt in Roman Lee's direction. "See if you can convince me that you have changed sides once and for all and are now on the side of good and righteousness with folks like the ranger and me."

He turned, tapped his gun barrel in the ranger's direction, and slipped it down into his holster.

"I will do that too," said Roman Lee. "I might be an outlaw, but after riding with these Cowboys, I've come to realize that even among outlaws, there're both good and bad."

"Oh," said Thorn, "did that time the ranger here put a bullet through your gullet and stuck you in Yuma prison for a couple of years rehabilitate you after all?"

"Don't start on that, Dan'l," the ranger cut in, looking up from starting a fire off the side of the trail where he'd cleared a spot.

"No, that's okay," said Roman Lee. "The fact is, taking a bullet in the chest might have had a lot to do with the way I think of things these days." He looked back and forth between the two. "What the bullet through my chest didn't change, riding with the two of you in Bad River made up for. It just took me some time to mull it over."

"Don't go getting sentimental on us, Roman Lee," Thorn said. "Sam might shoot you again."

"That's enough, Dan'l." Sam stepped onto the trail, took a small coffeepot from his holdings bag and took two of the dead outlaws' canteens from Thorn on his way back to the fledgling campfire.

While the coffee boiled, their horses were moved off the trail out of sight. Then the three of them dragged the dead off the opposite side of the trail and rolled their bodies over the edge and down the rocky slope. Their three horses were unsaddled and stripped of all tack and bridles and shooed away. But a few minutes later, as Sam, Thorn and Roman Lee sat around a low flame campfire drinking coffee from tin cups, the outlaws' horses eased out of the shadows into the soft circling glow of firelight. Gradually the horses gathered closer to the three men, their coffee and their banter as wolves began their searching howls in the distant darkness.

"Well, come on in, fellas. Don't mind us," Thorn said.

The ranger topped off Thorn's cup and set the coffeepot beside the low flames. Roman Lee Ellison leaned back against his saddle, a wool blanket beneath him, his battered Stetson brim down over his eyes.

Sam studied Thorn for a moment across the flicker of firelight. "If you're all through talking to stray horses, why don't you tell me what brings you out here on my trail?"

Thorn gave a nod toward Roman Lee as if to say that he might be listening.

Sam looked over at the tilted-down Stetson.

"Roman Lee, are you listening?" he asked loud enough to be heard.

"I hear every word being said," Roman Lee replied. "But I'm not listening."

"He's not listening," the ranger said to Thorn.

"Yeah, so I heard," said Thorn. "If you don't mind, neither am I." He reached inside his duster, pulled out an official-looking envelope and handed it around the fire to the ranger.

Sam gave him a questioning stare in the flicker of firelight. Sam gestured all around at the darkness and then down at the letter in his hand, unreadable in the night. "This is a joke, right?" he said.

"All right, give it back," said Thorn. "I'll tell you what it says and you can read it in the morning and suit yourself."

Sam withdrew the envelope before Thorn could reach it.

"I'll just keep it, read it in the morning, *then* give it

back," Sam said. He turned to Roman Lee. "How does that sound to you, Roman Lee?" Sam stuck the letter inside his shirt and patted it.

"Sounds good to me," Roman Lee said quietly under his hat brim.

"All right, here's what the letter will tell you in the morning," Thorn said to the ranger. "It'll say I'm working on bringing down a faction of the Arizona Cowboy Gang that was all set to take over Clement Melford's bank in Bad River and, with it, the members of the French business group that was siphoning off large amounts of both cash and gold from the mining operations across Mexico—"

"Who are you working for, Dan'l?" Sam asked, cutting in.

"We'll get to that later," Thorn replied.

Sam started to insist on knowing right then, but he would wait, he decided. Maybe that was too much to talk about in front of Roman Lee.

"All right," Sam said, "go on."

Thorn glanced at Roman Lee and lowered his voice. "That was good work you did in Bad River," Thorn said half under his breath. He got up into a crouch and seated himself a little closer to the ranger. "I hope you won't mind, but I sort of let some people think that I might have had something to do with all of it—"

"Hold it there, Thorn." The ranger raised a hand. In the same lowered voice he said, "I sort of did the same thing myself."

Thorn looked at him, confused.

"That's right, Dan'l," said Sam. "When I gave my report on Bad River to my captain, I told him you were a big help. Told him I might not have made it out of there had it not been for you keeping me in the know on things."

Thorn looked even more confused. "You told him *that*?" he said.

"I did," said Sam.

"Why?" Thorn asked as if he couldn't believe it.

"Because it's true, Dan'l," Sam said. "If it wasn't true, I wouldn't have said it."

"Well, I know that," Thorn said, "but I didn't—"

"Don't start second-guessing me on it, Thorn," Sam said in a firmer tone. "You didn't have to tell me you were on my side," Sam continued. "I saw it in every move you made. A lot of men died at Bad River. I might have been one of them if you hadn't been backing my play without anybody knowing it. I saw what you were doing for me without you telling me."

"It seemed like the right thing," Thorn said.

"It was," said Sam, "and when you and Irish Mike Tuohy showed up to back me with shotguns near the end, I knew that it was going to work out." He paused, then said, "Anyway, I did the right thing telling my captain."

Thorn grinned at Sam. "Don't forget crazy JR Claypool," he said. "He sure came through in a tight spot."

"Yes, he did," said Sam. "I hope he's doing well."

"He is indeed," said Thorn. "He's rich now!" He laughed and continued. "Funny how when you're poor and crazy, they chase you off the streets. But if you're rich and crazy, they name the streets after you!"

"So," said Sam, "I figure I owe you. If you're going up against the Cowboys, I'm with you as soon as I tell my captain about it."

"No need. The letter will tell you that the people I'm working for have already cleared it with your captain," Thorn said. He glanced again at Roman Lee and then said to Sam in almost a whisper, "Read it in the morning. They say everything looks better in light of day."